D1650749

Cal stood by the sitting room windows, taking in the frozen cityscape...

Devon's breath caught as she went to stand beside him. Buildings, trees, the statues on the bridge, the river itself...everything as far as the eye could see lay under a blanket of glistening white. Not a single car or bus or snowplough moved through the frozen stillness.

"Looks like most of the city must be shut down," Devon murmured, awestruck.

"Guess we'll have to resort to plan B," said Cal.

"Which is?"

"We talk politics. We try to guess each other's favourite movies. We wrap up in blankets and share our body heat. We have wild, uninhibited sex."

Her jaw dropped.

"We don't have to follow that precise order," he informed her solemnly. "We could start with the sex and work our way backwards."

His Expectant Ex
by Catherine Mann

"You're pregnant?"

"I'm fairly certain I'm two months along."

"We're having a child?" he asked in wonder.

It still seemed surreal to her, too. "If all goes well."

He pivoted hard and fast toward her. "Is something wrong?"

"I don't think so, but I only just took a home pregnancy test this morning."

Sebastian sat down beside her and slid his arm along the back of the sofa, almost touching her shoulders. "I still don't understand one thing."

She fidgeted, trying to ignore the warmth of him moving closer. She could not, would not let hormones muddle the waters between them. "What's that?"

"If you took a pregnancy test this morning, why didn't you tell me before the final divorce decree?"

Available in December 2009 from Mills & Boon® Desire™

THE CEO'S CHRISTMAS PROPOSITION

BY
MERLINE LOVELACE

HIS EXPECTANT EX

BY
CATHERINE MANN

⊚™ MILLS & BOON®

First published in Great Britain 2009
Harlequin Mills & Boon Limited,
Eton House, 18-24 Paradise Road, Richmond, Surrey TW9 1SR

The publisher acknowledges the copyright holders of the
individual works as follows:

The CEO's Christmas Proposition © Merline Lovelace 2008
His Expectant Ex © Catherine Mann 2008

ISBN: 978 0 263 87120 3

51-1209

Printed and bound in Spain
by Litografia Rosés S.A., Barcelona

THE CEO'S CHRISTMAS PROPOSITION

BY
MERLINE LOVELACE

A retired air force officer, **Merline Lovelace** served at bases all over the world, including tours in Taiwan, Vietnam and at the Pentagon. When she hung up her uniform for the last time, she decided to combine her love of adventure with a flair for storytelling, basing many of her tales on her experiences in the service.

Since then, she's produced more than seventy action-packed novels, many of which have made bestseller lists. Over ten million copies of her works are in print in thirty-one countries. Named Oklahoma's Writer of the Year and the Oklahoma Female Veteran of the Year, Merline is also a recipient of Romance Writers of America's prestigious RITA® Award.

When she's not glued to her keyboard, she and husband enjoy travelling and chasing little white balls around the fairways of Oklahoma. Check her website at www.merlinelovelace.com for news, contests and information about forthcoming releases.

Dear Reader,

If you've never visited Germany or Austria during the Christmas season, you've missed something really special. Think Kris Kringle, angelic choirs singing "Silent Night" and outdoor markets crammed with beautiful handicrafts and the most scrumptious eats imaginable. What better place to strand a heroine who's completely turned off by the way Christmas has been commercialised and a hero who decides on the spot she's all he wants under his tree!

Here's hoping you, too, enjoy the beauty of this season and the powerful message of love and joy that comes with it.

And be sure to watch for more HOLIDAYS ABROAD. *The Duke's New Year's Resolution* is coming next month from the Desire™ line, followed by *The Executive's Valentine Seduction*.

Best,

Merline Lovelace

To Pat, my college roomie who went off to Germany without me all those years ago but made up for it with four decades of friendship. Al and I still owe you and Norbert for the barn concert and dinner on the Elbe!

One

Shoulders hunched against the icy sleet pounding Germany's Dresden International Airport, Devon McShay grimaced at the Christmas carols belting from the outdoor loudspeakers.

"Okay," she muttered under her breath. "Call me Mrs. Scrooge. Call me the Grinchette. Call me the ultimate Krank. I hate this time of year."

Well, that wasn't totally true. The hopeless idealist in her still wanted to believe people might someday actually heed the messages of joy and peace the season signified. *If* they could get past the crass commercialization, that is. Not to mention the hole they dug for themselves every year by splurging on gifts they couldn't afford.

Her parents' increasingly bitter arguments over finances had always peaked this time of year and led eventually to an even more bitter divorce. Christmases after that had become a battleground, with each parent trying to outdo the other to win a daughter's love.

Devon's own holiday track record was just as dismal. As she sloshed through ankle-deep slush toward the terminal, she shook her head at her incredible idiocy in falling for a too-handsome, too-cocky newscaster at Dallas's Channel Six. Silly her, she'd actually thought she'd broken the Christmas curse when Blake caught her under the mistletoe and slipped a diamond on her finger. Exactly one year later, she'd walked into the station to find her husband with his hand under the miniskirt of a female Santa and his tongue halfway down her throat.

Devon had put her jerk of an ex out of her life, but even now, three years later, she couldn't work up any enthusiasm for colored lights or eggnog. That's why she'd jumped at the chance to avoid yet another season of forced Christmas cheer when her friend and business partner came down with the flu yesterday, mere hours before she was supposed to leave for Germany.

Devon, Sabrina Russo and Caroline Walters had been friends before they became business partners. They'd met while spending their junior year at the University of Salzburg. Filled with the dreams and enthusiasm of youth, the three coeds had formed a fast friendship.

They'd maintained that friendship long-distance in the years that followed. Until last May, when they'd met for a minireunion. After acknowledging that their lives so far hadn't lived up to their dreams, they'd decided to pool resources, educational backgrounds and interests. Two months later, they'd quit their respective jobs, relocated to Virginia and launched European Business Services, Incorporated. EBS for short. Specializing in arranging transportation, hotels, conference facilities and translation services for busy executives.

The venture was still at the risky stage. The three friends had sunk most of their savings into start-up costs. EBS now had an office, a small staff and a slew of international advertising. They'd landed a few jobs, but nothing big until the call from Cal Logan's executive assistant.

Turns out Logan had played football in college with one of Sabrina's old boyfriends. Said boyfriend had tipped his pal to EBS when Logan mentioned his people were scrambling to lay on a short-notice trip to Germany. Sabrina had worked twenty hours straight on the prep work and had been all set to hop a plane yesterday afternoon when the bug hit.

So here Devon was, her chin buried in a hot pink pashmina shawl, her toes frozen inside her stacked heel boots and her ears assaulted by a booming rendition of "O Tannenbaum," on her way to meet their first major client.

Again.

He'd been scheduled to arrive earlier this morning, but his assistant had called to say his corporate jet had been grounded due to icing. After considerable effort, she'd gotten him on the last commercial flight out before JFK shut down completely.

Ah, the joys of traveling this time of year! Conditions here in Dresden weren't much better. Sleet had been coming down all day. Praying her client's plane made it in before this airport closed, too, Devon hurried into the terminal.

Her breath whistled out in a sigh of relief when Logan exited Customs. She recognized him right away from the newspaper and magazine articles Sabrina had found on the Internet during her frantic prep work.

Caleb John Logan, Jr. Thirty-one. Six-two. With jet-black hair, laser blue eyes and a linebacker's shoulders under his charcoal-gray cashmere over-coat. His jaw-dropping good looks didn't score him any points with Devon, however. She'd learned the hard way not to trust handsome heartbreakers like Cal Logan.

But he was a client. An important one. And she was willing to give someone who'd served a hitch in the Marines before earning a B.S. from the University of Oregon, an MBA from Stanford and his first million at the ripe old age of twenty-six the benefit of the doubt.

Right up until he spotted the hot pink pashmina, that is.

Sabrina had indicated she'd be wearing it, and the

flash of color was certainly more visible than the sign Devon held up with his name on it. So she wasn't surprised when Logan picked her out of the crowd and cut in her direction. She'd just plastered on her best EBS smile when he whipped an arm around her waist. The next moment, she was sprawled against his cashmere-covered chest.

"Hello, Brown Eyes."

Swooping down, he covered her mouth with his.

Sheer astonishment kept Devon rooted to the spot for a few seconds while her mind whirled chaotically. Her first thought was that her client had downed a few too many drinks during the long flight. Her second, that he'd seriously mistaken the kind of escort and consulting services EBS provided. Her third shoved everything else out of her head.

Whoa, mama! The man could kiss!

His mouth moved over hers with a skill that ignited sparks at a half-dozen flash points throughout her body. Devon hadn't experienced that kind of spontaneous combustion in a while. A *long* while.

The sparks were still popping when she pushed off his chest, only now they fueled a flush of anger.

"Do you always greet women you don't know with a lip-lock, Mr. Logan?"

A smile crinkled the skin at the corners of his eyes. "As a matter of fact, I don't. That was from Don."

"Huh?"

"He said he owed you one from New Year's Eve two years ago and made me promise to deliver it."

She stared up at him in total incomprehension. Logan hooked a brow and attempted to prompt a nonexistent memory.

"He abandoned you at the Waldorf. Five minutes before midnight. To deliver twins."

"I don't have a clue who or what you're—"

Understanding burst like a water balloon.

"Wait a sec. Are you talking about Sabrina's old boyfriend? Your buddy, who's now an ob-gyn doc?"

It was Logan's turn to look startled. He recovered faster than Devon had, though. His smile widened into a rueful grin.

"I take it you're not Sabrina Russo."

"No, Mr. Logan, I am not. And if you'd listened to any of the voice mails we left on your cell phone in the past twenty-four hours," Devon added acidly, "you'd know Sabrina came down with the flu and couldn't make the trip."

"Sorry. I've been in the air for twenty-three of those twenty-four hours. I had to make a quick trip to the West Coast before turning right around and heading for Germany."

She knew that. Still, that was no excuse for his behavior. Or…what was worse…her reaction to it.

"My cell-phone battery crashed somewhere over Pennsylvania," he said, his smile holding an apology now. "I crashed somewhere over the Atlantic. Any chance we can erase what just happened and start again?"

Oh, sure. As soon as her lips stopped tingling and

her nerves snapping. Reminding herself that he was a client, Devon forced a stiff nod.

"Good." He shifted his briefcase to his left hand and held out his right. "I'm Cal Logan. And you are?"

"Devon McShay. One of Sabrina's partners."

"The history professor."

So he'd done some checking on the small firm he'd hired to work the details of his five-day, three-city swing through Germany.

"Former history professor," she corrected as she led the way toward the baggage-claim area. "I quit teaching to join forces with Sabrina and Caroline at EBS."

"Quite a career shift."

"Yes, it was."

She left it at that. No need to detail her restlessness after her divorce. Or her ex's very public, very mortifying attempt at reconciliation on the six o'clock news. Dallas hadn't been big enough for both of them after that.

That was when she'd quit her job and joined forces with her two friends. Now Devon the history prof, Sabrina the one-time party girl and Caroline the shy, quiet librarian were hard-nosed businesswomen. With pretty much the future of their fledgling enterprise hanging on how well Devon handled Cal Logan's trip.

After this rocky start, she thought grimly, things weren't looking real good.

Cal matched his stride to the staccato pace of the woman at his side. She was pissed, and no wonder.

He'd pulled some real boners in his time. This one ranked right up near the top of the list.

He'd never intended to follow through on his buddy's joking suggestion that he deliver a long-delayed New Year's Eve kiss. Then he'd exited Customs and spotted the woman he'd assumed was Sabrina Russo.

Tall and slender, with dark auburn hair caught up in a loose twist, she would have snagged any man's attention. Her high, sculpted cheekbones and the thick lashes fringing her brown eyes had certainly snagged Cal's.

Brown Eyes. Don's nickname for the woman he'd dated briefly. Except she wasn't that woman. And her eyes, Cal saw now, weren't brown. More like caramel, rich and dark, with a hint of gold in their depths.

Then there was that scarf. The hot color should have clashed with her red hair. Instead, it seemed to shout at the world to sit up and take notice.

Cal had noticed, all right. Now he'd damned well better unnotice.

Fun was fun, but he didn't need the kind of distraction Devon McShay could represent. Logan Aerospace had too much riding on the delicate negotiations that had forced him to cancel an entire week's appointments and hustle over to Germany.

"I confirmed your meeting with Herr Hauptmann for two p.m.," she informed him as suitcases began to rattle onto the baggage carousel. "I also requested early check-in at the hotel if you'd like to swing by there first."

"Definitely."

He scraped a palm across the bristles on his jaw. Given the time change, it was late morning here in Dresden but still the middle of the night U.S. time. Cal needed a shower, a shave and a full pot of coffee in him before his two o'clock meeting. As he waited for his leather carryall and suit bag to make an appearance, he gave Ms. McShay and EBS full marks for recognizing that fact.

Great start, Devon thought while her client filled out a search form for his missing luggage. *Just terrific.*

Logan had shrugged off the inconvenience with the comment that his American Express would cover the expense of delayed or lost luggage. Meanwhile Devon would have to scramble to supply him with everything from a clean shirt to pajamas.

Assuming he wore pj's. Maybe he went to bed commando. An instant, vivid image leaped into her head and refused to leap out.

Oh, for Pete's sake! She'd known the man for all of fifteen minutes and already she was imagining him naked. Disgusted, Devon tried to put the brakes on her runaway thoughts. The announcement that blared over the loudspeaker at that moment brought them to a screeching halt.

"Aufmerksamkeit, Damen und Herren."

Her head cocked, she listened as an official announced in German, English and Japanese that all flights in and out of Dresden were canceled until further notice. A chorus of groans went up inside the terminal.

By the time she escorted her client to the exit, a mile-long line of travelers was huddled in their over-coats at the taxi stand. To make matters worse, pick-up and drop-off traffic had snarled every lane. The limo Devon called on her cell phone couldn't get through the logjam.

Lord, she hated this time of year!

"The driver says he's stuck two terminals over," she related to Logan. "Traffic's not moving an inch. We can wait inside until he gets here. Or we could walk," she added with a dubious glance at the sleet still plummeting from a gunmetal-gray sky.

"I don't mind stretching my legs, but are you sure you're dressed warm enough to walk?"

"I'm fine."

Except for her boots, she admitted silently as she wove a path through the lines of frustrated travelers. Served her right for choosing style over practicality. The stacked heels and slick leather soles made for treacherous going on the icy pavement. Logan caught her as her foot almost went out from under her.

"At the risk of making an ass of myself for the second time in less than a half hour," he said solemnly, "may I suggest you hang on to me?"

Devon was only too glad to hook her elbow through his. She was also all too aware of the strength in the arm covered by layers of wool and cashmere.

He was her client. He was her client. He was her client.

She chanted the mantra over and over again as they dodged icy patches. When she finally spotted a stretch limo up ahead and confirmed it was theirs, her nose and ears tingled from the cold but Logan's solid bulk had shielded the rest of her from the worst of the knifing wind and sleet.

Devon sank into the limo's soft leather and welcome heat. Wiggling her frozen toes inside her boots, she offered Logan an apology. "I'm sorry about this hassle."

"You can't control the weather."

Or the traffic. It crawled along with the speed of a snail on Prozac. Seemingly unperturbed, Logan extracted a charger from his briefcase and plugged his cell phone into one of the limo's ports.

"Excuse me a moment while I check my calls."

He had a slew of them. The rueful glance he sent her confirmed that several were from EBS. He was still on the phone when the limo finally reached the airport exit. The slick roads made Devon grateful for the fact that Sabrina had somehow managed to wrangle last-minute reservations at the Westin Hotel across the river from the oldest part of Dresden. With any luck, efficient road crews would have the roads sanded before she and Logan had to tackle the Old City's maze of narrow, cobbled streets.

Devon had checked into the hotel yesterday afternoon and sunk like a stone into its heavenly feather bed. Hopefully, Cal Logan would decide on a power nap and do the same while she hit the shops for whatever he would need. She led the way through a lobby decorated with fragrant pine boughs and skirted a twenty-foot Christmas tree, only to have the desk clerk send her hopes crashing.

"I'm very sorry, Ms. McShay. The guest presently occupying Mr. Logan's suite hasn't yet departed."

"But you indicated there would be no problem with early check-in."

"I didn't think there would be, madam. Unfortunately, the present occupant's flight has been canceled, and he's requested a late checkout pending other arrangements."

"How late?"

"He's one of our platinum customers," the clerk said with a look that pleaded for understanding. "We have to give him until four o'clock."

Smothering an extremely unprofessional curse, Devon turned to her client. Logan had shrugged off the irritating glitches so far, but the crease between his brows suggested his patience was stretching thin.

Hastily, she dug in her purse for the key card to her room. It wasn't a VIP suite, but it did have a spacious sitting room, a separate bedroom and that incredible down comforter.

"Why don't you go up to my room and relax?" she said with determined cheerfulness. "You can give me a list of what you'll need until your luggage gets here, and I'll hit the shops."

If his luggage got here. Judging by his clipped response, Logan considered the possibility as remote as she did.

"All I need right now is a shirt that doesn't look like it's been slept in. White or blue. Neck, sixteen and a half, sleeves thirty-two."

Whatever that translated to in German. Devon had enjoyed several mild flirtations and one serious fling during her year at the University of Salzburg but hadn't gotten around to purchasing men's clothing. Sternly, she banished visions of sending Logan into his meeting with Herr Hauptmann wearing a shirt with a collar that choked him or cuffs that dangled well below his suit coat sleeves.

"White or blue," she repeated. "Sixteen and a half. Thirty-two. Got it."

Summoning a breezy smile, she handed him the key.

"It's room four-twelve. I need a few things, too. I'll look around the shops for a couple of hours. Stretch out and make yourself comfortable, Mr. Logan. I'll buzz the room before I come up."

His incipient frown eased. "We're going to be spending the next five days together. Please, call me Cal."

Devon hesitated. She and Sabrina and Caroline had all agreed they needed to maintain a strictly professional relationship with their clients. Especially ones as powerful and influential as Caleb John Logan, Jr.

On the other hand, he *was* the client. Refusing his

request wasn't really an option after the annoying glitches they'd encountered so far.

"Cal it is. See you in a few hours."

She dragged out the shopping as long as she could and dawdled over coffee in the lobby café until close to twelve-thirty. Just to be on the safe side, she called Herr Hauptmann's office to confirm the meeting was still on for two o'clock before searching out a house phone. Her client answered on the second ring.

"Logan."

"I'm sorry to wake you, but we'll need to leave soon."

"No problem. I've been crunching numbers."

"I have your shirt."

"Great, bring it up."

As the elevator whisked upward with noiseless efficiency, Devon's thoughts whirled. She'd ordered the limo for one. Hopefully the roads would be sanded and relatively clear. She'd better arrange backup transportation to Berlin tomorrow, too, just in case the airport was still shut down. She'd check the high-speed train schedules, she decided as she rapped on her room door, and...

When the door opened, her thoughts skittered to a dead stop. Cal Logan in cashmere and worsted wool could make any woman whip around for another look. Shirtless and bare-chested, he'd give a post-menopausal nun heart palpitations.

Two

As their limo crossed the centuries-old stone bridge leading into Dresden's Old City, Devon was still trying to recover. She couldn't remember the last time she'd gotten up close and personal with that much naked chest.

"What's going on?"

Logan's question banished her mental image of taut, contoured pecs and a dusting of black hair that arrowed downward. Blinking, she saw him lean forward to survey the town square just across the bridge.

It was one of the most beautiful in all Europe. Although almost eighty percent of Dresden had been destroyed during two days of intense bombing in World War Two, decades of meticulous restoration had resurrected much of the city's glorious architecture. The monumental Baroque cathedral with its openwork dome tower dominated a three-block area that included a royal palace, a magnificent state opera house and the world-famous Zwinger, a collection of incredibly ornate buildings surrounding a massive courtyard once used to stage tournaments and festivals.

It wasn't the architecture that had captured Cal Logan's attention, though, but the outdoor market in full swing despite the miserable weather. Shoppers bundled in down jackets, ski masks, stocking caps and earmuffs roamed rows of wooden stalls crammed with handicrafts.

"It's a *Christkindlmarkt*," Devon told him. "A Christmas market. Most towns and cities in Germany have one. The tradition dates back to the early 1400s, when regular seasonal markets took place throughout the year. The Christmas market evolved into *the* major event, where locals would gather to sell homemade toys, ornaments and foodstuffs."

Thus initiating the commercialization process that had expanded over the years to its present mania. As a historian, Devon admired the medieval atmosphere of this lively town square. The self-proclaimed Grinchette in her had to work to see past the throngs of eager shoppers.

"Dresden's market is one of the oldest in Germany. And that—" her nod indicated the wooden structure dominating the square "—is the tallest Christmas pyramid in the world."

Most traditional, multitiered wooden Christmas pyramids were tabletop size. Carved figures depicting the Nativity decorated each of the tiers. Candles sat in holders at the pyramid's base. When the candles were lit, warm air rose and turned the propeller-style fan at the top, causing the various tiers to rotate.

What had begun as traditional folk art designed to delight children with the dancing shadows cast by the rotating figures was now a multimillion-dollar industry. Wooden Christmas pyramids were sold all over the world, and less expensive versions were machine cut instead of hand carved. Dresden, however, had taken the traditional concept to new and ridiculous heights.

Okay, maybe not so ridiculous. As the limo inched along the jam-packed street leading past the markct, Devon had to concede the fifty-foot pyramid with its life-size figures was a pretty awesome sight.

Cal Logan evidently thought so, too. He twisted around for another glimpse of the busy square.

"I'd like to hit some of those stalls after the meeting with Herr Hauptmann." He settled back in his seat and caught her surprised expression. "I have nine nieces and nephews," he explained.

Nine? Devon made a mental adjustment to reconcile Cal Logan's public image as a jet-setting playboy with that of a doting uncle.

"How old are they?"

"Beats me. The littlest one is…little. The oldest just started high school. I think."

So much for the doting uncle!

"You'll need a better fix on their ages if you plan to shop for Christmas gifts."

"My executive assistant usually takes care of that," Logan admitted. "She'll have names, ages and personal preferences in her computer."

Devon got the hint. A quick glance at her watch confirmed it was still early back at Logan Aerospace corporate headquarters in eastern Connecticut. She'd bet the boss's executive assistant would be one of the first ones in, though. Luckily, Devon had added the woman's phone number and e-mail to her personal-contacts list.

"I'll e-mail her," she said, digging in her purse for her iPhone. "By the time we get out of the meeting with Herr Hauptmann, she should be at work and have access to the information."

With something less than enthusiasm, Devon worked the iPhone's tiny keyboard. She'd counted on this trip to provide an escape from the shopping frenzy back home. Now she'd have to brave the nasty weather and wade into a mob of shoppers to help her client find gifts for a whole pack of nieces and nephews. Thank goodness she'd had enough experience with German and Austrian winters to have worn her warmest coat.

Hauptmann Metal Works was located southeast of the Old City, in a section of Dresden that had been reconstructed along depressingly modern lines.

Remnants of East Germany's long domination by the Soviet Union showed in seemingly endless rows of concrete-block buildings. Some attempts had been made to soften their stark utilitarianism with newly planted parks and pastel color schemes, but the area held none of the old-world charm of other parts of the city.

Herr Hauptmann was awaiting their arrival. Big and beefy and ruddy cheeked, the German industrialist came out of his office to greet them. Devon had confirmed that he spoke fluent English, so she wasn't required to translate as he shook hands with his visitor.

"Welcome, Herr Logan. I have been looking forward to meeting you."

"Thank you, sir. This is Ms. Devon McShay. She's assisting me during my visit to Germany."

"Ms. McShay."

Devon had intended to make sure her client had everything he needed before fading into the woodwork with the other underlings, but Logan ushered her to a seat beside his at the long conference table.

Ten minutes of chitchat and a welcoming toast of schnapps later, she had plunged feet first into the world of high finance. The numbers Logan and Hauptmann lobbed back and forth like tennis balls left her breathless. They weren't talking millions, but billions.

The main issue centered on the massive, joint-European venture to build the Airbus, touted as the world's biggest passenger jet. A number of American companies were involved in it as well, including Logan Aerospace. Devon had to struggle to follow the discussion of the incredibly complex global aerospace industry. She grasped the bottom line, though, when Logan leaned forward an hour later and summed it up with surgical precision.

"We can argue the numbers all day, Herr Hauptmann, but we both agree your company is dangerously overleveraged. You borrowed heavily to hire additional people and invest in new production facilities to win your big Airbus contract. With Airbus behind schedule and facing major cost overruns, its potential customers are dropping like flies. You can go down with them, or you can accept my offer of a buyout, which will not only save your Airbus contracts, it will give you greater access to American aerospace giants like Boeing and Lockheed."

"At a significantly reduced profit margin."

"For the first three years, until we've recouped your investment outlay."

The tension in the conference room was almost palpable.

"This company has been in my family for four generations, Herr Logan. It goes very much against my grain to relinquish control of it."

Devon held her breath as the two men faced each other across the conference table. She saw no trace of the even-tempered client who'd shrugged off the irritations of travel delays and lost luggage in the steely eyed corporate raider who went straight for the jugular.

"You've already lost control, sir."

Hauptmann's ruddy cheeks took on an even darker hue. Devon gulped, hoping he didn't have a stroke as Logan delivered the coup de grace.

"I know you've had a similar offer from one of my competitors, Templeton Systems. I don't know the terms, of course, but I do know Templeton's standard practice is to replace key managers at every level with their own people."

The other executives present shifted uncomfortably in their seats. Logan swept a glance around the table before meeting their boss's gaze again.

"I'm willing to work with you on a restructuring plan that will mesh the skills of your people with any of my own I decide to put in place."

All eyes shifted to Hauptmann. Frowning, he worked his mouth from side to side for several moments.

"How long is this offer on the table?" he asked finally.

"I leave Dresden tomorrow for Berlin to finalize the financial arrangements. Then I plan to make a quick visit to the Airbus production plant in Hamburg before I fly back to the States on Friday. I'll need your answer by then."

"Very well. You shall have it."

Wow! These guys played hardball. Five days to make a multibillion-dollar decision. Devon was impressed.

With a visible effort, Hauptmann shelved his

company's fate and played the gracious host. "What a shame you have only one night in our beautiful city. Our Boys' Choir is giving a special Christmas performance at the opera house tonight. My wife and I would very much like for you to join us for the concert and a late dinner. And your lovely assistant, of course."

Devon fully expected Logan to make a polite excuse. He'd been traveling for twenty-plus hours and had spent the brief respite in her room prepping for this meeting. Surely he wanted to crash.

Or not.

Showing no sign of the fatigue he must be feeling, Logan accepted the invitation.

"Excellent." Hauptmann pumped his hand again and escorted him out of the office. "I'll send a driver to pick you up at your hotel at seven."

Devon waited until they were outside and in the limo to release a long breath. "Whew! That was pretty amazing. My father's an accountant, so I'm used to hearing him throw around numbers. Never any as big as those, though. Do you think Herr Hauptmann will accept your offer?"

"We'll know by Friday."

He was so nonchalant about it. If she hadn't just seen him going in for the kill, she might not have believed all those news articles Sabrina had found on the Web citing his lethal skills as a corporate raider.

"Do you still want to stop at the Christmas market?"

"If we have time."

It was almost four now. They would have to hustle to hit the jam-packed market, select gifts for an assortment of kids, check on Logan's luggage and get him moved into his suite in time to shower and change. Maybe, she thought hopefully, his executive assistant had decided to take the morning off and hadn't responded to Devon's e-mail requesting the names, ages and gift preferences of Logan's nieces and nephews.

No such luck. The response was waiting when she clicked on her iPhone. She scrolled through the list once and was going over it a second time when their limo slowed for the crowded streets of the Old City. Devon caught a glimpse of the market through a narrow alleyway. They could sit in the car while it crawled another quarter mile to the square or cut through the alley and meet the limo on the other side.

"Hier ist gut," she told the driver.

He pulled over to the curb and his passengers climbed out. The sleet had let up a little, thank goodness, but the air was still cold enough to make her teeth ache.

"I'll tell the driver to wait for us by the bridge, Mr.… Er… Cal."

He eyed her coat and the hot pink shawl she draped over her head and wrapped around the lower half of her face. "You sure you'll be warm enough? We can skip the market and go straight back to the hotel."

Devon was tempted to take the out he offered. *Very* tempted. All she had to do was fake one little shiver. But they were out of the limo now, and the market was only a short walk away.

"I'm good if you are."

Nodding, he hiked up the collar of his overcoat and pulled a pair of gloves from his pocket. When they started down the cobblestone alley, he took her elbow with same courtesy he had at the airport.

Devon wasn't sure how such a simple gesture could be so casually polite and so damned disconcerting at the same time. She made a conscious effort not to lean into his warmth as their heels echoed on the ancient stones.

The narrow walk wound around the back of the great cathedral. Thankfully, the cathedral walls blocked most of the wind. The gusts that did whistle through the alley, however, carried tantalizing scents. Devon's nose twitched at the aroma of hot chocolate, apple cider spiced with cinnamon and cloves, freshly baked gingerbread and the sticky sweet cake Dresden was so famous for.

"You'll have to try the stollen," she told her client. "It's a German specialty that's supposed to have originated right here in Dresden."

Sure enough, when they exited the alley and joined the throng in the main square, the first booth they encountered was selling slices of the cake still warm and steaming from the oven.

"When in Rome…"

Taking her at her word, Logan steered her toward the line at the booth.

Not Logan. Cal. Still struggling to make the mental adjustment, Devon dredged her memory bank for details of the treat so popular throughout Germany and Austria.

"The Catholic Church used to forbid the consumption of butter as part of the fasting in preparation for Christmas. Sometime in the sixteenth century, the Elector of Saxony got permission from the Pope for his baker's guild to use butter and milk when baking their Christmas bread. Dresden's stollen became highly prized after that, and every year the baker's guild would march through the streets to present the first, huge loaf to the prince in gratitude."

She could imagine the color and pageantry of that medieval processional, with trumpets sounding and the bakers in all their finery tromping through the snow with their thirty-six pound loaves. The tradition still continued, she knew, only now it was a mega-parade complete with floats, marching bands, a stollen queen and a five-ton loaf!

"Here you go."

Logan—*Cal*—passed her a paper-wrapped slice and a foam cup of something hot and steamy. He retrieved the same for himself before they lucked out and found space at one of the stand-up tables dotting the square.

Devon's first bite more than made up for the cold nipping at her cheeks and nose. Eyes closed in ecstasy, she savored the rich blend of nuts, raisins, candied fruits flavored with spices and brandy and, of course, tablespoons of butter.

The hot chocolate was also spiked, she discovered after the first sip. As a result, she was feeling warm both inside and out when they dumped their trash in a handy container.

"Ready to do some serious stall hopping?" she asked.

"Hang on. You've got powdered sugar on your lip."

He moved closer, and for a startled moment Devon thought he was going to repeat his performance at the airport and kiss away the sugar. Her heart speeded up, and she didn't know whether she was more relieved or disappointed when he tugged off a glove and brushed his thumb along her lip.

Then she looked up and caught the lazy half smile in his eyes. For the most absurd moment, the cold and the crowd seemed to fade away. She held her breath as his thumb made another pass. Warm. Slow. Caressing.

"There." He dropped his arm. "All clear."

With the brandy heating her stomach and his touch searing her skin, the best Devon could manage was a gruff "Thanks."

Sweating a little under her heavy wool coat, she edged her way into the crowd that snaked through lanes of brightly decorated stalls. Thanks to her client's efficient assistant, picking out gifts took little effort.

Four-year-old Andrew got a hand-carved train on wooden tracks. Seven-year old Jason scored a two-foot-tall nutcracker in a smart red coat. For the twins,

Julia and Bethany, Devon recommended denim skirts lavishly trimmed with filigree lace from Plauen. The more studious Janet received a glass globe of the world handblown and painted by a local artisan, while baby Nick got mittens and a stocking cap in a downy yarn that sparkled like spun gold.

Dusk was falling and the strings of lights illuminating the market had popped on by the time Cal and Devon rounded out the purchases with a doll in a fur-trimmed red dress, a wooden puppet and a chess set featuring incredibly detailed Prussian soldiers. Their arms full, they had started for the bridge and the waiting limo when a ripple of eager anticipation raced through the crowd. They turned just in time see the giant fir next to the wooden Christmas pyramid light up.

A chorus of collective ooooohs filled the square. It was followed by the sound of young voices raised in a joyous rendition of "O Tannenbaum."

Second time today, Devon thought. Strangely, though, the song didn't produce quite the same level of cynicism as when she'd heard it blasting through the loudspeakers at the airport.

Maybe because these voices were so young and angelic, or because she still felt the glow from the spiked hot chocolate. Certainly *not* because her lip still tingled from Cal Logan's touch.

"There's the car."

The driver had pulled into a cul-de-sac beside the bridge spanning the Elbe and was sitting with the engine idling. He jumped out to relieve them of their packages, but the magical view drew his passengers to the wall fronting the river's bank. Completely enchanted, Devon leaned both hands on the wall.

The ancient stone bridge spanned the Elbe in a series of graceful arches. Below the bridge, the river was a solid sheet of dark, glistening ice. Atop it, the statues of saints and kings along both sides had acquired a coating of frost that glittered in the glow of the street lamps, while the trees lining both banks were strung with white lights that turned the icy nightscape into a winter wonderland.

"Now that," Devon murmured, "is a sight."

Cal shifted his gaze to his companion's profile. The instant attraction that had prompted him to make a fool of himself at the airport this morning returned with a swift and unexpected kick.

"Yes," he agreed, "it is."

Interesting what a difference a few hours could make, he mused as he leaned an elbow on the cold stone of the wall. He'd arrived in Germany intent on acquiring a subsidiary that would cost him billions but make Logan Aerospace one of the top U.S. players in the European market.

He was still determined to acquire Hauptmann Metal Works. Betting on the outcome, he'd finalize the financial details when he met with his bankers in Berlin tomorrow. But the heat that stirred in his belly as his gaze lingered on Devon McShay was fast convincing him he should acquire her as well.

Three

"Logan kissed you?"

The question shot from Devon's two partners almost simultaneously. She nodded in response, wondering how the world had survived before digital videoconferencing.

"He did."

Her partners' images filled her laptop's split screen. She'd caught Sabrina at home, still flushed and feverish but on the road to recovery. Caroline was at the office. Devon knew without being told she'd been up since dawn and hard at it.

The two women couldn't have been more different. Sabrina Russo came from a privileged background and had partied her way through college.

Caroline Walters was quiet and withdrawn and had worked part-time jobs to earn spending money even during their shared year at the university. At this moment, however, their faces wore almost identical expressions of surprise.

"Logan thought I was you, Sabrina."

"Huh?"

"That was pretty much my reaction, too."

Swiftly, Devon explained about the long-delayed New Year's Eve kiss.

"That sounds like Don Howard." The blonde shook her head in mingled amusement and exasperation. "So how did you handle it?"

"I didn't slug our client on the spot," Devon drawled, "but I came close."

After she'd recovered from her near total meltdown, that is. She couldn't explain the ridiculous reaction to herself, let alone her partners. Nor did she mention the way her nerves tingled every time Logan took her arm. Shelving her completely irrational sensitivity to the man's touch, she ran through the string of disasters that had begun with his long-delayed flight and ended just minutes ago, when she finally moved him into his suite.

"At least I got him to his meeting with Herr Hauptmann on time. Believe it or not," she added with a grimace, "at Cal's request we also squeezed in some post-meeting Christmas shopping."

"Uh-oh."

Instant sympathy filled Caroline's forest green

eyes. She knew how this time of year scratched at Devon's old wounds. Sabrina had zoned in on another aspect of her comment, however.

"Cal?" she echoed.

"He insists we proceed on a first-name basis."

Devon glanced at her bedroom window. She hadn't even had time to draw the drapes before she dashed into the bathroom to freshen her makeup and change. Ordinarily, she would have found the illuminated spires across the river magical. Their coat of glistening ice instilled a less enthusiastic response tonight.

"On the negative side," she told her partners, "there's still no sign of his luggage, and the weather reports are grim. Everything's shutting down. The airport, the trains, the autobahn. We may be stuck in Dresden indefinitely."

"Logan can't hold you responsible for the weather," Caroline protested.

"Or EBS," Sabrina added briskly. Despite the party-girl persona she projected to the rest of the world, she was the partner with the most business sense. Only Devon and Caroline knew the personal hell she'd gone through to gain that knowledge.

"Has he made any noises about being dissatisfied with EBS's services?" she wanted to know.

"No complaints so far. That could change real fast, though. Between getting ready for this concert and dinner tonight and giving you guys an update, I didn't have time to work backup transportation and hotel reservations."

Caroline jumped in, as Devon had hoped she would. "I'll take care of that. We've got Logan's schedule and current itinerary on the computer. I'll work up a list of alternative options and have them waiting for you when you get back from the concert."

"Thanks, Caro. I didn't plan on an evening out."

"Good thing I talked you into packing your long velvet skirt."

That came from Sabrina, who firmly believed appearance and flexibility were as important in their business as organizational skills. All three were getting a real test tonight.

"What are you wearing with it?"

"The gold lamé number you also made me pack."

Devon leaned away from the computer's built-in camera to display the scoop-necked, cap-sleeved top in glittering gold. Lightweight and silky, it could jazz up a suit for an after-five cocktail meeting or provide an elegant stand-alone for an evening function like this.

"Perfect," Sabrina announced. "Now go eat, don't drink and be merry."

"Yes, ma'am."

Cal escorted her to the lobby and the car Herr Hauptmann had sent. His hair was still damp from his shower and the tangy lemon-lime scent of his aftershave teased her senses.

The two-hour concert provided another banquet for her senses. Dresden's opera house had been leveled during World War Two and damaged again when the Elbe flooded its banks in 2002. But huge infusions of funds had restored the theater to its former glory. Pale green walls, magnificent ceiling paintings and the ornate molding on its tiers of boxes made an incredible backdrop for the Dresden Boys' Choir. The ensemble rivaled Vienna's for the purity of the voices. The singers' notes soared high, sounding as though they flew on angels' wings

Dinner afterward was smaller and more intimate but every bit as elegant. Herr Hauptmann had reserved a corner table at Das Caroussel, located in a recently restored Baroque palace. Mindful of Sabrina's parting advice, Devon feasted on braised veal accompanied by a sauerbraten ravioli that made her taste buds want to weep with joy, but limited her alcohol intake to a few sips of a light, fruity Rhine wine.

Madam Hauptmann was a surprise. Vivacious and petite next to her husband's bulk, she spoke flawless English and was delighted to learn Devon had studied in her native Austria. She was also *very* impressed with Cal Logan. As dinner progressed and the waiter refilled her wine glass, Lisel Hauptmann's playful flirtation began to include seemingly accidental touches and sidelong glances her husband failed to note.

Devon noticed them, however. The beauty of the concert and the luxurious restaurant evaporated bit by bit. By the time coffee was served, her dessert of Jerusalem pear and artichoke vinaigrette tasted more like chalk with every bite.

She'd had to endure countless scenes like this during her short-lived marriage to Blake McShay. Tall and trim and salon-tanned, her husband had played his flamboyant good looks and TV-personality role for all they were worth. But only for PR purposes, or so Blake would argue when Devon objected to the way he let women fawn all over him.

To Cal Logan's credit, he appeared completely oblivious to Madam Hauptmann's less-than-subtle signals. That should have won him some brownie points with Devon, but the bad taste stayed with her after the Hauptmanns dropped them off at their hotel. She returned short, noncommittal responses to her client's comments during the walk through the lobby and said even less in the elevator.

The plush, patterned carpet lining the hall muted their footsteps as they approached Cal's suite. He stopped beside the double doors but didn't insert the key. Tapping the key card against his hand, he raked a glance over her face.

"You okay?"

"I'm fine," she lied.

In fact, she was anything but. Watching Lisel Hauptmann's performance had stirred too many nasty memories. All Devon wanted was to crawl between the sheets and let sleep wipe them away. Her client's long day gave her the perfect out.

"But you must be exhausted," she said. "I'll check the weather and call you in a few minutes with our revised itinerary for tomorrow."

"Why don't you bring me a printed copy? We can have a cognac while we go over the details."

"I don't care for cognac."

He cocked a brow at the stiff response. "I'm sure we can fine something else to suit your tastes. See you in a few minutes."

"Fine."

Devon could feel those blue eyes drilling into her back as she marched the few yards to her room and knew she had to get a grip here.

So Cal Logan was too damned hot for his own— or anyone else's—good? So he and this crazy time of year combined to throw her off balance? She'd darn well better get her head on straight before she trotted back to the man's suite.

The e-mail from Caroline didn't help in that regard. Her heart sinking, Devon skimmed the meager contents. European weather experts had already labeled this the ice storm of the century. Many airports had closed until further notice. Trains were running hours behind schedule, if at all. Road conditions were expected to worsen overnight. The experts predicted widespread power outages as trees groaning with the weight of ice cracked and toppled electrical lines.

Caroline's advice was to hunker down right where they were and wait out the storm. With great reluctance, Devon called down to the desk to check on room availability should they have to extend.

"It should not be a problem, madam."

Ha! She'd heard that before.

"If you and Herr Logan cannot depart because of this storm, our other guests most likely cannot arrive. In either case, we will work out suitable arrangements."

Vowing to hold them to that promise, Devon printed the e-mail and headed back down the hall.

"It's not looking good for travel to Berlin tomorrow," she announced when Cal opened the door.

"I heard."

Ushering her inside, he gestured to the plasma TV mounted on the wall. The screen showed a scene of almost eerie beauty. Like slender, long-limbed ballerinas, a row of ice-coated linden trees bowed almost to the ground.

"I caught the tail end of a CNN Europe broadcast. Evidently this front isn't expected to move any time soon. We need to discuss options."

He'd shed his suit coat and loosened his tie. He'd also popped the top buttons of his blue shirt and rolled up the cuffs. As he reached for the doors of the highboy that housed the suite's well-stocked bar, Devon caught the gleam of a thin gold watch on his wrist, all the more noticeable against skin tanned to dark oak.

It was a deep, natural color that couldn't have come from a bottle or the cocoon of a tanning bed. Devon should know. Her ex had spent megabucks on the latter. And those white squint lines at the corners of his eyes weren't the result of peering at spreadsheets. Cal Logan might run a corporation that employed thousands, but he didn't do it exclusively from the confines of a corner office.

"You said you're not a cognac devotee. What would you like?"

The dazzling array of bottles beckoned. She'd been careful to take only a taste of schnapps during the welcome toasts at Herr Hauptmann's office and a few sips of wine at dinner. With her client's trip coming apart at the seams, though, she decided on a shot of something stronger than the diet Sprite she started to ask for.

"Baileys would be good. On the rocks."

"One Baileys coming up."

While he splashed the creamy liqueur into a brandy snifter, Devon took a quick glance around. Since the suite's previous occupant had delayed his checkout, she hadn't been able to inspect it before Cal moved in. She needn't have worried. From what she could see, the King's Suite more than lived up to the hotel's proud claim that royalty had slept here, not to mention presidents, prime ministers and a good number of rock stars.

The luxurious apartment consisted of four rooms, each filled with what looked like priceless antiques. In the sitting room, gas-fed flames flickered in a marble fireplace with a mantel so ornate she guessed it had once graced a prince's palace. The adjacent dining area boasted gilt-edged wainscoting and a chandelier dripping crystal teardrops. Separate bedrooms flanked the two central rooms.

Through the open double doors of one, Devon caught a glimpse of a stunning headboard carved with hunting scenes and topped by a life-size wooden stag's head. Pale gold brocade covered the walls of the second bedroom. Bed curtains in the same shimmering silk were draped from the crown-shaped medallion centered above a magnificent four-poster.

"Wow," Devon murmured. "I've toured castles that weren't as richly appointed."

"Me, too." Cal came to stand beside her. Amusement laced his voice as he surveyed the decadent splendor. "Kind of makes you wonder what went on behind those bed curtains on cold, dark nights like this one."

Devon's back stiffened. She sent him a sharp glance, but there was nothing suggestive in the look he turned her way.

Or was there?

She was still trying to interpret his lazy half smile when he handed her the Baileys and retrieved his snifter of cognac from the marble-topped coffee table. With a ping of crystal on crystal, he tipped his glass to hers.

"Here's to Mother Nature. For better or worse, she's calling the shots."

"For the foreseeable future, anyway."

Devon lifted the snifter to her lips. Her first sip of the cool, creamy liqueur went down like a chocolate milkshake. The second hit with a little more punch.

"I called the front desk," she told Cal as she moved toward the high-backed sofa angled to face the fire. "If necessary, we can hole up here until the storm breaks."

His gaze went to the sitting-room windows. The drapes were drawn back to showcase Old City's illuminated spires and turrets. The sleet blurring the world-famous view gave it an impressionistic, almost surreal, quality.

"Looks like holing up is becoming more necessary by the moment."

Devon had to agree. "I'll call the people you were supposed to meet with in Berlin and Hamburg first thing in the morning and try to reschedule. Do you have any flexibility in when you need to return to the States?"

"I would prefer not to spend Christmas Day in Germany. Or in the air," he added with a wry smile. "As the only non-dad in the family, my sisters usually make me play Santa for my nieces and nephews."

"Beard and all?"

"Beard and all." He sank into the cushions at the other end of the sofa and stretched his feet toward the fire. "I'd hate to miss Christmas with my family and certainly wouldn't want to deprive you of being with yours."

"Not a problem for me."

Evidently Devon's shrug didn't come across as careless as she'd intended. Cal eyes held a question as he regarded her from a few feet away.

"No close family?"

"No brothers or sisters, and my parents divorced when I was a kid," she explained. "It wasn't an amicable parting of the ways."

To say the least. Devon hid a grimace behind a swallow of smooth, chocolaty liqueur.

"They fought over where I'd spend every holiday and vacation. I got so I dreaded school breaks."

"The fighting hasn't let up now that you're an adult?"

"If anything, it's worse. Now they lay the decision on me, along with the guilt. That's one of the reasons I was more than happy to step in and take this trip when Sabrina got hit with the flu."

"What about someone else?" Cal asked casually. "Someone special to catch under the mistletoe?"

Devon squirmed, remembering Blake's proposal under that damned sprig of green. No way she intended to relate the fiasco that had followed. Or her ridiculous, starry-eyed belief she'd finally broken the Christmas curse.

"No one special."

"Good."

"Excuse me?"

"I've been wondering about that since you picked me up at the airport this morning."

Calmly, he set his brandy snifter on the coffee table, reached across the cushions and removed hers from her hand. Devon went from surprised to instantly wary as he laid his arm across the back of the sofa.

"I've also been wondering if that kiss hit you with the same wallop it did me."

Oh, boy! Where had that come from? Hastily, Devon scrambled to get things back on a less personal basis.

"How it hit either of us is completely irrelevant, Mr. Logan."

"Cal."

"This is a business trip, *Mr.* Logan. For me as well as you."

"We took care of business this afternoon. Even hard-charging professionals are entitled to some downtime."

"*You* took care of business this afternoon. I'm still on duty."

His mouth curving, he rendered a snappy salute that reminded her that this sophisticated multibillionaire had once been a lowly private or lieutenant or whatever.

"Now hear this," he intoned. "This is your captain speaking. All hands are officially at liberty."

"It doesn't work like that," she said stubbornly.

"Sure it does. So answer the question, McShay. Did you feel the same kick I did?"

Every shred of common sense Devon possessed shrieked at her to lie like hell. Despite his blithe assurances to the contrary, her gut told her she should *not* mix business and pleasure. Especially with someone like Cal Logan. He was too powerful, too charismatic. Too damned sexy.

On the other hand...

Stop right there! There *was* no other hand. She'd been burned once by a handsome, charismatic charmer. She'd be a fool to stick her hand in the fire again.

"I repeat, Mr. Logan, how it hit either of us is completely irrelevant. I don't intend to—"

She broke off, blinking as the cityscape that had filled the windows behind Cal suddenly went black. Dresden's beautiful spires and turrets disappeared before her eyes. In almost the next second, the luxurious King's Suite plunged into darkness broken only by the flames leaping in the marble fireplace.

Four

"A major substation went down."

Cal hung up the house phone and confirmed what he and Devon already suspected.

"Power is gone to half the city, with more outages being reported as we speak."

The flickering flames from the fireplace painted his face in shades of bronze as he crossed the room. His shadow loomed large against the pale walls.

"The desk clerk says the hotel has a backup generator, but…"

Devon's heart sank. She had a feeling the "but" was a lead-in to something she didn't want to hear. Sure enough, Cal delivered the grim news.

"It provides only enough power for emergency-exit lighting."

Leaving the rest of the hotel in the dark.

"How long do they think the power will be out?"

"They have no idea. They're hoping it'll just be a few hours."

Terrific! What better way to end a day character-ized by more screwups and miscues than she wanted to count? Suddenly weary beyond words, Devon ached to sink into her featherbed and sleep right through this latest disaster.

"I think we should pack it in," she suggested. "There's nothing more we can do tonight."

Cal accompanied her to the door but leaned an elbow against the ornate molding. "Actually, there is. You could answer my question. Did you feel the same punch I did?"

As if she was going to admit he'd rocked her back on her heels at the airport this morning!

"I don't intend to answer it," she said primly.

"Coward."

The soft taunt held as much amusement as specu-lation. Devon responded to both with a lift of her chin.

"The kiss was a mistake. Or more correctly, a case of mistaken identity. Your friend asked you deliver it to someone he no doubt described as a good-time girl."

Which Sabrina Russo most definitely had been. Only Devon and Caroline knew how hard their friend had to work now to maintain her laughing, efferves-cent facade.

"In case you haven't noticed," Devon said coolly, "I'm not that woman."

"Trust me, I've noticed."

This far from the fire, the room was in deep shadow. She couldn't read Cal's expression, but the amusement was still there, lacing his deep voice.

"So here's the deal," he said. "I'm thinking we should try it again."

"What?"

"No mistakes or mistaken identities. Just you and me this time. We'll test the waters, see if we experience the same punch."

Devon gave an exasperated huff. Despite her every effort to maintain a businesslike attitude, her client wasn't going to let go of that ridiculous incident at the airport unless and until she killed it stone-cold dead.

Assuming she could. With him leaning over her, his features a contrast of light and dark, she had the mortifying suspicion she could lose herself in Cal Logan's arms.

The mere thought tightened the muscles low in her belly. For a dangerous moment, she indulged the fantasy of popping the rest of his shirt buttons. Sliding her palms over the contours of his chest. Locking her arms around the strong column of his neck.

Summoning every ounce of willpower she possessed, Devon wrapped her hand around the gilt-trimmed latch and yanked the door open.

"Good night, *Mr.* Logan."

* * *

Cal let her go. He'd heard the rusty edge of exhaustion layered under the irritation in her voice. She had to feel almost as whipped as he did.

He knew damned well his tiredness would have evaporated on the spot if she'd taken him up on his challenge. But would hers? His rapidly evolving plans for Devon McShay didn't include a sleepy, halfhearted seduction. He wanted her wide awake, her breath coming in short gasps, her body eager and straining against his.

Cal scraped a hand across his chin, trying to remember the last time a woman had roused this kind of hunger in him, this fast. From the first glimpse, Devon had stirred his interest. From the first taste, she'd dominated his thoughts. All during the meeting with Hauptmann, Cal had had to work to keep his attention on the acquisition details and off the woman sitting next to him.

He was damned if he understood why. Even with Alexis—beautiful, sensual, avaricious Alexis—a part of him had always remained detached. And more than a little cynical. He'd known from day one that the glamorous blonde had been more attracted to his millions than to him.

Yet prickly, stubborn Devon, who insisted on maintaining a professional distance, had Cal plotting all kinds of devious ways to get her in his bed. He had several in mind as he crossed the darkened room, intending to toss down the rest of his cognac before he hit the sheets. A sharp rap brought him back to the door.

When he opened it, his pulse spiked. Devon stood in the hall. For a wild moment, Cal was sure she'd come back to conduct the experiment he'd suggested.

"The key to my room doesn't work."

So much for his misguided hopes, he thought wryly.

"I used the house phone to call the front desk. They think the sudden power outage sent a jolt through the computer that electronically resets the hotel's door locks."

The only lighting came via the red emergency-exit signs. It was more than enough for Cal to note her thoroughly disgusted expression.

"Until they get the computer back online, not even security or housekeeping can let me in. So I thought... Since you have two bedrooms... Maybe we could..."

"Share?"

"Yes."

"Sure. Come in."

He stood aside, careful to keep his expression neutral as she swept by him. She was clearly upset by this latest turn of events. That didn't stop him from feeling a whole lot like the big bad wolf when Red Riding Hood appeared with her basket of goodies.

She halted in the sitting room, her slender figure silhouetted against the glow from the fireplace. "Which bedroom are you using?"

He gestured to the one on the right. "I went for the stag's head instead of the crown."

"Okay." She hesitated. "Well, uh, I guess I'll turn in."

He had to fight a grin. He shouldn't be enjoying her predicament so much. "'Night, Devon. I'll see you in the morning."

"Good night."

He waited to see if she'd tack on another *Mr.* Logan. She didn't.

When the door closed behind her, a fierce satisfaction gripped Cal. He was halfway home. He had Devon here, in his lair. That was progress enough for tonight.

Or so he thought.

An hour later he was forced to admit he'd made a serious error in judgment. With the electric heat out, the room temperatures had gone down like the *Titanic*. The thick comforter provided sufficient protection against the cold, but all Cal could think of was how much warmer he'd be with Devon curled up beside him. The fact that she slept less than a dozen yards away kept him awake and aching long into the cold, dark night.

Devon woke to sunlight so bright and dazzling she had to put up an arm to shield her eyes. Squinting through her elbow, she saw she'd neglected to draw the pale gold brocade drapes. No surprise there. She'd whacked a shin on a chair leg and bumped into the dresser while stumbling around in the inky blackness last night.

Still squinting, she lowered her arm. That's when she discovered that dazzling sunlight didn't necessarily equate to warmth. The elegant bedroom was as cold as the inside of an Eskimo's toolshed. Each breath brought icy air slicing into her lungs. It came out a second later on a cloud of steamy vapor.

Gasping, Devon dragged the covers up to her nose. Obviously, the hotel's power was still out. She knew zero about substations and transformers and such, but suspected the city that had gone dark right before her eyes last night was probably still powerless.

So where did that leave her? More to the point, where did it leave her client? Until she had a fix on the situation, she wouldn't know how to handle it.

She huddled under the covers, trying to work up the nerve to make a dash for the bathroom. The mere thought of planting her bare feet on the icy bathroom tiles kept her burrowed in.

"Devon?"

Her startled gaze flew to the door. "Yes?"

"You decent?"

"I… Uh…" She scrunched down until only her eyes showed above the fluffy comforter. "Yes."

The door opened and a man she almost didn't recognize entered the room. The cashmere overcoat and hand-tailored suit were gone. So was the boardroom executive.

This Cal Logan looked more like a cross-country Nordic skier. He wore a cream-colored turtleneck and bright blue ski jacket with the collar turned up.

Matching ski pants emphasized his muscular thighs. The pants were tucked into microfiber boots cuffed by thick thermal socks Devon would have killed for at that moment.

Luckily, she didn't have to resort to murder. Cal carried a shopping bag across the room and dumped it on her bed.

"Good thing the hotel caters to the winter sports crowd. I had the manager open the ski shop. I figured we'd both need some cold-weather gear if the power stays off for more than a day or two."

"A day or two?" Gulping, Devon tugged the covers down a few inches. "Surely they'll restore it before that."

"Maybe, maybe not. The manager said at least two-thirds of the city and most of the surrounding countryside have been affected. And it's still happening. Lines are coming down right and left."

Her gaze went to the uncurtained windows. The suite was on the sixth floor, too high up to afford more than a glimpse of the ice-coated trees lining the Elbe. From what Devon could see of them, however, most had bent almost to the ground under the unrelenting weight of the ice.

"I had to guess at your size." Cal's blue eyes skimmed down the covers and back up again. "If anything doesn't fit, I'll take it down and exchange it."

"Thanks. Er, I don't suppose you were able to scrounge some hot coffee along with the ski clothes."

"Sorry. The hotel kitchen is temporarily out of operation. The staff was scrambling to put together a cold breakfast for the guests, though." He headed for the door. "We'll go down as soon as you're dressed."

Devon dove into the shopping bag and extracted a thick pair of socks. Only after her toes were encased in thermal warmth did she grab the bag handles and make a run for the bathroom.

The toilet seat almost gave her freezer burn. The icy stream that gushed from the water taps made washing her hands and face a challenge of epic proportions. Thankfully the hotel's amenities included spare toothbrushes and a complimentary tube of toothpaste. Shivering and hopping from foot to foot, she brushed away the overnight fuzz, then shimmied into black-silk long johns so thin and sheer she wondered how the heck they could retain any heat. Her bikini briefs showed clearly through the almost-transparent silk. So did her demi-bra.

A V-necked sweater in pale lavender went on over the thermal silk undershirt. The ski pants and jacket were a darker shade of amethyst trimmed with silver racing stripes. Cal, bless him, had thought to include gloves and a headband in the same rich purple.

Ears, fingers and toes all warm and toasty, she zipped on a pair of microfiber boots and left the bathroom with a last glance at the woman in the mirror. She could use some lip gloss and a hairbrush. Hopefully, the hotel's computer whizzes would figure out some way to operate the door locks so she could get back into her own room soon. If not, she'd have to conduct another raid on the downstairs shops.

After she got some coffee in her. Preferably hot, although she'd take an injection of caffeine however she could get it right now. And food. Any kind of food. With her body's basic need for warmth satisfied, her stomach was starting to send out distress signals.

Cal stood by the sitting-room windows, taking in the frozen cityscape across the Elbe. Devon's breath caught as she went to stand beside him. Buildings, trees, the statues on the bridge, the river itself…everything as far as the eye could see lay under a blanket of glistening white. Not a single car or bus or snowplow moved through the frozen stillness, although a few brave pedestrians were making their careful way across the bridge into the Old City.

"The manager didn't exaggerate," Devon murmured, awestruck. "Looks like most of the city must be shut down."

"Looks like." He didn't sound particularly concerned as he turned and skimmed a glance over her new uniform. "How does everything fit?"

"The boots are a little loose, but you did good otherwise. Very good, actually."

The comment was more of a question than an endorsement. Logan responded with one of his quicksilver grins.

"That's what comes of having four younger sisters. We'll exchange the boots downstairs."

"We don't need to exchange them. I'll fill the space with another pair of socks."

"You sure?"

"I'm sure."

"You'd better bring your purse with you," he advised. "With the electronic locks on the fritz, we can get out but the keys won't get us back in. We'll have to leave the door propped open."

There went her lip gloss and hairbrush.

"What about your laptop and briefcase?" she asked. "Are you just going to leave them?"

"I took them downstairs earlier. They're secured behind the desk."

"We might need them to work your revised schedule if I can't get to mine."

"I think we'd better shelve any idea of work until we know the extent of the storm."

"But—"

"No buts. I'm declaring today an official holiday. All set?"

Since she didn't appear to have much choice in the matter, Devon stuffed the little evening bag she'd taken to dinner last night inside a jacket pocket and pressed the Velcro flap closed. This, she predicted silently as she and Cal descended six flights of cold, dank stairs, was going to be a looooong day.

Long, she amended some ten hours later, and inexplicably, incredibly magical.

Looking back, she saw that she and Cal had shed

their respective roles with their business suits. No longer travel consultant and client, they became co-conspirators in a determined effort to beat the cold.

Their first act was to down a surprisingly lavish breakfast. With a fervent murmur of thanks, Devon accepted a mug of the hot cocoa the hotel staff had brewed over a can of Sterno. The rich, frothy chocolate paved the way for a cold buffet of cheeses, fruits, yogurt, smoked salmon and thick slabs of Black Forest ham. Smoked over pine and coated with beef blood to give it a distinctive black exterior, the moist ham tasted like heaven slapped between two slices of pumpernickel cut from a wheel-size loaf.

After breakfast Cal insisted they don knitted ski masks and get some exercise. Devon had her doubts when the ice crusting the snow broke under her weight and she sank to her ankles. To her relief, the water-resistant microfiber boots kept her feet dry. What's more, the depressions provided just the traction she and Cal needed to join the other hardy souls who'd ventured out into the winter wonderland.

They'd gone only a few yards when what sounded like a rifle shot split the air. Instinctively, Devon hunched her shoulders and grabbed Cal's arm. He stopped her before she could drag them both facedown in the snow.

"It's just a tree cracking under the ice. Look, there it goes."

She followed his pointing finger to one of the graceful lindens lining the Elbe's banks. It was bent almost double, its branches sweeping the frozen earth. As Devon watched, the trunk groaned and split right down the middle. One half crashed to the ground. The other stood mutilated, a wounded sentinel silhouetted against the blue sky.

"Oh, how sad."

"Even sadder when you think how many other trees have split like that and brought down power lines." Cal shook his head. "Crews will have to clear tons of debris before they can repair the lines."

Keeping her arm tucked in his, he steered clear of any trees that might crack and come down on them. They made it as far as the bridge and were thinking of turning back when a lone snowplow cleared a path across the ancient stone spans.

Cal and Devon followed in its wake, as did dozens of others. They were drawn by the unmistakable tang of burning charcoal and the yeasty, tantalizing scent of fresh-baked stollen.

They followed their twitching noses to Dresden's oldest bakery. Only a block off the main square, Der Kavalier had already drawn a crowd of resilient natives and tourists determined to make the best of the situation.

Munching on the sweet, spicy bread baked in a wood-fired brick oven, they wandered down the Long Walk. The columned promenade had been erected in the sixteenth century to connect Dresden's castle with the building that had once housed the royal stables. The history buff in Devon felt compelled to point out the incredibly detailed, hundred-yard-long frieze depicting a progression of Saxon kings and nobles.

"Those are Meissen tiles. All twenty-four thousand of them. The originals were fired in the porcelain factory just a few kilometers from Dresden. Most of them had to be replaced after World War Two."

Cal dutifully admired the frieze and pumped her for more information on the city's colorful history. He did it so skillfully that Devon ran out of narration before he ran out of patience.

By then it was well past noon. They stumbled on a tiny restaurant tucked away on a side street with a kitchen powered by a loud, thumping generator. It took a thirty-minute wait but they finally feasted on steaming bowls of potato soup and black bread. Stuffed, they strolled back across the bridge only to find a wide swath of frozen river fronting their hotel had been cleared to provide space for an impromptu winter carnival.

Vendors roasted chestnuts and sizzling shish kebabs over charcoal braziers. A one-legged man muffled to the ears in scarves and a lopsided top hat cranked a hand organ. Skaters glided arm in arm to his wheezy beat. Several enterprising youngsters had overturned a wooden box and offered to rent their family's skates for the princely sum of two euros.

Over Devon's laughing protests, Cal plunked down the requisite fee. He wedged his feet into a pair of hockey skates at least one size too small and selected a pair of scuffed figure skates for Devon. When he went down on one knee to tie the laces, she made a last attempt at sanity.

"I haven't been skating since I was a kid."

"Me, either." Pushing to his feet, he dusted the snow off his knees. "Ready?"

"As ready as I'll ever be," she muttered.

He gave her a few moments to test her wobbly ankles. The next thing Devon knew, strong, steady hands gripped her waist and propelled her across the ice.

One of those hands was nestled at the small of her back when they finally returned to the hotel a little after five-thirty.

The kitchen staff had pooled its collective ingenuity to prepare another remarkable meal for the guests. Mostly cold meats and salads, with a few hot selections cooked over cans of Sterno. Spicy goulash filled the air with the tang of paprika, while bubbling cheese fondue hinted at the dry white wine and kirsch that had gone into it. For dessert, the guests were offered a choice of prefrozen Black Forest Cake and Bananas Foster flamed at the tableside.

Devon's taste buds were still sighing in ecstasy over the combination of rum and cinnamon in the flambéed bananas when she and Cal went upstairs.

They'd already been advised the electronic key-card system was still inoperable. Maintenance offered to force the lock on Devon's door, but Cal suggested she give the system another couple of hours to come online. Meanwhile, she could warm her toes in front of the fire in his suite.

When they entered the King's Suite, the rooms were as dark and as cold as a witch's tomb, yet Devon felt as though she'd come home. She couldn't believe how much she'd enjoyed her day in the bracing fresh air. Almost as much as she hated for it to end.

She could have blamed that bone-deep reluctance for what happened next. Or the hot, spiced wine she'd guzzled after skating. Or the alcohol spiking the cheese fondue and Bananas Foster.

She didn't resort to any of those excuses, however. All she had to do was look into Cal's eyes to know the day they'd just spent was merely a prelude for the night to come.

Five

After a day filled with dazzling sunlight, the night brought darkness, isolation and a swift escalation of the sexual tension that had been building between Devon and her client since their first meeting.

An intense awareness of his every move nipped at her nerves as he adjusted the gas fire. Housekeeping had been in sometime during the day and set it to burn low and steady. Cal soon had the flames leaping higher, shedding some light but little warmth beyond a radius of a few feet.

He solved that problem by dragging the heavy sofa closer to the fireplace. While he angled the sofa to catch the maximum heat, Devon lit the candles the hotel had provided its guests, along with extra blankets and a complimentary bottle of schnapps.

The schnapps she left on the sideboard but the extra blankets and two plump pillows came with her when she joined Cal on the sofa. Draping one of the blankets around her shoulders, she eyed a cordless phone nesting in its cradle on a nearby table.

"Do you think the house phones still work? I really should call my office and let them know what's happening. Or rather, not happening."

Her cell phone was in the purse stuffed in the pocket of her ski jacket. Unfortunately, she hadn't charged it before leaving for dinner last night and the freezing temperatures today had drained what little was left of the battery. Cal's mobile phone had taken a similar cold-weather hit. Between the weak signals and the saturated airways caused by so many land-lines going down, he hadn't been able to place any calls, either.

"You can give it a try," he replied, "but the cradle charger requires electricity. I'm guessing it's dead, too."

He guessed right.

They might have been alone in the universe. No TV blaring the latest financial news. No music to disturb the stillness. No phones or laptops to connect them with the rest of the world. Just the two of them. Together. With hours of quiet isolation ahead.

"This is so weird," Devon muttered, hiking the blanket up around her ears. "I never realized how much we depend on electricity. Heat, light, cooked

food, hot water, every form of communication…
They're all gone or severely restricted."

"Makes you appreciate the things we take for
granted every day," Cal agreed.

Kicking off his boots, he stretched his stocking
feet to the fire. Devon admired his seemingly philo-
sophical acceptance of the situation even as she
worried about its impact on his business. And hers.

"You told Herr Hauptmann you need to finalize
arrangements with your bankers in Berlin before
you fly back to the States on Friday. That's three
days from now. What if we're still stranded here in
Dresden, without any way to communicate with
the banks?"

"With this much money on the line, the banks will
be more than happy to work with me."

"So you were bluffing to force his hand?"

"I was taking a calculated risk. As you heard at the
meeting yesterday, Templeton Systems also made
Hauptmann an offer, but they haven't locked in the
financing yet. I want this deal signed, sealed and delivered before they do."

She blew out a silent whistle. She'd left that meeting
convinced the banks had Logan's back to the wall.

"Remind me not to get into any high-stakes poker
games with you."

His rich chuckle carried across the crackle and spit
of the gas-fed flames. "And here I was thinking a
little five-card stud might be one way to pass the
time tonight. Guess we'll have to resort to Plan B."

"Which is?"

"We talk politics. We try to guess each other's favorite movies. We wrap up in these blankets and share our body heat. We have wild, uninhibited sex."

Her jaw dropped.

"We don't have to follow that precise order," he informed her solemnly. "We could start with the sex and work our way backward."

The sheer audacity of it took her breath away. Then she saw the laughter glinting in his blue eyes, and her lungs squeezed again. Despite the wicked glint, she knew he wasn't kidding.

More to the point, she knew darn well she wanted what he was offering. Devon didn't even try to deny it. The mere thought of stretching out beside him, of feeling his body press hers into the cushions, had her heart ping-ponging against her ribs.

"What do you think, McShay?" He reached across the back of the sofa. Burrowing under the blanket draped over her shoulders, he curled a palm around her nape. "Are you up for Plan B?"

She swiped her tongue over suddenly dry lips. Her fast-disintegrating common sense shrieked at her to end this dalliance, right here, right now.

Because that's all it was. All it could be. She'd fallen for a stud like Cal Logan once and still had the scars to show for it. No way she was going to set herself up for another tumble.

So don't.

The blunt admonition came compliments of her

alter ego. The one with shivers rippling down her spine from the slow stroke of his thumb on her nape.

Have some fun, dummy. Enjoy a mind-blowing orgasm or two. Then you and Logan can go your separate ways, no harm, no foul.

Since every hormone in Devon's body was screaming at her to agree, she wet her lips again.

"I, uh, think we should start with a modified Plan B."

His thumb stilled. The gaze that had been locked on her mouth lifted to hers.

"I'm listening."

"We conduct the experiment you suggested last night. See what happens. Take it a step at a time from there."

A slow grin spread across his face. Devon's alter ego was whooping with joy even before he agreed to her proposed modification.

"Sounds good to me."

His hand tightened on her nape and tugged her closer. In the flickering light of the fire, his face was like a painting by one of the old Flemish masters, all strong planes and intriguing shadows. Then Devon's lids drifted shut, his mouth came down on hers and all thoughts of old masters, Flemish or otherwise, flew out of her head.

This kiss was slower than yesterday's. More deliberate. Despite that—or maybe because of it—the sensual movement of his lips over hers packed even more of a wallop. Devon angled her head to give him better access before surrendering to the urge she'd been battling since her first glimpse of the man shirtless.

Tugging down the zipper on his ski jacket, she flattened her palms against the broad expanse of his chest. She could feel his pecs under his turtleneck, and the jackhammer beat of his heart.

Or was that her heart pounding like a rock drummer on steroids? At this point, Devon wasn't sure and didn't particularly care. All she knew was that her other self almost wept when Cal broke the contact and lifted his head.

To her profound relief, his breath came as hard and fast as hers. The hand at the back of her neck held her steady. His eyes burned into hers.

"Well? What's the verdict? Do we progress to the next step?"

"Yes!"

She flung her arms around his neck, shedding the blanket draped over her shoulders along with any and all remaining doubts.

Cal made a sound halfway between a growl and a grunt of fierce satisfaction. His free hand tunneled under her hips. With one quick maneuver, he had her flat on her back.

His mouth was harder now, more demanding, but Devon's hunger matched his. She locked her arms around his neck and strained against him. Hip to hip, mouth to mouth, they explored the feel, the taste, the texture of each other.

He didn't ask for permission to progress to step

three. Probably because Devon was already there. Fighting free of her ski jacket, she relieved him of his, then yanked up the hem of his turtleneck and silky thermal shirt. Her hands were hot and greedy as she planed them over his back and waist and the hard, taut curve of his butt.

He wasted no time in following suit. Her lavender sweater and black silk long-john top came up and over her head with a couple of swift tugs. Her boots hit the floor next. With a speed that left her breathless, Cal peeled off her ski pants and long-john bottoms.

His hot, hungry gaze roamed from her breasts to her belly. The flesh mounded so enticingly by her black lace demi-bra brought an appreciative growl, but the matching thong stopped him cold.

"Were you wearing that thong under your dress when we went to dinner with the Hauptmanns?"

"Yes."

"And you slept it in last night?"

"Since I couldn't get back in my room, I didn't have anything else to sleep in."

"Good thing I didn't know that," he said, his voice rough, "or you wouldn't have made it out of bed this morning."

That drew a husky laugh from Devon. She wasn't any more immune to flattery than the next girl, and the expression in Cal's eyes as they devoured her nearly naked flesh was *extremely* gratifying. It almost made up for the goose bumps popping out all over her skin.

Her ensuing shiver could have been caused by the

cold air. Or the liquid fire that spread through her when he got rid of his own ski pants and long johns. Or the erection that pushed against the front of his shorts.

Her groan of dismay, however, was most definitely due to the latter. Cal's startled look prompted another groan from her, this one of embarrassment.

"I didn't mean… It's not you… Well, it is but…" As flustered now as she was aroused, she blurted out the problem. "Oh, hell! I don't have a condom. I hope you do."

"No, I don't." His lips twisted in a rueful grin. "I don't usually pack a supply for short business trips."

Unlike her ex, Devon couldn't help remembering. Blake had never left home without an emergency stash.

"I could make a quick trip down to the lobby," Cal commented. "Or…"

"Or what?"

The wicked glint returned. "We could improvise."

Devon's pulse stuttered and skipped. Oooh, boy! She was asking for trouble if the mere thought of taking him in her mouth could turn her on and her common sense off.

"You want to improvise first?" Her voice husky, she rose up on her knees and pressed her palm against his rock-hard erection. "Or shall I?"

His breath hissed out. That was all the answer she needed.

"Me," she murmured, sliding her hand inside his shorts. "I'll go first."

With a small grunt, he reached for the blanket,

whipped it around them both and followed her back down onto the sofa cushions.

They were cocooned in darkness and a heat fueled by desire. Devon used her hands and teeth and tongue, licking him, teasing him, driving him almost to the brink.

His salty taste was on her lips when she felt his body go taut. The engorged shaft in her hand seemed to pulse and swell even more. She bent her head, intending to finish what she'd started. Cal stopped her by the simple expedient of pulling free of her hold.

"Not yet," he rasped. "Not until I have my turn."

With the blanket still tented around them, he rolled her onto her back and inched downward. Slowly. As Devon had moments ago—or was it hours?—he used his hand and teeth and tongue on her eager flesh. Her nipples ached when he finished with them. Her belly quivered under his nipping kisses.

Then he spread her legs and found her hot, wet center. Once again he moved slowly. So slowly. His tongue rasped her sensitive flesh. His fingers worked sensual magic. Soon waves of exquisite sensation streaked through every part of Devon's body.

She could feel the climax coming. She tried to delay it, fought to contain the spiraling tension. She might as well have tried to contain the snow and sleet that had stranded them. Despite her determined efforts, her vaginal muscles coiled tight, then tighter still. Her head went back. A groan ripped from far back in her throat. Giving up the fight, she rode the burst of blinding pleasure.

For the second day in a row, Devon woke to dazzling sunlight. Only this time she wasn't lying in a bed topped by a majestic crown. Nor was she swathed like a mummy in a warm, insulating duvet. This time the warmth emanated from the very large, very heavy body squashing her against sofa cushions.

She lay on her side, she discovered when her sleepy haze cleared. Her back was tucked against Cal's front, with her knees bent and her bottom cradled on his thighs. Sometime during the night they'd both dragged on their thermal silk long johns. After her second earth-shattering orgasm, Devon thought lazily. As memories of the night just past came rushing back, her mouth curved into a smile. The little huff that escaped her lips was part sigh, part mewl of remembered pleasure.

As soft as it was, the sound produced a rumble in the solid wall of chest pressed against her back.

"'Bout time you woke up, Cinderella."

The blanket covering them rustled. Calloused fingertips brushed the tangled hair from Devon's cheek. Prickly whiskers rasped against her cheek as Cal scrunched around to nibble on her earlobe.

"Or was it that Snow White chick who slept for a thousand years?" he muttered between bites.

Laughing, she hunched a shoulder against the invasion of his hot, damp breath in her ear. "Someone with nine nieces and nephews should know that was Princess Aurora, aka Sleeping Beauty. And it was a hundred years, not a thousand."

"Yeah, well, Disney lost me after I had to watch a talking teapot and candlestick do their thing a half-dozen times one long, agonizing weekend."

With a final nibble, he disengaged and departed the sofa. A blast of cold air hit Devon's fanny before he tucked the blanket around her again. Only then did it register that the hotel's electricity must still be out.

"I waited for you to wake up before mounting a scouting expedition," Cal said. "Stay here and keep warm. I'll go downstairs and see if I can scrounge up some hot coffee or chocolate."

She rolled over and watched while he gathered his ski jacket, pants and boots. His cream-colored silk long johns fit him like a second skin, which made the watching a delight. As Devon's gaze roamed his broad, tapered back and trim backside, her delight ripened to a feeling of intense, almost physical, pleasure.

The front view was even more arousing. The cool, in-command executive looked more like a rough-and-tumble hockey player. His short black hair stood up in spikes. The whiskers that had rasped Devon's skin showed dark against his cheeks and chin. The spandex ski pants molded his muscular thighs, while the half-zipped jacket showed the strong column of his throat.

"Don't move," he ordered, dropping a kiss on the tip of her nose. "I'll be right back."

She fully intended to follow his instructions and remain huddled under the blanket until he returned. Unfortunately, the bathroom beckoned with increasing urgency. Dreading the prospect of another session on the icy toilet seat, Devon held off as long as she could. Nature finally conquered the cold. Shivering, she shoved her feet into her boots and dragged on her ski jacket, then sprinted for the bathroom.

When she went to wash her hands and face, the woman looking back at her from mirror gave a small shriek. Her hair was a bird's nest of dark, tangled red. Her face was devoid of all color. Except, she noted ruefully, for the whisker burn on the side of her chin. She leaned forward and fingered the tiny abrasion, then dismissed it with a shrug.

What the heck. It was small enough price to pay for the mind-bending pleasure Cal had given her last night.

See, her alter ego smirked. *What did I tell you? Is the man hung, or what?*

"No arguments there," Devon muttered.

And if the electricity doesn't come back on, you and El Stud can spend another night or two between the sheets before you go your separate ways, no harm, no foul.

"No harm," she echoed, frowning at the face in the mirror, "no foul." Somehow that didn't sound as bracing as it had last night.

Oh, come on! Don't get all hung up here. One night does not a commitment make. For you or for him.

Okay, okay! She wasn't going all gooey over the guy. Well, maybe a little, but not enough to do anything too stupid. Like fall in love with him.

She almost had herself convinced when the bathroom lights blinked on. A half second or so later, the plasma TV in the other room came to life.

"Hallelujah!"

Whooping, Devon happy-danced through the bedroom and into the sitting room. She had no idea how long it would take for the heat to kick in, but relief had to come soon. And hot water! She could shower. She could wash and blow-dry her hair. She could—

The jangle of the house phone interrupted her joyous list making. Thinking it was Cal calling from the lobby, she snatched up the receiver.

"Hello?"

A surprised huff was her only response. Maybe it was a repairman, testing the lines without expecting an answer. Someone who didn't speak English. Swiftly, Devon switched to German.

"Hallo? Ist jemand da?"

"I'm sorry. They must have put me through to the wrong suite." The voice was female, the accent decidedly American. "I'm trying to reach Cal Logan."

"This is Mr. Logan's suite."

That produced a sharp silence, followed by an even sharper query. "Who is this?"

Uh-oh. Obviously the caller hadn't expected another woman to answer Cal's phone. Then again, Devon hadn't expected to be here at this early hour of the morning answering it. Scrambling to recover, she infused her reply with crisp professionalism.

"This is Devon McShay. I'm Mr. Logan's travel consultant."

"Is that what they're calling it these days?"

The sneering comment had Devon gritting her teeth. "May I ask whom I'm speaking to?"

"Alexis St. Germaine." The reply was as glacial as the ice coating the trees outside. "Mr. Logan's fiancée."

Six

Cal balanced a cardboard tray in one hand and inserted a new key card into his suite's door lock. With the hotel's electricity restored, the computer that controlled the locks was back in operation.

Cal had mixed emotions about the return to full power. He could certainly use a hot shower and a shave, but he wouldn't have minded being left in the dark with Devon McShay for another night or two or three.

Just thinking about how he'd left her, wrapped in that blanket with her hair a tangled cloud of red and her brown eyes sleepy, got him rock hard. Which explained why he'd raided the sundries section of the lobby gift shop for condoms. With or without electricity, his plans for Devon included several more sessions under the blankets.

"The hunter returns," he announced to the woman standing beside the sofa, her arms folded across the front of her ski jacket. "We have coffee. We have fresh, crusty rolls. We have butter and strawberry jam."

She didn't leap on the hot coffee. That was his first clue something was wrong.

"We also have electricity," he said, commenting on the obvious.

"So I noticed," she said stiffly. "I'll go downstairs, retrieve a key for my room and get out of your hair."

When she started for the door, Cal deposited the tray on a side table and stopped her. "Whoa! What's going on here, Devon?"

"Nothing."

The look she flashed him said exactly the opposite. Baffled, he couldn't figure out what had caused her transformation from sleepy and sexy to ice maiden.

"Something was definitely going on last night." He tried to coax a smile out of her. "I was kind of hoping for more improvising this morning."

"I'm sure you were."

The swift retort shot up his brows. She saw his reaction and offered a strained apology.

"I'm sorry. That was uncalled for. What happened last night was as much my fault as yours."

"Fault?"

Well, Christ! Talk about being slow on the uptake.

He was dealing with a major case of morning-after regrets here.

"It was a crazy situation." She refused to meet his eyes. "The cold… The dark…"

"Funny," Cal said, attempting to smooth away the regrets, "I remember more heat than cold."

Instead of the smile he'd hoped for, all he got was a lift of her chin and a barbed reply.

"We had some fun while the lights were out, Mr. Logan. Let's leave it at that. Now it's back to business for both of us."

"The hell you say." He was starting to get pissed. "When you know me better, Devon, you'll discover I don't turn it on and off that easily."

"Don't you?" Disdain and something very close to disgust darkened her eyes. "Oh, before I forget, your fiancée called a few minutes ago. She heard about the ice storm on the news. She's been worried about you and wants you to call her back as soon as possible."

"That's interesting," Cal said, his eyes narrowing, "since I don't happen to have a fiancée."

"You'd better inform her of that. Now if you'll excuse me, Mr. Logan, I'll leave you to make your calls and go make mine." Her chin came up another notch. "Assuming you still want EBS to work your travel arrangements, that is."

The realization that she thought he was the kind of slime who would sleep with one woman while engaged to another pissed Cal even more.

"Yes, *Ms*. McShay, I do."

"Fine. I'll work the revised itinerary and get back with you."

This wasn't over between them, Cal vowed as she made for the door. Not by a long shot. He'd make that clear shortly. First, he had to deal with Alexis.

His temper simmering, he had the phone in hand almost before the door snapped shut behind Devon. He punched in the country code for the U.S., followed by the number of the Park Avenue apartment he'd leased for Alexis St. Germaine some months ago.

"It's Cal," he bit out when she answered.

"Darling! I've been so worried about you. The news has been running the most awful stories of derailed trains and fifty-car pileups all across Europe."

The husky contralto brought back instant memories of the first time Cal had heard it. He'd been dragged to one of his sisters' charity soirees. It was a crowded, noisy affair, but Alexis St. Germaine had turned the head of every male in the room.

Cal had walked off with the prize, although even then he'd suspected the stunning blonde was more interested in his bank balance than in him. After a particularly energetic tussle, he'd teased her about it. Alexis had laughed and admitted she had extravagantly expensive tastes and always made it a point to marry well. She'd also admitted she'd lined Cal up in her sights as husband number three the moment he'd walked into the charity ball.

For several months, he'd almost convinced

himself they might make a go of it. Alexis was smart, sophisticated and the center of attention at every party. Only gradually did Cal realize his fiancée craved an audience like a junkie craved a fix. After an endless round of cocktail hours, dinners at expensive watering holes and pre- and post-theater gatherings, he'd called it quits.

He'd insisted she keep the four-carat solitaire and arranged to transfer the Park Avenue apartment into her name, but Alexis wanted more. She hadn't come right out and threatened a breach-of-promise suit, but just last week her lawyer had dropped a hint that Cal might want to consider a reconciliation.

"I called your office," she told him. "When they said they hadn't heard from you, I envisioned you in the hospital or trapped in train wreckage somewhere."

"I'm fine."

"I know. Now. Your, ah, travel planner assured me you'd both survived the storm."

The casual comment contained a question Cal had no intention of answering.

"I miss you, darling. When are you coming home?"

"What do you want, Alexis?"

He knew damned well there was more to her call than concern for a stranded ex-fiancé. Sure enough, her husky laugh came over the line.

"You know me so well. We really should try again. Why don't we get together for the holidays?"

"I don't think so. You'll be partying, and I've got a deal to close."

"What company are you trying to buy now?"

"One you've never heard of."

"Well, don't spend all your billions on it, darling. I went a little crazy at Bergdorf's the last few weeks we were together. The bill arrived in the mail yesterday."

So that was it. Cal's mouth curved in a sardonic grin.

"Send it to my office. I'll take care of it."

"I knew you would," she purred.

"Consider this a Christmas present, Alexis. And just so we're clear, this is the last 'gift' from me until you nail husband number three. That will certainly merit a wedding present."

The unsubtle warning produced another rippling laugh.

"Don't count yourself out of the running yet."

"Idiot!"

Devon stalked across the lobby, still kicking herself for the conversation in Cal's suite.

She'd handled it all wrong. She'd intended to play it cool, not brittle and bitchy. So he was engaged? Or not, depending on who she listened to. So he cheated on the woman who still obviously loved him? That was his problem. His, and Alexis St. Germaine's.

There was no reason Devon should feel like The Other Woman. But she did, dammit. She did!

As she skirted the giant Christmas tree by the front desk, all she could think of was that awful evening she'd walked into her husband's office and found him getting hot and heavy with a giggling

Santa. Only this time, she was the getter and Cal was the gettee.

God! How stupid could one person be!

"Devon McShay," she told the desk clerk. "I need a new key for my room."

"Right away, Ms. McShay." The young woman was muffled to her ears in a heavy coat and wool scarf and obviously relieved to have the power back on. "It's good, yes? To have the lights and the computers again?"

"It is."

"And the tree," she added, nodding to the giant fir dripping handcrafted ornaments and silver garlands. "What is Christmas without colored lights?"

Devon returned an inarticulate response and pocketed the key. She'd hoped this trip would keep her less-than-joyful memories of the holiday season at bay. Instead, she'd have a whole new set to add to the grab bag.

"Idiot," she muttered again.

The hotel's heating system was starting to chase away the chill when she let herself into her rooms. Her junior executive suite was a fourth the size of Cal's palatial arrangement. Yet after the tumult of the past two days and nights, Devon reveled in the privacy and having access to her own things.

Shrugging out of the lavender ski jacket, she made a beeline for the bathroom. Her number-one priority was a shower. Cautiously, she tested the water. It was gloriously, deliriously hot.

"Thank God!"

Stripping, she adjusted the oversize showerhead to full force and stepped into the glass cubicle. The stinging jets needled into her skin. She stood with her face upturned for long moments, letting the punishing stream pour over her, before lathering up and washing away the sticky residue of the night spent in Cal's arms.

Scrubbed, shampooed and near scalded, she wrapped a towel around her head and one of the hotel's plush terry-cloth robes around her tingling body. The superfast heating coil Europeans used to boil water produced an almost instantaneous mug of coffee. Sipping the life-restoring brew, Devon padded to the desk and flipped up her laptop.

Number-two priority was reworking Cal Logan's itinerary. The sooner she got him to Berlin and Hamburg and on that flight back to the States, the sooner she could put this whole sorry episode behind her.

The screen came to life, and the e-mail icon that popped up indicated forty-three incoming messages. At least half were from her partners, she saw as she scrolled through them. Sabrina and Caroline had both become increasingly worried about how Devon was faring through the storm and blackouts affecting most of Western Europe.

She zinged off responses that her partners wouldn't read for some hours yet. It was still the middle of the night back in the States. Sabrina and

Caroline were both sawing z's. Unlike Ms. St. Germaine, who'd stayed up until the wee hours trying to reach Cal.

Fingers flying, Devon searched the Internet for status reports on the travel situation in and around Germany. Her pulse leaped when she saw the high-speed trains between Dresden and Berlin were once again up and running.

The train station was only a few blocks away. If the streets had been plowed and sanded, they could get a taxi and catch the eleven-fifteen express. A quick call to the front desk assured her a few hardy taxi drivers had braved the weather and were parked outside. She booked the last two first-class seats on the express and was about to call the Berlin hotel to make sure they still had rooms when a sharp rap on her door interrupted her feverish activities.

Devon squinted through the peephole and bit back a curse. She wasn't prepared for Cal yet. Not with her hair wrapped in a towel turban and the rest of her naked under the terry-cloth robe. For a cowardly moment, she was tempted to ignore his knock.

Oh, hell! She had to face the man sooner or later. Might as well get it over with. Summoning a cool, businesslike smile, she unhooked the chain and opened the door.

"Good timing. I was just about to call you with an update."

She could hardly brief him in the hall, but the mere thought of inviting him inside ratcheted up her stress level. He'd showered and changed, too. His black hair gleamed with dampness. Above the open collar of the blue dress shirt she'd purchased in the gift shop, his face was clean-shaven. Recalling the red mark left by his raspy whiskers, Devon clutched the collar of her robe with one hand and gestured him inside with the other.

"I've booked us on the eleven-fifteen express train for Berlin. I'll confirm our hotel reservations for tonight and we'll be good to go."

"Not quite. We need to clear the air first."

"You're right. We do." Dragging in a deep breath, Devon took the lead. "I apologize. Again. I had no right to get all huffy with you earlier. We're both adults. Last night was…"

Incredible. Mind-boggling. The wildest sex she'd ever experienced.

"…fun," she finished, wincing inside at the total ridiculousness of the adjective. "You may not believe this after our, uh, activities, but I'm not usually into one-night stands."

Her stiff little speech stirred his temper. She could see it in his eyes, hear it in his drawled retort.

"You may not believe this, but I'm not, either."

She scrubbed the heel of her hand across her forehead. He wasn't exactly making this easy, dammit.

"Look, whatever arrangement you have with Ms. St. Germaine is between you and her. I'd just rather not be part of it. I had enough of that sort of thing with my ex."

Hell! She hadn't meant to let that out. Her brief marriage and its sordid demise were no one's business but hers.

She could see her slip had registered with Cal, though. His expression lost a little of its hard edge as he hooked his thumbs in the pockets of his pants.

"First, Alexis St. Germaine and I are not engaged. We were, but we called it off before I left on this trip."

"The woman must be delusional, then. She seems to think you're still a twosome."

"She's not delusional, but she is extravagant. I paid the bills she ran up when we *were* a twosome. She just got a few more in she needed help with."

Devon bit her lip. Evidently Cal hadn't scored any better in his choice of a mate than she had.

"Second," he continued, his gaze drilling into her, "the last word I'd use to describe our activities last night is 'fun.'"

That brought her chin up. "Really? Then how would you describe them, Mr. Logan?"

"How about the start of something that could lead us down any number of paths, *Ms*. McShay?"

She rubbed her forehead again and tried to sort through her jumbled emotions. Her lascivious alter ego was jumping for joy over the fact that Cal was not, in fact, engaged. Her other, more rational self was every bit as relieved but far more cautious.

"About last night being the start of something," she said finally. "I'm not sure this is the right time for either of us. You've just ended a relationship."

More or less. Ms. St. Germaine obviously still needed convincing.

"And my partners and I are just getting our new business off the ground," she said doggedly. "With you, I might add, as our first major client."

"I don't see a problem."

"Then you're a lot better at compartmentalizing than I am," she retorted. "I'm having some trouble shifting back and forth between Cal Logan the client and Cal Logan the stud."

"That last bit is a compliment, right?"

His hopeful look drew a huff of reluctant laughter from Devon. "Mostly."

"Good. You had me worried there for a moment."

He was doing it again, she realized. Using humor to bypass her doubts and undermine her resolve. Her laughter fading, Devon pressed her point.

"The very fact that you weren't sure if it was a compliment only emphasizes how little we know each other."

"What do you want to know?" He leaned his hips against the back of the sofa and crossed his arms. "Ask me anything. Age. Weight. Shoe size. Whether I prefer sausage or pepperoni on my pizza."

"I'm serious, Cal."

"So am I. Ask away."

"Much as I would like to take you up on your offer, I have to remind you we're booked on the eleven-fifteen express to Berlin. I still need to confirm our hotel rooms and get packed. And," she added, her mind clicking on the tasks ahead, "I need to take the gifts you bought for your nieces and nephews down to the business office for packing and FedExing. And see what's happening with your lost luggage. And call for a taxi. And get us checked out."

And blow-dry her hair.

And put on some makeup.

And scramble into some clothes.

With a small rush of panic, Devon had a sudden mental image of the silver bullet express pulling out of the station while she ran after it, screaming at the damned thing to wait.

"Okay," Cal conceded. "We'll table this discussion for the time being."

She heaved a sigh of relief as he shoved away from the sofa.

"You work the phones and pack," he instructed, shifting into executive-decision mode. "I'll take the kids' stuff down to the business office, get us checked out of the hotel and have the front desk call a taxi."

He shot back his cuff, checked his watch and whistled. "Can you be ready in a half hour?"

Like she had a choice? "I can."

He crossed to the door and yanked it open, then paused.

"By the way, the correct answers are thirty-one, one-eighty, size ten and pepperoni." His grin came out, quick and slashing. "And just for the record, I don't consider getting to know you better and getting you into bed again to be mutually exclusive."

Seven

They made it to the train station with exactly twenty minutes to spare.

Miracle of miracles, Cal's leather carryall and suit bag had been delivered and were waiting at the front desk when he went down to check out. He'd managed a quick change into a fresh suit, a crisp white shirt and a red tie for the three-hour trip to Berlin. Devon had scrambled into her stacked-heel boots, gray wool slacks, an off-white turtleneck and her heavy winter coat. The hot pink pashmina fluttered behind her like a cape as she and Cal jumped out of the cab and hit the crowded station.

Stranded travelers thronged the ticket booths, all anxious to get to their chosen destinations for Christmas after the horrendous delays caused by the storm. Since Devon had booked their tickets online and printed them at the hotel's business center, she and Cal didn't have to fight the crowds at the booths. There was another logjam at the gate, but they got through it just as the two-minute departure warning sounded.

The high-speed bullet train hummed on its track, as eager as a thoroughbred at the starting gate. Cal slung his suit bag over his shoulder and shifted his carryall and briefcase to one hand so he could relieve Devon of her roller bag while she made a dash for the first-class coaches. With his longer legs, he kept up with her easily.

Mere seconds after they jumped aboard, a final warning sounded and the doors glided shut. Devon led the way to their reserved seats and flopped down, breathless.

"We made it!"

"So we did," Cal said as the train started to move.

He stashed their bags in the overhead compartment and swiveled his airline-style seat around to face hers. They had a small table between them and, when the train pulled out of the station, a bird's-eye view of Dresden's Old City through the wide windows.

The spires and turrets rose above the frozen River Elbe, a sparkling, ice-coated panorama Devon knew she would never forget. She propped her chin on her hands and drank in the view until apartment buildings obscured it. Sighing, she swung around to face Cal.

"Quite a city," he commented, shrugging out of his overcoat. "If this deal with Hauptmann Metal Works goes through, I'll have to make several return trips." The skin at the corners of his eyes crinkled. "Think you can work it so we don't get buried under ice next time?"

Devon didn't know which pronoun carried more interesting implications. The "you" that indicated he wanted EBS to handle his future trips to Germany or the "we" that suggested she would be traveling with him.

"I'll do my best to skirt the ice," she replied. "You didn't have a message from Hauptmann waiting on your cell phone?"

"No, but I didn't expect one. If it were me, I'd wait until the last minute and try to work some extra concessions in terms of salary adjustments and stock options."

He helped Devon out of her coat and hung it alongside his on the hooks attached to their seats. The train was picking up speed now and zipping through the city's outskirts. The urban sprawl soon fell away, giving passengers glimpses of the fascinating blend of culture and history that had prompted UNESCO to declare this strip of the Elbe river valley a World Heritage Site.

Elegant eighteenth- and nineteenth-century suburban villas with terraced gardens and elaborate facades perched atop the riverbanks. Ironwork bridges from the dawn of the Industrial Revolution spanned the frozen Elbe at several crossings. Small towns and villages dotted the landscape. From the distance, the stucco and half-timbered farmhouses appeared much as they must have in previous centuries.

"Hungry?"

The question drew her gaze from the rolling countryside. They'd missed breakfast in the rush, or at least Devon had. Cal may have feasted on the crusty rolls and strawberry jam he'd brought up to the suite before she'd marched out in a huff.

"I'm starving," she admitted, "but they won't start serving lunch in the club car until noon."

"That's only twenty minutes from now. Hang tight. I'll scrounge a couple of menus. We can check 'em over while we wait."

He headed for the door to the next car, moving with an easy grace that accommodated for the swaying motion of the train. Devon wasn't the only one who followed his progress. Several people looked up as he passed. The men's glances soon returned to their newspapers. The women's tended to linger several seconds longer.

With good reason, Devon admitted ruefully. His suit had obviously been tailored by a master. The red silk tie had probably cost more than her entire outfit. It wasn't just the clothes that snagged those lingering glances, however. It was the way he wore them, the way he carried himself. That air of unmistakable self-confidence and power turned most women on, big time. Devon included.

Hey, she told her sniggering other self. *I'm only human.*

The problem now was what to do about the contradictory emotions Cal Logan roused in her. In the flurry of frantic, last-minute activities, she hadn't had time to process what he'd told her about his fiancée. Make that ex-fiancée.

Nor had she let herself think about the zinger he'd tossed out just before he'd left her hotel room. That bit about getting to know her and getting her into bed again not being mutually exclusive now jumped to front and center in her mind. It was still there when Cal returned with the menus, two cups of hot chocolate and two slices of stollen.

"First seating in the club car is all booked up. I reserved a table for the second seating. I figured this would tide us over until then."

They attacked the sticky-sweet Christmas bread and hot chocolate with equal fervor. Devon was savoring her last bite when Cal stretched out his legs and regarded her across the littered table.

"So tell me about this jerk you were married to."

She threw him a startled glance. "Did I say he was a jerk?"

"I extrapolated. So tell me."

Sighing, she fiddled with her fork. "There's not much to tell. We met, we married, we discovered we had different interpretations of monogamy. I thought it meant one mate for life. Blake thought it meant one wife but lots of mating on the side."

She stabbed at the crumbs on her plate. Even now, she kicked herself for not picking up on the signs sooner.

"How long were you married?"

"Less than a year." Her mouth twisted. "We got engaged on Christmas Eve and flew to Vegas for a quick wedding three weeks later. The following Christmas Eve I walked into the television station where he works and found him, uh, exchanging gifts with the station manager."

"Male or female?"

"Female," she said with a small laugh. "Thank goodness! My ego took a bad-enough bruising as it was."

As soon as the words were out, Devon realized their truth. She'd been hurt and furiously angry, but looking back she could see her pride had been dinged as much as her heart.

"Is that when you decided to go into business with Sabrina Russo?"

"No, I hung around Dallas for a few years. The idea of starting EBS didn't come up until Sabrina and Caroline—our other partner—and I got together for our annual reunion last spring. The three of us were roommates in college," she explained. "Only for one year. At the University of Salzburg, as part of a study abroad program."

"Salzburg, huh? That must have been an incredible experience."

"It was!"

Devon jumped on the change of subject.

"The whole time we kept thinking we'd landed smack in the middle of a remake of *The Sound of Music*. When we walked to classes each morning, we went past the convent featured in the movie. I swear to goodness, you could hear the nuns chanting on their way to Mass."

Smiling, she shared her memories of that year in the fairy-tale Austrian city.

"I was a history major, so I dragged my poor roommates to every castle and museum in or around the city. Caroline's an opera buff. She made sure we didn't miss a performance at the Salzburg Opera House. Sabrina, on the other hand, got us personally acquainted with most of the city's *Biergartens* and *Ratskellers.*"

Cal chuckled. "Brown Eyes, also known as the good-time girl. That's how my pal, Don Howard, described her. Guess the shoe fits."

"It did then," Devon admitted, bristling a little in defense of her friend. "Sabrina's changed. All three of us have. That's why we decided to start EBS. We needed to refocus our lives and couldn't think of a better way to do it than by combining our resources and the experience we gained while living abroad."

"I hope the combination works for you."

"Why wouldn't it?"

"You said your dad's an accountant. I'm sure he's told you that in any partnership, someone always ends up having to make the tough financial decisions. I'll bet he's seen a lot of friendships sacrificed to the bottom line. I certainly have."

"You won't see these."

"I'll take your word for it," he said easily. "Now to the important stuff. What do you like on your pizza?"

* * *

By the time the train pulled into Berlin's new glass-and-steel megastation, Devon knew she was dangerously close to falling for Cal Logan, and falling hard.

He was so damned easy to be with. He'd entertained her for a good part of the journey with stories about his various sisters and brothers-in-law and their numerous progeny. She'd reciprocated by telling him a little more about her parents and their still-stormy relationship years after the divorce. Yet even as she and Cal lingered over dessert and coffee in the luxuriously appointed club car, swapping family histories, the physical hunger the man roused in her increased with every shared laugh, every seemingly casual touch.

There was nothing the least casual about the protective arm he put around her shoulders as they wove through the jostling crowds inside the station, however. Or the possessive hand he nestled against the small of her back to steer her toward the rank of taxis. She'd intended to call from the train and order a limo, but Cal nixed the idea since their hotel was only a few blocks from the station.

As soon as the cab pulled away from the terminal, the hustle and bustle of Germany's vibrant capital enveloped them. Devon knew from news reports that the ice storm hadn't hit Berlin as hard as it had Dresden. She saw the truth of that in the traffic and pedestrians clogging the sanded streets and sidewalks.

Unlike Dresden, which had been restored to its earlier glory after the devastation of World War Two and the bleak years of Communist domination, a new city had risen from the ruins of Berlin. The ultramodern skyscrapers of Pottsdamer Platz dominated the skyline. The Sony Center's towering, circus-tent–like dome of glass and steel sparkled in the bright afternoon sun. Windows in the pricey shops and department stores lining Friedrichstrasse showcased designer boots and bags and clothing—all displayed against backdrops of silver snowflakes or green-and-red Christmas paraphernalia, of course.

Devon tried not to let the crass commercialism dampen her pleasure at returning to a city brimming with history and world class museums. And even she caught her breath at the hundreds of live poinsettias lining the magnificent staircase leading up to the lobby of their hotel. More poinsettias were tiered to form a thirty-foot-high Christmas tree in the center of the lobby.

"We'll have to hustle," Cal warned after they'd checked in and hit the elevators.

He'd called ahead to set up a late afternoon meeting with his contacts in Berlin. That barely left them time to dump their bags and freshen up.

"I'll meet you in the lobby in fifteen minutes," Devon promised.

Her room was on the eighth floor, his suite on the tenth. When the elevator door pinged open, she grabbed her roller bag and started to exit. Cal held the door with a bent arm, but blocked her way. A crooked grin tugged at his mouth as he resumed his stated campaign to get her into bed again.

"Sure you don't want to share a room? We did pretty well the last two nights."

Oh, yeah, she wanted to share! After those hours on the train, with the easy conversation and comfortable camaraderie, Devon had advanced *her* stated goal of getting to know Cal better. So much better, the mere thought of kissing that smiling mouth and exploring the hard, muscled body under the hand-tailored suit made her throat go dry.

"We're down to fourteen minutes and counting," she said a little breathlessly. "How about we make that decision when we get back?"

Cal's grin when he dropped his arm and stepped back into the elevator told her the decision was already made.

The grin stayed with Devon as she hurried down the hall to her room. Once inside, she flung her suitcase onto a luggage rack and dropped her briefcase onto the desk before dashing to the bathroom. Hair combed, face scrubbed and makeup reapplied, she had time for one quick call and a voice mail for her partners on her way out.

"In Berlin. Off to a meeting with Logan. More later."

Much more later, she thought as she hurried back down the hall. The question of just how much had her pulse pounding and anticipation singing along her veins.

* * *

The taxi delivered Devon and Cal to the Daimler-Chrysler Center, a mini-city of towering high-rises interconnected by walkways, parks, shops and restaurants. Although it was barely four-thirty in the afternoon, the tall buildings crowded out the sun and threw deep shadows across the plaza. To counter the early evening gloom, white lights blinked everywhere—in leafless tree branches, in shop windows, in restaurants. Her arm tucked in Cal's, Devon hurried through the tunnel of lights toward the skyscraper housing the German headquarters of Bancq Internationale.

As he had at the meeting with Herr Hauptmann, Cal included her in the session with the financial advisors. Devon might as well have remained in the outer offices while the half-dozen men and three razor-sharp women hammered out the details of the proposed acquisition. They threw out so many numbers and terms like minority equity stakes and venture capital line of credit she was soon lost.

The meeting lasted for several hours. It was a working session, with suit jackets discarded, ties loosened and sleeves rolled up. Although Devon was more of an observer than a participant, she felt as whipped as the other men and women at the table when Cal finally called a halt.

"We've got the basic structuring down. I'll e-mail these figures to my people so they can go over them tonight. We'll make any necessary adjustments when we get together again tomorrow afternoon. By then," he added as he unrolled his sleeves and shrugged into his suit coat, "I should have heard one way or another from Herr Hauptmann."

Since they hadn't been sure when they would arrive in Berlin, Cal had already declined an offer of dinner and an evening on the town with the firm's senior executives. That, too, was rescheduled for tomorrow.

"Leaving us free tonight," he murmured provocatively to Devon as the elevators whisked them down to the plaza.

Like she needed reminding!

The sudden spike in her pulse erased the mind-numbing effects of three-plus hours of financial analyses. She could feel her heart thumping against her ribs when she and Cal emerged into a night that had come alive with big-city vibrancy.

Diners were jammed elbow-to-elbow in the pubs and restaurants, while last-minute Christmas shoppers packed the pricey boutiques. Carolers in Victorian-era costumes occupied a raised platform in center plaza. Their voices amplified by speakers, they sang of shepherds keeping watch over their flocks and wise men traversing great distances.

For the first time in more Christmases than she could remember, Devon found herself actually enjoying the carolers and the crowds. Much of that, she admitted silently, had to do with the man at her side.

Okay, all of it. The eagerness she'd felt as a young child, before her parents' acrimonious fights had turned the holidays into a war zone, didn't come *close* to the anticipation now zinging through her veins.

She had no idea where this…this association with Cal Logan might lead. As he'd said, it could take them down any number of paths. Or it could end in Hamburg, when they boarded their separate flights back to the States.

But that wouldn't happen until Friday morning. They still had two full days, and two nights, together. She was reminding herself of that fact when Cal stopped and sniffed the air.

"I smell tomatoes and garlic and…"

"Pepperoni," she finished, laughing. "Why do I have the impression pizza is your favorite food group?"

"Maybe because it is. I pretty much lived on junk food when I was a teenager. After I joined the Marines, I'd slop up my SOS and try like hell to convince myself it was hot, crusty pizza."

"What's SOS?"

"You don't want to know." He tugged on her arm. "Come with me, woman. I think it's only fair I wine and dine you before I have my way with you."

She had to protest, if only for form's sake. "I thought we deferred that decision."

"You deferred, I decided."

That sent Devon's simmering anticipation to a near boil. She felt its heat as they made for the lively, crowded Italian restaurant across the plaza. They were shown to a table after only a short wait. By then their imminent return to the hotel so dominated her thoughts she was amazed she could get down a single slice, never mind the three Cal insisted on heaping onto her plate.

He was just as generous with the wine. It was a rich, full-bodied Dornfelder that more than held its own against the spicy pizza sauce. Although by no means a wine connoisseur, Devon had spent enough time in Germany to know the hybrid red Dornfelder grape was grown mostly in the Rheinhessen and Pfalz regions, but was gaining in popularity throughout the country.

With good reason, she decided when she and Cal returned to their hotel. The buzz was mild on its own, but potent as hell when combined with the heat that roared through her the minute the elevator door swished shut and Cal backed her against the rear wall.

Eight

"People get arrested for this sort of thing," Devon panted.

"Only if they get caught."

Her back was to the mirrored elevator wall. Her mouth was greedy under Cal's. Her breath coming in eager gasps, she popped the buttons on his overcoat and burrowed under the layers.

She'd tried to put the brakes on. Tried to rein in her hunger for this man. Now the walls had come down and she didn't even think about holding back. The taste of him, the feel and the scent him, torched every one of her senses.

She didn't feel the elevator slow, but Cal did, thank God. He disengaged a half second before the doors slid open. Devon had a good idea what she must look like, though, with her lip gloss smeared, her cheeks flushed and her hair tumbling free of its clip. Still, she managed a smile and a nod for the elderly couple that stepped into the elevator.

"Guten abend."

The silver-haired woman returned the greeting. Her husband glanced from Cal to Devon and back again. Cal returned his knowing smile with a bland one of his own, yet his unbuttoned coat and lopsided tie told its own tale.

A moment later the elevator glided to a stop on Devon's floor. Mere moments after that, the door to her room slammed shut and she and Cal were tearing at each other's clothes.

Mouths hot, hands impatient, they left a trail of outer garments from the door to the bed. Cal kept an arm banded around Devon's waist as he yanked down the duvet, then took her with him to the satiny-smooth cotton sheets.

The first time they'd made love had been in the cold and dark. Huddled under a tented blanket, Devon had explored with her hands and mouth and tongue. This time she intended to feast on the sight of the powerful body pressing her into the mattress.

Attacking his shirt buttons, she dragged it free of his pants. Her palms felt the heat as she moved them over his chest, his shoulders. The tight, bunched muscles set her heart hammering against her ribs. She could almost feel the endorphins shooting into her bloodstream as the muscles low in her belly clenched.

With an impatience that matched Devon's, Cal stripped off the rest of his clothes and went to work on hers. Her boots hit the floor with a thud. Her wool slacks and turtleneck followed a moment later.

"Well, damn!"

The low exclamation brought Devon up on one elbow. "What's the matter? Oh, no!" Groaning, she answered her own question. "Please don't tell me we're condomless again."

"No, I laid in a good supply."

"Then what…?"

"I didn't think anything could turn me on more than that black thong and bra you were wearing the other night." His grin came out, quick and delighted. "I was wrong."

Shifting her under him, he slid a palm inside the waistband of her lacy hipsters. Her stomach hollowed under his touch, and every nerve in her body snapped to attention when he slowly tugged them down. Her bra went next. Then he was all over her, teasing, tormenting.

He used his tongue and teeth to bring her nipples to tight, aching peaks. The heel of his hand cupped her mound. His thumb pressed her hot flesh, and his fingers…his fingers worked sheer magic!

Eager to give as good as she got, Devon wrapped her hand around the erection poking at her hip. It filled her palm, hot flesh over hard steel, and made her crazy to feel it fill the rest of her.

"Now," she panted. "Now is a good time to find that supply you mentioned."

Grinning, Cal thrust off the bed and snagged his slacks. Devon was wet and ready and impatient as hell as he ripped open a condom. When he repositioned himself between her thighs, she hooked her legs around his calves and took him into her body.

It wasn't until the next morning that she realized she'd also taken him into her heart.

Sometime during the night, Cal had kicked down the last of her protective barriers. Maybe during their second supercharged session, when she'd straddled his hips and ridden him to an orgasm that ranked right up at the top of her all-time-great list. Or just before dawn, when he'd nudged her awake and made slow, lazy love to her.

Whenever it had happened, Devon felt happily, ridiculously content as Cal leaned over her and dropped a kiss on her cheek.

"I'm going up to my room to shower and change."

"Mmmm."

"You sleep in for a while. I'll take your key and bring you breakfast in bed."

Devon snuggled for a little while longer before realizing she couldn't lie there and wait for him all sticky and fuzzy from sleep. She dragged to the bathroom, turned on the shower and leaned against the glass stall. Eyes closed, she let the jets pelt life into her boneless body. With the tingling came memories of the night just past and a silly, goofy grin.

Watch it, kiddo. You were just supposed to have some fun.

She'd definitely had that!

Remember what happened the last time you fell for a charmer like Logan.

This was different. *Cal* was different.

You met him all of...what? Three days ago? How do you know he's different?

She knew. She wasn't sure how she knew, but she knew. Or so she told herself as she cut off the pesky thoughts along with the shower jets.

She emerged from the bathroom sometime later dressed and ready to face the day. Her first order of business was to update her partners. It was well past one in the morning back in the States, so Devon flipped up the lid of her laptop, intending to type out a detailed e-mail. To her surprise, she saw that Sabrina and Caroline were online and conducting a video chat. Quickly, she keyed in her password and joined the session.

"Hi, guys. Why are you both up so late?"

"We're talking business."

Sabrina's face filled one half of the laptop's screen. Her long blond hair was pulled back in a scrunchie, and her eyes were bright. Not with fever, Devon was relieved to learn, but with excitement.

"We got a new contract this afternoon," Sabrina

related. "A big one, but it's another quick turnaround. Caroline and I have been working the prelims."

"Who's the client?"

"Global Security, International. From what we've uncovered so far, the company started out as a band of mercenaries hired to provide personal protection for top Iraqi government officials. It's since evolved into one of the largest—and most lethal—security agencies in operation around the globe."

Devon was as anxious as her partners for their fledgling company to succeed, but she wasn't particularly thrilled at the idea of donning a helmet and flak vest.

"They don't want us to work their travel and provide escort service in and out of Iraq, do they?"

"No, thank goodness. We've been tasked to scout out locations and finalize arrangements for an off-site gathering of their key personnel in late January or early February."

"They specified Italy or Spain," Caroline put in. "Something close to the ocean. We're thinking the Amalfi Coast south of Naples as one possibility, Barcelona or the Costa Brava as the other."

Devon thought fast. She was supposed to fly back to the States on Friday, the same day Cal departed. She could change her reservations and travel by way of Naples or Barcelona or both.

The click of the door lock distracted her momentarily. She glanced over her shoulder, waved to Cal and turned back to the screen.

"Do you want me stay over in Europe?" she asked

her partners. "I could fly from Germany to Italy, scout out possible locations for this conference and hit Spain on the way home."

"Oh, Dev." Caroline's forest green eyes filled with sympathy. "I know how this time of year scratches at old scars, but you don't want to spend Christmas shuttling between countries. Come home and spend it with us."

"Sorry." The deep voice came from just over Devon's left shoulder. "As it turns out, I'm going to require EBS's services longer than originally anticipated. If Devon agrees, she'll be spending Christmas with me."

Startled expressions crossed the two faces on the split screen.

"That's Cal," Devon explained.

She could feel her cheeks heating and was fumbling for an explanation for his presence in her bedroom this early in the morning when he bent down. The camera in her laptop's lid merged his face with hers.

"Hello, ladies."

Caroline merely nodded in response to this unexpected intrusion into their business, but Sabrina gave a low, gurgling laugh.

"So you're Don's buddy. Thanks for delivering the long overdue—if completely misdirected—kiss."

"It was my pleasure."

His warm breath stirred the hairs at Devon's temple and sent little shivers rippling down her spine.

"I'd better go," she told her partners. "I'll send

you an e-mail with this potential change in our client's schedule."

Signing off, she slewed around in her chair. "As soon as said client tells me what it is," she added pointedly.

He leaned forward and planted his hands on the arms of her chair. Caged, she looked up into blue eyes blazing with the satisfaction of a hunter who's just bagged his prey.

"I had a message from Herr Hauptmann when I checked my calls a little while ago. He's agreed to my terms for the buyout."

"Cal! That's great! Congratulations."

He tugged her out of the chair for a celebratory kiss. Devon gave it joyously. After sitting in on the meetings in Dresden and here in Berlin, she almost felt part of the Logan Aerospace team herself.

"Hauptmann wants to set up another meeting to sign the necessary paperwork and work the final details of the merger. We agreed on the first week in January. I thought I'd bring my key staff over then to tour the plant and confer with their counterparts."

"So you want EBS to work your travel arrangements?"

"I want EBS to work my *staff's* travel arrangements. I've decided to stay in Europe over the holidays. I'm hoping you'll stay with me."

"But… But… You said you always spend Christmas with your family. All those nieces and nephews. What happened to playing Santa?"

His mouth curved. "You happened."

Her heart stuttered, stopped and started again with a painful thump.

"I've been to almost every major city in Europe," he added, tucking a stray curl behind her ear, "except Salzburg. After listening to you describe it yesterday, I thought we might spend Christmas there."

Beautiful, magical Salzburg. In midwinter, when it was dressed in snowy white. With Cal Logan. Devon melted into a puddle of want on the spot.

Cal's smile widened as he read the answer in her face. "We could fly down to Austria after the meeting in Hamburg tomorrow. Think you can work the travel arrangements and a hotel room on short notice?"

She noted his suggestion of a single room even as her head whirled with yet another change in plans. All they had on the schedule today was a second meeting with the finance people this afternoon and dinner with the firm's senior execs tonight. She had until then to work the arrangements.

"You go play with your numbers." Waving a hand, she shooed him away. "I'll hit the computer."

Devon zinged off a quick e-mail to her partners detailing the latest developments. The rest of the morning she was on her laptop, arranging the trip to Salzburg and laying the initial groundwork for a meeting between Cal's key staff and that of Hauptmann Iron Works.

The mood was jubilant when she and Cal met

with his financial wizards that afternoon, and the thrill of victory imbued the air during dinner at one of Berlin's finest restaurants.

The same high spilled over to a more private and *much* more erotic celebration when Devon and Cal returned to the hotel. Seemingly inexhaustible, he took her to the edge of the precipice three or four times before intense, unstoppable pleasure finally drove her over.

They left Berlin early the next morning for Hamburg, Germany's second-largest city. It was only a few hours away by high-speed train. Called the Venice of the North, the city was situated on the wide mouth of the Elbe. The river that meandered across Germany and provided such a scenic setting in Dresden provided Hamburg with direct access to the North Sea. As a result, it had been a rich sea-trading center and leading member of the Hanseatic League as early as the Middle Ages.

Cal's sole purpose for the visit was to tour the massive Airbus production facility located on the banks of the Elbe. Logan Aerospace had several contracts for navigational aids used in the aircraft. In addition, Cal wanted to see firsthand the extent of Hauptmann Metal Works contracts. Devon had arranged for a limo to meet them at the train station and deliver them directly to the Airbus plant.

The tour ran longer than expected. During lunch in the executive dining room, the plant manager offered Cal the opportunity to meet with the engineers responsible for integrating all navigational aids. That might have presented a problem if Cal hadn't canceled his plans to fly back to the States that afternoon as originally scheduled. Luckily, Devon had reserved seats on an early evening flight to Salzburg.

She wasn't too thrilled at the idea of another four or five hours at the Airbus production facility, however. The discussion had veered into techno-speak well beyond her comprehension and had deadened her initial awe.

Cal must have noticed the way her eyes glazed over at the prospect of spending the rest of the day listening to him talk product specifications and redesign. When they finished lunch, he asked for the use of an office to make some calls. Devon used the time to make a few of her own. Their respective business taken care of, he offered her an escape.

"You don't need to hang around here all afternoon. Why don't you take the limo and go downtown? Since you'll be staying in Europe several weeks longer than planned, I'm sure you need to pick up a few things."

More than a few! She could use hotel laundry and dry-cleaning services for the outfits she'd brought with her, but two pants suits, four tops, one long skirt and the skiwear Cal had purchased in Dresden weren't going to hack it for an extended stay.

She almost salivated at the thought of hitting Hamburg's famous Mönckeberg Strasse. The Mö, as the natives liked to call their favorite shopping street, rivaled New York's Fifth Avenue and Beverly Hills' Rodeo Drive for high-end boutiques and ultra-elegant department stores.

She'd been a backpacking student traveling on a Eurorail Pass and a limited budget during her only other visit to Hamburg. She still couldn't afford to shop the designer boutiques, but she *could* do some serious damage in the department stores.

She was happily making a mental list when Cal reached into his suit pocket for his wallet and extracted several bills.

"This should cover what you need. If not, just give me a call and I'll authorize a line of credit."

As Devon stared at the bills, her little bubble of anticipation fizzled and went as flat as two-day-old champagne. Only yesterday he'd told her about picking up the tab for his extravagant former fiancée. Now he was offering to do the same for her.

"That's…" She swiped her tongue over suddenly dry lips. "That's very generous, but I don't need you to pay for my personal necessities." She lifted her gaze to his. "Or anything else."

He looked at her blankly for a moment. Then his brows snapped together. "Christ, Devon. I hope to hell you're not implying what I think you are."

When she didn't answer, his eyes went cold.

"I've asked you to extend your stay in Europe to handle the meeting between my staff and that of Hauptmann Metal Works. Naturally, Logan Aerospace will cover your expenses."

Confronted with his obvious anger, she tendered an apology. "I'm sorry if I jumped to the wrong conclusion, but…"

"If?"

The acid comment stiffened her spine. "I told you I'm not as good at compartmentalizing as you are. I'm still trying to separate the client from the…"

"Stud," he finished, his jaw tight.

He didn't appear to find the label as amusing as he had yesterday. Neither did Devon.

"I'll spell it out for you." He dropped the bills in her lap. "Logan Aerospace will cover any expenses you incur incidental to the business portion of this trip. Make sure you get receipts. My accountants will expect an itemized listing when EBS submits its final bill."

Nine

Dammit all to hell!

Cal administered a swift mental kick as he accompanied his escort down the mile-long corridors of the Airbus production facility.

He'd handled that scene with Devon wrong. He shouldn't have lost his cool or acted like such a stiff-necked jerk. After what he'd told her about Alexis, no wonder she'd jumped to the wrong conclusion.

Still, the fact that she *had* mistaken his motives put a severe dent in his pride. It also pissed him off. Royally. Did she really think he'd intended to buy her? Or that he would be stupid enough to mix his personal finances with that of his business?

The dig hit at something deeper, though. Something he hadn't stopped to analyze until this moment. He'd wanted Devon McShay from their first meeting, when he'd tugged her into his arms and delivered Don's kiss to the wrong woman. Cal hadn't exaggerated when he'd told her about the kick to the gut he'd experienced there at the Dresden airport. If anything, he'd understated the issue.

In the days since, his hunger for her seemed to have taken on a life of its own. Every touch, every stroke of his hands over her warm, smooth flesh, fed the beast in his belly. He got hard just remembering her taste, her scent, the feel of her slender body under his.

Yet the craving wasn't simply physical. Sometime in the past few days it had gone beyond mere attraction. He knew now he wanted more from Devon than the admittedly intense pleasure she gave him.

The problem was, he couldn't decide what that "more" constituted. Just weeks ago he'd ended an engagement to a woman he'd felt the same kind of hunger for...at first. Alexis was nothing if not stunningly seductive. And to her credit, she'd made no secret of the fact she considered Cal's wealth and power among his chief attractions.

By contrast, Devon went to almost the opposite extreme. The woman was as stubborn as an Arkansas mule when it came to the business side of their relationship. So stubborn, she couldn't—or wouldn't—separate the client from the man.

Correction. Stud.

Cal's simmering irritation took a sardonic turn. Okay, he had as much ego as the next guy. He'd made a joke of the tag when Devon first laid it on him. Truth be told, it had put a little strut in his walk. He wasn't strutting now.

Which brought him back full circle. Why the hell was he so pissed? And what did he want from Devon?

He'd better figure that out before he met up with her again in a few hours.

What did Cal want from her?

More to the point, Devon thought as she threaded through the shoppers thronging the Mö, what did she want from *him?*

Shoulders hunched against the damp fog that rolled in from lake across the boulevard, she paid little attention to the store windows festooned with Christmas displays. Cal's wad of bills burned a hole in her coat pocket.

Her rational mind knew he was correct in insisting Logan Aerospace cover expenses incident to her extended stay in Germany. Her less rational and wholly emotional self couldn't shake the nasty thought he was paying for services unrelated to EBS.

She caught her reflection in a shop window and made a moue of disgust. She looked as miserable and confused as she felt.

"It's this time of year," she muttered under her breath to her reflection. "It always makes you crazy."

Yeah, it does. So what are you going to do about this particular crazy?

If she had an answer to that, she wouldn't be standing on the sidewalk, talking to a store window!

What she needed, she decided, was to talk to her business partners. They had the distance, the separation, to view this issue objectively. That they were also her closest friends might muddy the water a bit, although Devon didn't see how it could get any muddier.

She checked her watch and saw it was almost three o'clock here in Hamburg. That would make it close to nine in the morning back in Virginia. Caroline and Sabrina had stayed up late last night working the new contract, but, knowing her partners, she bet they were both up and at it again.

Eager to talk to them, Devon cut over a block and pushed through the revolving doors of Alsterhaus, Hamburg's most famous department store. The multistory facility was large and elegant and a favorite with locals and visitors alike. It offered all kinds of products, from stationery and fashion and fine wines to the latest electronics and CDs. The top-floor restaurant featured a superb view of Lake Alster and the canals and waterways.

Devon lucked out and got a corner table by the windows. It was private enough for a conversation with her partners but still offered an incredible view. Although she'd consumed a working lunch with Cal and the Airbus brass in their executive dining room, she couldn't resist a bowl of Hamburg's famous eel soup.

She'd sampled it on her previous visit and knew the soup base was a clear broth flavored to a sweet-and-sour edge by vinegar and sugar. Finely sliced carrots, leeks, dried plums, pears, apples and small dumplings simmered with the broth. The eel, sliced a half-inch thick, weren't added until the last minute. Devon wasn't real big on eels, but the ones fished from the northern reaches of the Elbe tasted more like chewy chicken than fish.

She chose a dry white Rheingau to sip while waiting for her soup, then hit the speed-dial number for the office. Both Sabrina and Caroline were already at work. Wishing she had her laptop so she could see their faces, Devon responded to Caro's demand to know where the heck she was now.

"Still in Hamburg. Cal's meeting with Airbus is running later than anticipated."

Sabrina chimed in, her voice filled with her ready laughter. "Good thing we decided on flexibility as one of our primary operating parameters. Will you have to rework your connections to Salzburg?"

"Yes. No. Maybe."

"What does that mean?"

"It means I don't know if I'm going to Salzburg."

"Why not? I thought it was all set."

"I thought so, too." Sighing, Devon stared unseeing at the glass-topped tour boats plying the gray waters of Lake Alster. "That was before Cal opened his wallet and handed me a stack of bills to buy whatever I needed for our little play date in the Alps."

Stark silence greeted her statement. Sabrina was the first to break it. "Surely he wasn't that crass."

"No. He couched the gesture as a cost of doing business. He thinks Logan Aerospace should cover any expenses I rack up as a result of staying over to work the conference of his key personnel."

"Okay, now I'm officially confused. What are we talking here? The conference or your play date in Salzburg, as you so delicately term it?"

"*You're* confused!"

Out of deference to the other diners in the busy restaurant, Devon managed to refrain from wailing into the phone. Barely.

"Everything's happened so fast. I feel as though I've been riding a nonstop bullet express since the moment I met Cal Logan."

"Can't you slow the express down?" Caroline asked, her voice warm with concern.

"I've tried! Believe me, I've tried. I told Cal I wasn't any good at mixing business and pleasure. I insisted we should get to know each other better before jumping into the sack again."

"That didn't work?"

"It did and it didn't. We talked for hours on the train between Dresden and Berlin." She let out a long sigh. "Then we hopped right back into bed."

"Is he that hot?" Sabrina wanted to know.

"And then some," Devon said on a half laugh, half

groan. "He's also funny and thoughtful and smart and very take charge."

"Uh-oh."

"Exactly! Every time I think I have a handle on where things are going between us, he'll say or do something that throws me completely offtrack. Like this business with the cash. Do you think I over-reacted to his offer to pay my expenses?"

"No!" Caroline said with swift, fierce loyalty. She, too, carried the scars left by the one man she'd let herself love. Hers went deeper than Devon's, though, and at her express wish were never discussed.

"Yes!" Sabrina countered just as swiftly. "You're staying over in Europe at Cal Logan's request to set up a conference. Logan Aerospace should cover any business-related costs."

"Which doesn't include a holiday tryst with the CEO," Devon pointed out.

"It's your call, Dev," Sabrina said, her voice softening. "Don't go to Salzburg *or* work the conference if either one will cause you grief."

"I second that," Caro said staunchly. "With the contract we just landed, EBS doesn't need Logan Aerospace."

All three women knew that was a gross exaggeration. Even with the new contract, their fledgling business was a long way from recovering the initial start-up costs and turning a profit.

"Sabrina and I trust your judgment explicitly. Do what your heart and your head tell you is right."

* * *

Devon's head and heart debated the issue right up until it was time to go back for Cal.

In a last-minute compromise, she used her personal credit card to purchase a few necessities. They were stuffed in her roll-on when the limo pulled up at the visitor's entrance to the Airbus production facility.

She remained in the car, waiting for Cal, her gaze on the Elbe. This far north, the river was broad and flat and gray, its midchannel current too strong to freeze over as it had in Dresden. Across the river, the ruins of a watchtower and castle sat atop a strategic hill. Lining the bank below were pricey condos and small resort hotels, interspersed with boat docks and rowing clubs.

A flurry of movement at the front entrance caught her attention. Cal strode out, his cashmere overcoat slung over his arm. The wind ruffled his dark hair as he said goodbye to the Airbus execs. Watching him, Devon tried to sort through the welter of contradictory emotions the man stirred in her.

It wasn't just his physical presence, although she'd be the first to admit he gave new meaning to tall, dark and gorgeous. It was more his unique blend of sophistication and humor, of power and personality. She'd seen him in action in the boardroom, knew he could go for the jugular. Yet she'd also seen him in secondhand skates, the tip of his nose red from the cold and his eyes alight with laughter as he propelled her across the ice.

Then there was the instant heat he ignited with every touch, every kiss. Her hormones had been working overtime since that first meeting in the Dresden airport. And that was the problem, pared down to its core.

Devon had mistaken lust for love once. She wouldn't—*couldn't*—make the same mistake again.

Briefcase in hand, Cal headed for the limo. When he slid into the seat beside her, his expression showed none of the anger of a few hours ago. But his glance held a distinct challenge when it met hers.

"Did you find everything you needed?"

"That depends," she said carefully as the driver put the limo into gear.

"On?"

"On what we decide after you hear what I have to say."

She smoothed her gloved hands over the flaps of her black wool coat. She'd had plenty of time to rehearse her speech on the way back to the Airbus plant.

"Here's the deal. We've already established that I'm not as skilled as you are when it comes to separating personal and professional relationships. The misunderstanding earlier this afternoon made that painfully obvious. So I think we choose which of the two relationships we want to nourish."

"I thought I'd made *that* painfully obvious. I want you, Devon."

The answer caused a flutter just under her ribs but didn't tell her what she needed to know. With a swish of the soft leather seat, she angled around to face him.

"I want you, too. So much I can't think straight. Which is why I can spend the weekend with you in Salzburg or I can arrange your conference, but I can't do both."

"Can't, or won't?"

"Okay, won't."

He accepted that with a small nod, his gaze thoughtful as he studied her face.

"Just to clear the air," he said slowly, "I'm not trying to buy you by throwing a little business your way. Having you work the conference seemed like a win-win situation for both EBS and Logan Aerospace."

It was, Devon admitted silently, until the lines between lust and love began to blur and left her feeling her way blindfolded through a potential minefield.

"I know that's how it's done in the business world," she conceded. "It was the same in academia. You scratch my back by helping me research my article in the *Journal of Medieval History.* I'll scratch yours by reworking the outline for next semester's graduate course on the Italian Renaissance. Things have a way of getting complicated, though, when the back-scratching turns physical."

A gleam of amusement softened his eyes. "More complicated for you than for me, apparently."

"If that's your way of saying I'm being overly cautious, you're right. A botched marriage has a way of doing that to a girl. Not that we're talking marriage," she added hastily. "Or anything close to it."

Maybe *she* wasn't, but Cal had spent the past few

hours analyzing more than product specifications and redesign parameters.

The more he'd thought about his irritation at Devon's response when he'd offered to pay her expenses, the more he realized how arrogant he must have sounded. Consciously or un, he'd placed her in the same category as Alexis. As though she was someone whose career he might boost. Someone he could assist financially. Someone who needed him.

Only gradually had the hard truth sunk in. Unlike Alexis, Devon McShay was dead set on making it on her own. Her stubbornness had annoyed the hell out of him at first. Irritation had given way to grudging acceptance, then an admiration that got all mixed up with the other feelings the woman roused in him.

He wanted her with a hunger that seemed to feed on itself. The wanting grew with every hour in her company, every smile she sent his way, every stroke of his palm over the curve of her breasts or belly. Cal had walked out of the Airbus production plant determined to keep Devon in his life—and in his bed—for the foreseeable future.

Now she'd drawn a line in the sand. He could have her or her professional services, but not both.

"So who's supposed to make the decision?" he asked. "You or me?"

"I've already made it." Her gaze held his, clear and unwavering. "I'd rather spend Christmas with you than land a million in new contracts."

"Good." Grinning, Cal slid a hand under the soft

fall of her hair and hooked it around her nape. "If the answer had been any different, I wasn't letting you out of this car until I'd changed your mind."

He tugged her close for a kiss that left her breathless and him hurting like hell. Flushed and obviously relieved that he'd acquiesced so readily to her decision, she flopped back against the leather seat.

Cal didn't burst her bubble. He had acquiesced. To a point. He wouldn't push the issue right now, but during the next few days he *would* employ every one of the skills he'd acquired over the years to convince Devon she couldn't put him—or herself—into nice, neat boxes.

He came with Logan Aerospace attached. She was EBS. When they merged, so would their business interests.

During the drive to Hamburg airport, Cal began to contemplate a completely different sort of merger. The idea took shape slowly as he listened to Devon's bubbling, infectious enthusiasm over spending a few days in her all-time favorite city.

"Salzburg any time of year is wonderful, but it's absolutely magical in winter. I can't wait to show you all my favorite haunts."

"I hope that doesn't include all those museums and ruined castles you told me about."

"Only a few," she admitted, laughing. "I'll go easy on you. Thank goodness the city doesn't get as jam-packed with tourists in winter. Especially over the holidays. They're all home, doing the family thing."

She hesitated, her eagerness tinged with a touch of guilt.

"Are you sure you don't mind not playing Santa for all those nieces and nephews?"

"I'm sure. What about your folks?" he asked, searching her face. "Were they disappointed that you won't be with one of them for Christmas?"

"Not particularly." She hunched her shoulders in a mock shudder. "Each of them would have spent the entire time griping about the other, so I'd already decided to spend the holidays with Caro and Sabrina instead. They're my real family."

Something twisted inside Cal. He'd grown up surrounded by the large, boisterous Logan clan. Even in the Marines, when he'd been stationed halfway around the world and couldn't get home for the holidays, his parents and sisters had inundated him with letters and phone calls and packages crammed full of goodies he'd shared with his entire platoon.

He thought of the lonely Christmases Devon must have spent while he listened to her plans for their time together.

"I want to take you to the Opera Haus. And maybe we can get in some skiing. Caro and Sabrina and I spent every hour we could on the slopes during our year in Salzburg."

"Either one sounds good."

"Oh, Cal! You're going to fall in love with Salzburg, just as I did."

Smiling, he curled a knuckle under her chin and tipped her face to his. "I'm already there."

She looked a little startled, but before he could elaborate, the limo glided to a stop at the terminal. Devon snagged a cart for their few pieces of luggage while Cal tipped the driver.

"We'd better hustle," he said, slinging their cases onto the cart. "We don't want to miss the flight."

Ten

The joyful clanging of Salzburg's cathedral bells pulled Devon from sleep. She lay still, her backside tucked against Cal's thighs, his arm a dead weight on her waist, and savored the happiness that spread through her. She'd returned to her favorite place in the world. Birthplace of Mozart. Home to one of the world's great music festivals. Repository of her eager, youthful dreams.

She couldn't believe she was back after all these years. Or that she was sharing the magic with Cal.

Rather than stay at one of the big chains, she'd booked them into a small hotel in the historic heart of the city. The hotel nestled right up against the old Roman walls, almost in the shadow of the castle that rose high above the copper roofs and cupolas of the *Altstadt*.

They'd arrived too late yesterday evening to do more than feast on Wiener schnitzel and pan-fried potatoes at the hotel's restaurant and take a stroll through the brightly illuminated Christmas market that filled the main square.

Ah, but today, Devon thought as the bells sang to her, today she'd show him the city she'd fallen in love with so many years ago. Almost quivering with anticipation, she wiggled her butt.

"Hey, big guy! You awake?"

"I am now."

His voice was lazy and amused. The rest of him, it turned out, was anything but.

His arm tight, he drew her closer. She could feel him hardening against her rear, feel his breath warm on the back of her neck.

"I can't think of a better way to start the day," he murmured, inserting his knee between hers.

She thought about protesting for all of two or three seconds. She needed to hit the john, splash the sleep from her face, attack her teeth. Those minor considerations evaporated when Cal leaned forward and nipped the tendons in her neck. Her little shivers of delight had him fumbling for one of the condoms on the nightstand.

"We're going to run through your whole supply at this rate," Devon muttered.

"I'll restock," he promised as he slipped his arms around her waist again.

He slid in. Slowly. Stretching her. Filling her. Pulled out. Slowly. Until just the tip tormented her eager flesh.

Then in again. Out again. The pace was maddening, but the sensations incredible. They spread from Devon's belly, one piling on top of the other, making her grind her hips against his and squeeze every one of her muscles as tightly as she could.

She felt Cal go rigid behind her, heard his breath hiss out. She squeezed harder. He went over the edge with a long, low grunt. She fell off a few seconds later.

Devon lay in his arms, her body joined with his, until the world stopped spinning. "Heck of a way to start our first day in Salzburg," she got out after a minute or two.

"Heck of a way to start *any* day," he agreed, nuzzling her hair.

Her energy seeped back in slow degrees. With it came her eagerness to show Cal her favorite city. Rolling over, she dropped a loud, smacking kiss on his chin and pointed a stern finger at the bathroom.

"Okay, fella. You first. And make it quick. We have things to do and places to go."

Fortified by a hearty breakfast, they bundled up in their ski gear and sallied forth.

After the beautiful but treacherous ice of Dresden and the cold, drizzly fog of Hamburg, Salzburg offered sparkling sunshine and a blanket of clean snow. The steep peaks ringing the city wore skirts of white. More snow dusted the church steeples and copper roofs of Old Town. Designated a UNESCO World Heritage Site for its cultural and historical significance, the city was divided into two halves by the winding Salzach River. And from every street corner was a view of the magnificent Hohensalzburg Fortress high atop a hill overlooking the city.

Christmas added a special, festive air. Colored lights twinkled in every window. Garlands fashioned from fragrant pine boughs wrapped every streetlamp. The resiny tang provided a sharp counterpoint to the mouthwatering aromas of roasting chestnuts and sizzling sausages, while the scent of fresh baked bread poured from every bakery and corner café.

People thronged the streets. Skiers with their skis and poles over their shoulders brushed elbows with native Salzburgers in traditional loden green coats and alpine hats sprouting pins, feathers or brooms. A scattering of hardy tourists craned to see the sights while huddling under blankets in open, horse-drawn carriages. Shoppers jammed the main squares and multitude of Christmas markets, snatching up last-minute gifts and goodies.

Avoiding the crowds, Devon took Cal to her favorite places. The library at the university with its incredible collection of illuminated manuscripts, which she'd spent so many hours pouring through when she should have been cramming for exams. Salzburg's monumental baroque cathedral, where Mozart was baptized and later composed many of his sacred works. The tiny *Weinstubbe* tucked away on a narrow street that served the best goulash in the city.

They departed the restaurant in late afternoon with their bellies full and their palates on fire from the paprika in the goulash. Arm in arm, they descended a flight of snowy steps. Devon had intended to take him to the funicular for the ride up to the castle and its panoramic views of the city, but the small crowd gathered outside a narrow building at the base of the stairs caught Cal's attention.

"What's this?"

Devon skimmed the plaque beside the door of the modest eighteenth century house. "Joseph Mohr was born here. He wrote the poem that later became the lyrics to 'Silent Night.' His house is a museum, but it's closed now."

"So why the crowd?"

She made a polite query and got several enthusiastic responses.

"This group is taking a sleigh tour to the chapel in Oberndorf where 'Silent Night' was first performed. A local choir does a special Christmas Eve performance there each year."

"You talked about taking a sleigh ride. Why don't we go, too?"

Just in time, Devon managed not to grimace. She wasn't into organized tours at the best of times, and schmaltzy tours like this one held even less appeal. But this was Cal's first visit to Salzburg, and it *was* Christmas Eve. He'd given up being with his family for her. She could go schmaltzy and touristy for him. Still, she felt compelled to issue a word of warning.

"They say the chapel in Oberndorf is miniscule. It only accommodates fifteen or twenty people. So the performance is held outside."

He skimmed a glance over her knit cap, pink pashmina and down-filled ski gear. "Will you be warm enough?"

"I'm good if you are."

"Great. Let's see if they can squeeze us in."

Devon fully expected the tour leader to shake his head regretfully. Special tours like this were no doubt sold out months in advance. The group had four no-shows, however, and the organizer promised Devon and Cal a seat in one of the sleighs if the missing four didn't turn up in the next ten minutes.

They didn't.

Sternly quashing her doubts, Devon climbed into a minivan with Cal for transport to a farm on the outskirts of the city. There the group transferred to horse-drawn sleighs that held six passengers in addition to a driver perched on a high front bench. Supplied with flasks of hot chocolate and snuggled under warm blankets, they set off with a stomp of hooves and the merry jingle of harness bells.

The track cut through a stand of snow-draped pines, and someone two sleighs back started singing. Soon the whole group was belting out "O Tannenbaum." Devon buried her chin in the folds of her scarf to hide another grimace.

* * *

Three hours later, she knew she'd broken the Christmas curse forever. No matter where she was or what happened in the years to come, this night would always, *always,* remain in her mind and her heart.

Her breath steamed on the cold evening air as she stood hand in hand with Cal among a crowd of several hundred. They formed a semicircle in front of the tiny chapel. Spotlights illuminated the hexagonal structure with its cupola dome. Tall pines, their branches heavy with snow, formed a dramatic backdrop behind it. Above, stars gleamed in a sky turning from dark blue to black.

A local priest had said Mass in the open air, accompanied by a choir in Austrian dress singing traditional hymns. With the Mass over, the choir began the carol everyone had come to hear. The famous strains of "Silent Night" lifted to the star-studded sky.

The choir sang the first few choruses in the original German, inviting the crowd to join in. Other languages followed. Devon had no difficulty with the German and Italian versions and picked out most of the French phrases. Cal's rich baritone soared during the English chorus.

Standing there in the cold, her hand gripped in his, Devon felt the painful memories from years past fade into insignificance. One by one, her old hurts dissipated. Layer by layer, her cynicism peeled away.

This was what she'd always longed for, she

realized. Not the gifts her parents had heaped on her in their never-ending competition to buy her love. Not the endless parties and spiked eggnog.

Just this cold, starry night. This quiet joy. A man like Cal to share it with.

The last notes of the last chorus faded into the night. No one moved. The stillness was as beautiful and consuming as the singing. Finally, someone stamped their feet against the snowy earth and the crowd began to drift toward the tour buses and sleighs. Cal needed to make a pit stop, so he and Devon joined the horde heading for the gift shop/museum set well away from the chapel.

While she waited for him, it occurred to her that he'd just given her the most remarkable gift of her life, but she didn't have anything to give him in return. She scanned the trinkets and souvenirs but couldn't find anything that suited her. Hoping she'd have time to hit a shop or two in Salzburg, she met Cal at the entrance.

Once they had climbed into their sleigh, he put his arm around her shoulders and pulled her close. The driver checked to make sure his passengers were all aboard and snuggled in before flicking the reins and calling to his team. The two plow horses stomped their hooves, snorting gusts of air through their nostrils, and strained against the harnesses. Bells jingling, they fell into an easy gait.

The village of Obendorf soon faded into the night, and the track once again cut through thick stands of pine. The trip out had been filled with laughter and song. The return was quiet.

Devon leaned against Cal, wrapped in his warmth. Her chin was tucked deep in the folds of her borrowed pink scarf. His lips nuzzled her temple.

"Thank you for tonight," she said softly. "I needed it. I didn't know how much until I stood there, listening to the choir."

"You're welcome."

Devon spent the rest of the ride back to the farm reflecting on this incredible night. She climbed into the van for the trip to town, absolutely convinced it couldn't get any better.

She was proved wrong the moment she and Cal walked into the restaurant at their hotel. She stopped dead, her disbelieving gaze locked on the two people at a table close to the stone hearth.

One of the occupants spotted her at almost the same moment. With a glad cry, she tossed down her napkin and shoved back her chair.

"Devon!"

Leaping up, Sabrina rushed across the room. Caroline followed a moment later. The three friends fell into each other's arms for a noisy, laughing group hug.

"I can't believe it!" Devon exclaimed when she got her breath back. "When did you guys get here?"

"A few hours ago. We would have been here flight out of Frankfurt got delayed."

"But... But I thought you were flying into Rome,"

she said to Sabrina, as confused as she was delighted. "And Caro was supposed to head for Barcelona to check out sites for our new contract."

"We changed our reservations after Cal's call," Sabrina informed her.

"Cal's call?" Devon repeated stupidly.

"He wanted it to be a surprise." Her friend's sparkling glance went to the man standing a little to one side. "Looks like we pulled it off."

"Looks like we did," Cal agreed. "By the way, Brown Eyes, I have something for you. This is from Don."

Grinning, he dropped a kiss on Sabrina's cheek before turning to the third member of the group.

"And you must be Caroline."

Caro took the hand he held out. Quiet and reserved by nature, she was slower to open up to strangers than the effervescent Sabrina. Cal got one of her rare, unguarded smiles, though.

"I am."

She started to say more but was interrupted by the arrival of another group of guests.

"We'd better move out of the way." She led the way back to the table. "We waited to order dinner. You haven't eaten yet, have you?"

"No," Cal answered. "We joined a Christmas tour and took a sleigh ride out to the country. We just got back."

Two pairs of astonished eyes turned toward Devon.

"A Christmas tour?" Sabrina echoed. "You? The

original Ms. I-don't-have-time-for-all-this-holiday-hype?"

An embarrassed flush warmed Devon's cheeks. Shrugging, she returned a sheepish grin. "I'm resigning my membership in Grinchettes Anonymous."

Caro reacted to the news by reaching over to squeeze her friend's hand. Sabrina merely shifted her glance from Devon to Cal.

"Well, well." A teasing smile tugged at her lips. "So there *is* a Santa. Where's your beard?"

"I'm going for a more generic look. How are you feeling?"

"All recovered. Sorry I canceled out on you at the last minute."

"I'm not."

He leaned back in his chair and hooked an arm over the back of Devon's. The possessive gesture wasn't lost on either of the other two women. Their almost identical expressions told Devon to expect an intense grilling later.

She had another matter to clear up first. Angling around, she faced Cal. "When did you call Caro and Sabrina?"

"The day after you agreed to spend the holidays with me here in Salzburg."

"But… I thought…"

"I know. We were supposed to use this time to get to know each other." Raising a hand, he tugged on a strand of her hair. "I keep telling you, Ms. McShay. I know all I need to know."

Across the table, Sabrina and Caro exchanged two very speaking glances.

"You mentioned your friends were flying over right after the holidays," Cal continued, his smile tender. "You also mentioned the three of you are closer than sisters. So I thought this would be a good way for you to have your family with you at Christmas."

Devon's heart melted into mush right there at the table. He'd given up being with the family he obviously adored but had arranged for her to be surrounded by those she loved. Which, she realized on a hot rush of emotion, included Caleb John Logan, Jr.

What an idiot she was! She'd been so afraid to trust her heart, so worried her instincts were flawed after the fiasco of her marriage. Instead of reaching out and grabbing love with both hands, she'd tried to hold it at arm's reach while she analyzed and dissected her feelings.

No more, she vowed fiercely. No more! From now on, she'd take her chances on life *and* love.

"You couldn't have given me a more perfect gift," she said with a catch to her voice. "Thank you. Again."

"You're welcome. Again."

While she basked in the utter joy of the moment, a rueful gleam entered his eyes.

"I have to confess I had ulterior motives. I still want EBS to work the Logan Aerospace conference. I thought this would be a good way for me to meet your business partners. And," he added with a wicked grin, "for them to convince you it doesn't make sense to turn down a lucrative corporate contract just because you have a thing for the CEO."

Devon gave a sputter of helpless laughter. She knew darn well she should be pissed over this blatant end run. It was hard to work up a good mad, though, when Cal had dressed the maneuver up with such a big red bow.

"I'll discuss the matter with my partners," she conceded.

"You do that." He gave her hair another tug. "Now how about we order? I'm starving."

The restaurant offered a set menu that night featuring traditional Austrian Christmas Eve specialties, with fried carp as the main course and chocolate-and-apricot Sacher torte for desert.

The four Americans weren't the only ones who lingered over coffee and the sinfully rich torte. Visitors from other countries shared the flickering glow from the fireplace. Devon listened with half an ear to a spattering of French, Sicilian-accented Italian and what she thought was Portuguese. Her mind wasn't on the murmured conversations going on around her, though.

Her chin propped in her hands, she watched her friends and Cal interact. Sabrina, with her tumble of sun-streaked blond hair and laughing eyes, engaged him in a lively give-and-take. Even dark-haired and usually-so-serious Caro responded to his teasing with lighthearted quips.

As her gaze roamed the small circle, Devon knew

she didn't want this night to end. Ever. She understood, though, when the inn's owner came by each table to wish his patrons a blessed Christmas and remind them the restaurant would close several hours early so the staff could spend the rest of the evening with their families.

Cal must have sensed her reluctance to abandon her friends. As he retrieved her jacket from the back of her chair, he checked his watch.

"It's still early back home. Why don't I go up to the room and make a few calls while you three have some girl time?"

"Some girl time would be good," Sabrina replied, hooking her arm through Devon's before she could wiggle out of the intense grilling she knew would follow. "We'll send her up in a little while."

Nodding, Cal gave Devon a quick kiss and said good night to her friends. He'd barely disappeared around a corner before Sabrina dragged Devon to a cluster of armchairs in a corner of the lobby.

"Sit!" she commanded. "Talk! Omit no detail!"

Eleven

Devon thoroughly delighted Cal when she wedged into the small shower with him on Christmas morning and insisted on soaping him down. And up. And down again.

The sudsy activities led them right back to bed. Flushed and eager, she pushed his shoulders flat on the mattress and straddled his hips. Her auburn hair was a wild tangle of wet curls from the shower. Her skin was slick and smooth and so creamy he wanted to lick her like a cherry-vanilla triple-dip ice-cream cone. She licked him instead.

The third gift didn't arrive until breakfast. Cal and Devon were down before Sabrina and Caroline and had the small dining room to themselves. A fire already danced in the hearth. A sweet, yeasty aroma wafted from the kitchen. In honor of the occasion, the owner of the small hotel was dressed in his Sunday best. Sporting a ruffled shirt, bright red suspenders and a gray jacket with brass buttons and the green traditional facings, he bustled out of the kitchen with a carafe of coffee and a plate of braided bread bursting with raisins and currants.

"Fröliche Weinachten!"

Smiling, Devon returned the greeting. "Merry Christmas to you, too."

"My wife bakes this stollen herself for our guests. We are happy to have you with us on this blessed day."

"Thank you."

"We prepare only a light breakfast this morning, yes? Then, after church, we have the goose."

"Served crisp and still sizzling," Devon told Cal as the manager went back to the kitchen. "With dumplings, potatoes, curly kale, brown gravy and steins of dark, foaming beer."

His stomach did a happy roll in anticipation of the feast. The rest of him was as delighted when she reached for his hand and threaded her fingers through his. Her warm brown eyes were luminous in the early morning light. Her smile made him want to bundle her right back upstairs.

"In case I forget to tell you later," she said softly, "this is my best Christmas ever."

That hit Cal like a fist to the gut. He thought of the chaos that would ensue when his boisterous clan descended the stairs of his parents' Connecticut home in about eight hours. The kids would squeal and attack the mounds of presents. His sisters and brothers-in-law would try to keep some semblance of order for two or three minutes before giving it up as hopeless. His folks would revel in the noise and mess.

From the little she'd told him, Devon had never experienced that kind of exuberant celebration. She would, he vowed fiercely. Next year.

Lifting their entwined hands, Cal brushed a kiss across the back of hers. "It's one of my all-time greats, too."

He'd planned to wait, give her the time she kept insisting she needed. Trouble was, he'd never been good at marking time. If he hadn't jumped at opportunities when they came along, he wouldn't have turned a small electronics firm into a multinational corporation. And this opportunity was just too good to pass up.

"I'm thinking we should to do this on a more permanent basis."

Her startled glance met his. Cal saw confusion in her face, along with a sudden wariness that made him want to pound the bastard who'd hurt her into a bloody pulp.

"I want more holidays with you, Devon. Easter. July Fourth. Groundhog Day."

Her hand jerked in his. Reflex action, Cal thought, until her nails dug in. He saw what he was hoping for in her golden brown eyes. He couldn't have received a gift that thrilled him more.

"I want the other days, too," he warned, raising her hand for another kiss. "Lazy Sunday mornings reading the paper. Thursday evenings at our favorite restaurants. Weekends once in a while with my folks. And yours, if they can—"

"Merry Christmas, you two!"

Sabrina's cheerful greeting floated across the small dining room. She punctuated it with a waggle of her brows when she noted their joined hands.

"Uh-oh! Looks like I'm interrupting something. Want me to go away?"

Cal smothered a curse and reminded himself that he was the one who suggested Devon's friends fly to Europe a few days early. Rising, he pulled out a chair for her.

"Yes, you're interrupting," he said with a grin, "and no, we don't want you to go away. Devon and I were just talking about holidays."

Sabrina plopped down and tore off a piece of the still-warm bread.

"God, this is good!" Between bites, she picked up on Cal's comment. "And speaking of holidays, what's the plan for New Year's? I'm booked at the resort I want to check out south of Naples, and Caroline's supposed to zip over to Barcelona, but we could both reschedule and stay here in Salzburg."

Caught in a trap of his own making, Cal left it to Devon to answer. He'd wanted to make Christmas special for her but hadn't planned on sharing her right through New Year's.

To his relief, she shook her head. "I appreciate you coming over early more than you can know, but you'd better take care of business next week."

"The perfect segue," Cal commented. He started to say more but held off when he spotted Caroline coming toward them.

She reminded him very much of his sister Rebecca. Same dark hair, same intelligent eyes, same quiet air. Becky's calm, unflappable nature had served her well as the middle of the five Logan offspring. She'd fallen naturally into the role of peacemaker and negotiator between her younger and older siblings.

From the little Devon had told him about her partners, however, Cal sensed Caroline's reserve owed less to birth order and more to some traumatic event that had turned her inward and forced her to draw on a reservoir of hidden strength. Whatever the crucible was, it had molded her into a woman he suspected could more than hold her own against her partners' more outgoing personalities.

He rose to greet her and pull out a chair. When she was settled and four coffee cups had clinked together in a Christmas toast, Cal made a casual comment.

"Devon mentioned you're an opera buff. I saw something about a candlelight performance of Mozart's works at St. Peter's tonight."

"The Mozart Dinner Concert. It's world renowned." Caroline's eyes lit up. "The singers dress in traditional costume and perform excerpts from his most famous works. The food is supposedly traditional, too. Authentic dishes from Mozart's era."

Cal blinked at the transformation. When she shed her reserve and opened up, Caroline Walters was a knockout. The warm glow faded almost as quickly as it had come, however.

"I wanted to go the year Devon and Sabrina and I were at the university, but the tickets were way out of a lowly student's price range."

"That's the *only* concert she didn't drag us to," Sabrina said with a chuckle. "We had Mozart oozing out our pores that year."

"Maybe we should correct the omission," Cal suggested.

"I wish!" Caroline said fervently. "Unfortunately, the dinner concerts are sold out months in advance."

"That's what they told me when I asked about tickets."

"When did you do that?" Devon wanted to know.

"Last night, when you were having your girl time." He scratched his chin. "All they had left were seats at the prince's table. We'll have to share it with some ambassador and his entourage. I hope that's okay."

Three glances zinged his way. Caroline's expressed astonished delight. Sabrina's glinted with approval. Devon's held a glow that made Cal's chest squeeze.

Damn! He had it bad. If he hadn't already decided on a very personal, very intimate merger with Ms.

Devon McShay, he would have drawn up the articles of incorporation on the spot.

Too bad they'd been interrupted a few moments ago. He might have had the deal already signed and sealed. Later, he promised himself. First, they had another piece of unfinished business to take care of.

"We were just discussing plans for next week," he said to Caroline. "I understand you're flying to Barcelona, and Sabrina's heading to Italy to scout locations for a new contract EBS just landed. That leaves Devon to work the Logan Aerospace conference." He shifted his gaze to the woman beside him. "You *are* going to work it, aren't you?"

Devon felt the last of her defenses crumble. Like she was going to leave Cal in a lurch after all the trouble he'd gone to for her?

"I am. Sabrina and Caro and I talked about it last night."

"Good."

She still had reservations about mixing personal with professional. As she'd told Cal repeatedly, she wasn't good at compartmentalizing. But—as he'd told *her*—it didn't make sense to turn down a lucrative corporate contract just because she had a thing for the CEO.

Make that a major thing, she amended. She wasn't sure whether Cal's speech a few moments ago about spending Sunday mornings together had been a proposal or a proposition. At this point, she didn't really care.

She could admit it now. She'd fallen completely, helplessly, wholly in love with the man—as she intended to tell him when they had a few minutes alone to resume their interrupted conversation.

That might not be for a while, she realized when Cal offered a suggestion.

"Should I fly some of my people over to help with the arrangements?"

"No!"

The protest came from all three women simultaneously. Amused, he glanced from one to the other before addressing Devon.

"Are you sure? With Sabrina in Italy and Caroline in Spain, you might need assistance."

"I can handle it," she said firmly.

"Maybe the three of us could sit down with you for a few hours," Sabrina suggested. "If we hammer out some of the details, Caro and I could help Devon with the preliminary legwork before we leave tomorrow afternoon. I know it's Christmas, but…"

"No problem," Cal said easily. "Do you want to do it now?"

"Not now," Devon said with a quick glance at her watch. "I haven't given you your Christmas present yet. Sabrina and Caro helped me pick it out."

He waggled his brows. "You mean I'm getting more than what you gave me in the shower this morning?"

"Yes, you idiot." Devon ignored her friends' wide grins and pushed back her chair. "But only if we get our butts in gear. If we don't hurry, we'll miss it."

"Miss what?"

"You'll see." Like a general marshalling her troops, she barked out orders. "Everyone get their coats, hats and gloves. Be down in the lobby in ten minutes."

Cal pestered her like a kid shaking an un-wrapped present, but Devon refused to give him a hint about where they were going. His got his first clue when they rounded a corner and stopped at a ticket booth.

"Wait right here," Devon ordered.

She was back a few minutes later with four tickets for the old-fashioned, cogwheel train that took visitors to the fortress perched high above Salzburg.

"Perfect timing," she announced as the train came rattling down the steep incline.

"You're sure about this?" Cal asked, eyeing the iron cars and narrow track doubtfully.

"We're sure."

When she pointed a finger at the entry gate, Caro and Sabrina hooked their arms in his and marched him forward. Their breath steamed on the frosty air as the cog train creaked and groaned its way up the steep incline. Eight nerve-wracking minutes later, they emerged onto the battlements of the fortress perched high above Salzburg.

"The fortress was constructed in 1077," Devon told Cal. "It's the largest in Europe to remain intact."

"I can see why. These rampart walls must be twenty, thirty feet thick. Who built them?"

"The archbishops who used to rule Salzburg in princely splendor. Unfortunately, the museum and the archbishop's apartments are closed today."

"Trust me," Sabrina murmured in an aside to Cal. "Closed is good. Otherwise a certain former history professor would keep you here all day."

"Philistine," Devon said, making a face at her friend.

"If the museum's closed, what's the big attraction?"

The three women exchanged smug looks and steered him around a corner.

"This."

"Good God!"

Cal's stunned reaction was exactly what Devon had hoped for. She'd wracked her brains for something to give him. Choosing a gift for a multibillionaire wasn't easy, particularly since most of the stores had shut down before she and Cal returned from their excursion to Oberndorf. Sabrina and Caro's unexpected arrival had nixed any hope of last-minute shopping, but Devon knew she *had* to give him something after all he'd given her. After consulting her friends, she hit on the perfect gift.

"This is amazing," Cal murmured as he took in the breath-stealing view.

All of Salzburg lay below, showcased against snow-covered Alps. The ramparts gave them an eagle's-eye view of the copper roofs, the narrow streets, the magnificent palaces lining the ice-coated river, the royal riding stable that hosted the world-famous music festival.

"It's our favorite place," Devon told him happily. "Caro's and Sabrina's and mine."

"Thanks for sharing it." He took her gloved hand in his and speared a glance around the small group. "All of you. It's a gift I'll always treasure."

"This is only part of it." Devon checked her watch again. "Wait five more minutes."

They spent the short wait roaming the castle walls and stamping their feet to keep out the cold. Devon's nerves ratcheted up another notch with each sweep of the second hand. Would the experience be as remarkable as she remembered? Would Cal feel the same magic she had?

Then the church bells began to toll, summoning the faithful for Christmas morning services. The great, deep-throated cathedral bells rang out first. Slowly, majestically, their booming thunder rose from the city. Then came the molten, golden knell from St. Sebastian's. Mere seconds later, silver notes poured from the bell towers of the university's four chapels. The twenty or so other churches in the city soon joined in.

This high up there weren't any buildings to block the sounds. No thick walls or double-paned windows to mute the reverberations. Every note rose liquid and clear, until the air came alive with the clang and clatter and clamor of bells.

Cal spun in a slow circle, speechless with amazement. Good thing, since Devon couldn't have heard ᴀᴀᴠᴇ the joyous symphony. It lasted for a good five minutes before gradually tapering off.

"That," Cal said when the last echoes finally died, "was incredible."

Devon beamed, Caroline let out a contented sigh and Sabrina raised a gloved hand for a high five.

"Mission accomplished," she announced. "Now let's head back down. I'm freezing my ass off."

The rest of the day passed in a blur of whirlwind activity. The Christmas dinner prepared by the innkeeper's wife more than lived up to expectations. Stuffed to the gills, Cal and Devon set up a temporary command post in their room and spent three hours hammering out preliminaries for the Logan Aerospace/Hauptmann Iron Works conference. They broke at five to get ready for the Mozart concert and their second feast of the day. Sabrina and Caro had just left when Cal's cell phone rang.

He glanced at the number on the caller-ID screen. Devon saw his brows snap together and wondered why he didn't answer but hesitated to ask.

The phone rang again a few minutes later. This time Cal swore under his breath. When he lifted his gaze to Devon's again, his blue eyes held a combination of resignation and regret.

"It's Alexis. I'm sorry. I need to take this."

"No problem. I'll get cleaned up."

She headed into the bathroom to give him some privacy but had to conduct a fierce inner struggle before conquering the nasty urge to leave the door open a crack.

She wasn't worried about a call from his former fiancée. Cal said it was over between him and Alexis St. Germaine. Devon believed him.

There was no reason for the old doubts to surface while she freshened her makeup and dragged a brush through her hair. Even less reason for her throat to close when she emerged from the bathroom to find Cal shrugging into his overcoat.

"What's going on?"

"Alexis is here."

"In Salzburg?"

He jerked the coat to settle it over his shoulders. The movement was impatient, almost angry.

"One of my sisters told her I'd decided to spend the holidays skiing."

"So she flew over to join you on the slopes?"

"She says she has an urgent business matter to discuss." His gaze locked on hers. "One that concerns you."

"Me?"

"She's at the Emperor Charles Augustus Hotel," he said brusquely. "I remember seeing it when we were out walking yesterday."

"It's just two blocks from here," Devon confirmed, wondering what the heck this was about.

Did Alexis St. Germaine want to utilize the services of EBS? If so, why hadn't she contacted Devon directly? And what would be so urgent about that?

Or was that just an excuse to lure Cal away? If so,

she thought with a sudden catch in her breath, he'd taken the bait quickly enough.

"I'll find out what she wants and be back as soon as I can. If I'm delayed, you and Sabrina and Caro go on to the dinner concert. I'll join you there."

He dug out his wallet and extracted a credit card. Devon stiffened, but Cal was in too much of a hurry to notice.

"I've already paid for the tickets. They're waiting at will-call. You'll need this to pick them up."

He pulled her close for a fierce, hard kiss. She didn't resist, but after the door closed she folded his American Express card in a fist so tight the edges cut into her palm. A desperate mantra kept repeating inside her head.

This wasn't the Christmas curse revisited.

Cal didn't love Alexis St. Germaine.

He'd settle this "business matter," whatever it was, and join her at the concert.

He *would!*

Twelve

Cal cursed under his breath for most of two-block walk to the world-renowned hotel situated on the banks of the Salzach River.

He knew damned well what Alexis was up to. She'd made it plain enough. She'd uncovered some information about Ms. Devon McShay. Information Cal needed to know. She'd flown to Austria to share it with him.

She would share it, all right. For a price. Cal had no illusions when it came to his seductive, sultry former fiancée. He knew how her mind worked. What he didn't know was what the hell she'd dug up on Devon.

As he approached the entrance to the Emperor's two-story, glass-enclosed lobby, Cal kicked himself for not ordering a more detailed background dossier when his buddy Don recommended a firm that could handle all the arrangements for Cal's short-notice trip to Germany. The brief his people had scrambled to put together on EBS had covered only the basics. Length of time in operation. Current corporate assets. Educational background and experience levels of the three owners.

Cal believed in giving small businesses a break. Hell, that's how he'd gotten his start. The personal recommendation from Don had cinched the matter.

He knew now he should have had his people dig a little deeper. Or pumped Devon for more information about herself. If he had, he might have been better prepared for whatever Alexis was going to hit him with.

Instead, he'd gone with his gut. He'd wanted Devon McShay since the moment he'd spotted her at the Dresden airport. Intent on having her, he'd brushed aside her protests that things were moving too fast, that they needed to get to know each other. Arrogant ass that he was, he'd forged ahead with his campaign to get her into his bed and keep her there.

That arrogance may well have put her at risk. Cal's prominence in the aerospace industry had provided great fodder for the media over the years. His engagement to high-profile Alexis St. Germaine had generated far more intrusive and gossipy articles.

Devon would be subject to the same intrusive scrutiny. The tabloids would dive into her past, speculate on her broken marriage, probably interview her ex, maybe even the parents she said were still so bitter and angry with each other.

Cal should have warned her, should have made sure she was ready when word of their holiday abroad leaked, as it surely would. And *he* sure as hell should have been prepared for someone to dig up a little dirt. That the someone was evidently Alexis only added to his self-disgust.

Kicking himself all over again, Cal strode up to the hotel's grand entrance. A doorman uniformed in a red jacket and black top hat swished open the brass-and-glass door.

"Fröliche Weinachten."

His scowl easing, Cal returned the man's greeting.

"Merry Christmas. Could you point me to the house phones, please?"

"Yes, sir. They are just there, beside the concierge's desk."

"Thanks."

Cal barely noted the combination of soaring glass windows, crystal chandeliers and elegant nineteenth-century antiques as he strode to the bank of phones and asked to be connected to Alexis's room.

"It's Cal," he bit out when she answered.

"Come up." Her husky contralto flowed like dark velvet. "I'm in three twenty-five."

"You come down." He glanced around, spotted a casual gathering place showcased by the two-story windows. "I'll meet you in the lobby bar."

"Oh, darling." Amusement rippled through her

smoky voice. "Don't tell me you're afraid to be alone with me."

"The lobby bar, Alexis."

He snagged a table by the windows and ordered a scotch. From long experience he knew his ex-fiancée would take her time making an appearance.

Impatience ate at him while he waited. Outside the brightly lit bar, traffic had picked up. A steady stream of cars and taxis moved along the wide boulevard fronting the river. Many, Cal guessed, were headed for the concert hall.

He checked his watch, smothered a curse and downed a swallow of scotch. Thankfully, Alexis stepped out of the elevators a moment later.

Heads turned as she crossed the lobby. Tall, silvery blond and movie-star glamorous in a peacock blue cape trimmed in fur dyed to match, she swept into the bar.

"Merry Christmas, darling."

"You, too, Alexis."

Her scent enveloped him as she stretched up for a kiss. Cal brushed her cheek instead of her lush red lips. Her eyes mocked him as she took the chair he held out for her.

"I wish you'd told me you were planning on a skiing break," she said, arranging the cape in graceful folds. "You know I love to ski. Remember the week we spent in St. Moritz?"

"I remember."

Cal signaled to the waitress and took his seat.

Once she'd taken Alexis's order for a champagne cocktail, he cut straight to the chase.

"What's this about?"

"So direct," she murmured, her red lips forming a little moue. "So abrupt. You don't have time for more than a hello and goodbye after I flew all this way to see you?"

"Actually, I don't." He relaxed into a wry grin. "I'm doing Mozart tonight."

"Darling!" The moue became a teasing pout. "And here I had to promise you all kinds of carnal delights to convince you to escort me to a concert."

Not quite, but Cal let that pass.

"Your little travel planner must be quite something to get you to a Mozart concert."

"She is, and her name is Devon. Devon McShay, as you know perfectly well."

"Yes, I do."

The waitress arrived then with the champagne. Alexis held up the crystal flute, clinked it against his glass and took a sip. Over the rim of the glass her glance was amused and just a little malicious.

"The question is, how much do you know about her?"

"All I need to."

"Are you sure?"

"Before this conversation goes any further, Alexis, I want to make one thing clear."

He kept his smile easy and his tone even but made damned sure she got the message.

"I'm not paying you for whatever dirt you've dug up on Devon. And I strongly suggest you don't sell it to the tabloids."

"Oh, Cal. You wound me. Do you think I would do that?"

Her limpid, wide-eyed innocence was so exaggerated he had to laugh.

"I know damned well you would. For the right price. Just remember, it's not too late to stop the transfer of the Park Avenue apartment into your name."

A blood-red nail tapped against the champagne flute. Once. Twice. Three times. Then she gave a low, throaty laugh that drew the interested glance of every male in the bar.

"Ah, well. It was worth a try."

Her amusement fading, she took another sip of champagne. Cal waited, guessing that she couldn't resist dropping whatever bombshell she'd come to deliver. He knew he'd guessed right when she slanted him a sly glance.

"Did Ms. McShay happen to mention her father is an accountant?"

"As a matter of fact, she did."

"Did she also happen to mention that he's with Pendleton and Smith?"

Cal's eyes narrowed. "No," he said slowly, "she didn't."

Her mouth curved in a smile of malicious satisfaction. "I thought not."

P&S was one of the largest accounting firms on the

East Coast. Among their most prominent clients was Templeton Systems, Logan Aerospace's chief competitor in the drive to acquire Hauptmann Metal Works.

"Is that what you flew all this way to tell me, Alexis? That Devon's father works for my competitor? If so, you're too late. I've closed the deal I was working."

Disappointment etched hard lines into her face, making it look years older for a moment. Her nail tapped the champagne glass again.

"Well, I was going to share a few details of her rather messy divorce, but I think I'll let you ferret those out for yourself."

"Wise decision."

She inclined her head, acknowledging defeat with a careless grace that took the edge from his anger. Softening his expression, Cal pushed back his chair.

"I'm sorry to leave you alone on Christmas night, but…"

"I know, I know. You're doing Mozart."

Her sultry charm returned as she rose with him. "Go," she ordered with another of her throaty chuckles. "I won't be alone for long."

Her glance swept past him to engage that of the silver-maned gentleman at the next table. The seductive smile she sent the man almost made him choke on his bourbon.

"No," Cal agreed with a grin. "You won't. Goodbye, Alexis."

"Goodbye, my darling."

She made sure he didn't take this kiss on the

cheek. Framing his face with both hands, she surrounded him with her unique aura of sex and sin.

He caught her wrists. Intent on extracting himself, Cal didn't notice the traffic backed up on the street outside the brightly illuminated bar, much less Caroline's white, shocked face framed in the rear window of a taxi.

Thirteen

Devon barely registered Caroline's dismayed gasp, quickly smothered. Nor did she pay any attention to Sabrina's soft "Damn!"

She sat frozen, her entire being focused on the two people on the other side of the soaring glass windows. The image imprinted itself on every brain cell. She could see it with excruciating clarity even after the stalled taxi began to move and her two friends swung toward her.

"Dev?"

She shook her head, too numb to speak. Sabrina swore again, viciously. Caro groped for her hand and squeezed so hard the bones ground together.

"Oh, Dev. It's not what it looked like. It can't be."

Still she couldn't speak. Caro leaned across her to throw an agonized glance at Sabrina.

"Tell her! Cal isn't Blake. He's not anything like Blake."

"Bull." Sabrina was too angry to pull her punches. "All men have one thing on their minds. You know it. I know it. Devon, unfortunately, has now experienced a double dose of reality."

"There's... There's probably a perfectly good explanation for what we just saw," Caro said stubbornly.

"Yeah, sure."

"Dammit, Sabrina! You're not helping here."

"I don't want to help. I want to pound Cal Logan's face into steak tartare."

"Oh, for...!"

Caro swung back, her face reflecting some of the anguish piercing Devon's chest.

"He's not Blake, Dev. You said it yourself. He's funny and smart and kind and—"

"I know." Devon tried to swallow past the brick in her throat. "I know. Just... Just give me a minute."

The minute stretched into two, then three. The numbness went away. The ache in Devon's chest didn't. It was still there, sharp and stabbing, when the taxi swept past the bridge spanning the Salzach and joined the stream of traffic turning into the yard of the concert hall.

The line of vehicles inched to the colonnaded entrance. An attendant in a white wig and blue satin knee breeches stepped forward to open the door.

Sabrina took care of the fare and joined her friends at the entrance.

"Cal's already paid for the tickets," Devon said, forcing each careful word. "They're at the will-call window."

They claimed the tickets and mingled with the crowd in the richly decorated foyer. The minutes stretched out again, slow and agonizing. Sabrina snagged glasses of champagne from a bewigged waiter and downed hers in a few angry swallows. Caro kept up a soft commentary about the pieces played by the costumed string quartet that entertained the pre-dinner crowd.

Devon's fingers tightened on the stem of her champagne goblet when a gong resonated at the top of the wide marble staircase. A footman in shining satin and white lace stepped forward with a sonorous announcement.

"Dinner is served."

She dug two tickets out of the envelope they'd picked up at the window. "You and Caro go on in. I'll wait for Cal here."

"No way!" Sabrina countered. "We'll wait with you."

"*Please.*" She thrust the tickets into her friend's reluctant hand. "Go in."

When Sabrina looked like she might balk, Caro grabbed her arm and yanked her toward the stairs.

The crowd mounted the wide marble steps and were greeted by a costumed soprano singing one of

Mozart's most famous arias. The lilting strains followed Devon as she moved to the windows at the far end of the now-empty foyer.

Outside the window, the illuminated towers and church steeples formed a timeless nightscape. Above them, spotlights lit up the majestic fortress that had guarded the city for ten centuries.

Salzburg. The city of her youthful hopes and dreams. The magical place she'd ached to share with Cal.

She hugged her arms to her chest, her gaze on the castle ramparts. And just like that her world righted itself.

The doubts faded. The hurt went away. She didn't need Caro to remind her Cal wasn't anything like Blake. She knew it. The shock of seeing him locked in an embrace with his one-time fiancée had shaken her to her core. Worse, it raised the ghosts of Christmases past.

But all Devon had to do was recall the wonder of last night at the Oberndorn chapel. Think about the calls Cal made to her friends. Remember the awe on his face when the bells sang out this morning.

He was more generous than anyone she knew and had given her more joy than she'd ever thought to experience. She knew with every fiber of her being that she couldn't be wrong about him or the feelings he roused in her.

"Devon!"

She spun around, saw him thrust his overcoat at

an attendant. Impatience and regret was stamped across his face as he hurried toward her.

"I'm sorry I'm late. Damned traffic got snarled at the bridge. Why didn't you go on in?"

"I was waiting for you."

"Are we too late for dinner?"

"Not yet." Grinning like a fool, she hooked her arm through his. "We'd better hurry, though, or we'll miss the potato soup."

"Hold on. Don't you want to hear why Alexis flew over to Salzburg?"

"Not tonight."

"Are you sure? It concerns you and—"

She stopped him by the simple expedient of laying a hand over his mouth.

"Not tonight, Cal. It's Christmas. I have food, music and friends waiting inside. And you're here, with me. That's all I want or need or care about. Everything else can wait until tomorrow."

"Not everything."

Tugging her hand aside, he smiled down at her. "About those Sunday mornings reading the paper...?"

Her heart bumped. "Yes?"

"That was my clumsy way of saying I love you."

"Glad you clarified that." Happiness spread through her, warming her from the inside out. "'Cause I love you, too."

He swept an arm around her waist and tugged her against him. Devon went into the kiss eagerly, joyfully, while Mozart's glorious aria floated from the hall above. She was breathless when he lifted his head and grinned down at her.

"You do know we're coming back to Salzburg on our honeymoon, don't you?"

"I'll work all the arrangements," she promised, laughing.

* * * * *

HIS EXPECTANT EX

BY
CATHERINE MANN

RITA® Award-winner **Catherine Mann** resides on a sunny Florida beach with her military flyboy husband and their four children. Although after nine moves in twenty years, she hasn't given away her winter gear! With more than a million books in print in fifteen countries, she has also celebrated five RITA® finals, three Maggie Award of Excellence finals and a Bookseller's Best win. A former theatre school director and university teacher, she graduated with a master's degree in theatre and a bachelor's degree in fine arts. Catherine enjoys hearing from readers and chatting on her message board – thanks to the wonders of the wireless internet that allows her to cyber-network with her laptop by the water! To learn more about her work, visit her website at www.CatherineMann.com or reach her by snail mail at PO Box 6065, Navarre, FL 32566, USA.

Dear Reader,

Thank you for picking up my book. Writing *His Expectant Ex* touched my heart on a number of levels. Reunion stories have long been a favourite of mine. After all, how awesomely romantic is it to see a man fall in love with his wife all over again on an even deeper level? I also enjoyed the opportunity to revisit characters from my WINGMEN WARRIORS series.

And lastly, including Sebastian and Marianna's dogs in the story was a special treat. Over the years, my husband and I have gone to local animal shelters to choose our dearly loved pets – Trooper (basset/beagle), Cooper (orange tabby) and Sadie (Boston terrier/pug). I would like to encourage you to visit and support your local animal shelter or humane society. There are so many abandoned animals out there hungry for affection and a home. For a peek at the Mann family's precocious pets, check out the photos on my website, www. catherinemann.com or at MySpace, www.myspace. com/catherinemann.

Thanks for following THE LANDIS BROTHERS novels. Stay tuned for the next instalment, featuring military hero Kyle Landis!

Happy reading!

Catherine Mann

To my parents, Brice and Sandra Woods, a beautiful testament of enduring happily-ever-after at over forty-five years of marriage and still going strong!

One

Hilton Head Island, South Carolina—
Two months ago:

Sebastian Landis had been in courthouses more times than any hardened criminal. He was one of South Carolina's most successful lawyers, after all. But today he'd landed a front-row seat for how it felt to have attorneys hold complete power over *his* life.

He didn't like it one damn bit.

Of course getting divorced ranked dead last on his "things I like to do" list. He just wanted to plow through all the paperwork and litigation so the judge could make it official.

Gathering files off the table in one of the court-house conference rooms, he barely registered his goodbyes to his attorney and polite handshakes with Marianna's counsel. Power ahead. Eyes on the finish line. Clipping his BlackBerry to his belt again, he kept his eyes off his wife, the only woman who'd ever been able to rattle his cool—his calm under fire being a renowned trait of his around courthouse circles.

At least they'd completed the bulk of the paper-work with their lawyers on this overcast summer day, leaving only the final court date. The settlement was fair, no easy feat given his family's fortune and her thriving interior decorating career. They hadn't even fought over the dissolution of their multimillion dollar assets—probably the first time they hadn't argued.

The only wrinkle had come in deciding what to do with their two dogs. Neither wanted to lose Buddy and Holly, or split the sibling pups up. Ultimately, though, they had each taken one of the Boston terrier/pug/mystery parent mutts they'd rescued from the shelter.

What would they have done if he and Marianna actually had children?

He backed the hell away from that open wound fast. Not going there today, no way, no how, because even a brief detour down that path kicked a hole in his restraint on one helluva crap day.

Which left him checking on Marianna in spite of his better judgment.

She rose from the leather chair, too damn beautiful for her own good, but then she always had been. With dark eyes and even darker long hair, she'd been every guy's exotic fantasy when they'd met on a graduation cruise to the Caribbean.

Thinking about that sex-slicked summer would only pitch him into a world of distraction. Scooping up his briefcase, he put his mind on what he could accomplish back at his office with the remainder of the afternoon. Of course he could also work into the evening. It wasn't like he had anything to go home to now, living in a suite at his family's compound. He reached the exit right in step with Marianna.

He held the door open, her Chanel perfume tempting his nose. Yeah, he knew a lot about his soon-to-be ex, like what scents she chose. Her favorite morning-after foods. Her preferred lingerie labels. He knew everything.

Except how to make her happy.

"Thank you, Sebastian." She didn't even meet his gaze, her lightweight suit skirt barely brushing against him as she strode past and away.

That was it? Just a thank-you?

Apparently he could still feel something besides attraction for her after all, because right now he was ticked off. He didn't expect they would celebrate with a champagne dinner, but for heaven's sake, they should at least be able to exchange a civil farewell. Not that civility had ever been one of his volatile wife's strong points. She'd never been one to run from a potentially contentious moment.

So why was she making tracks to the elevator, her designer pumps clicking a sprinter's pace? God, she made heels look good with her mile-long legs. She'd always been a shoe hound, not that he'd minded since she modeled her purchases for him.

Naked.

Damn it all, how long would it take for the flashes of life with Marianna to leave his head? He wanted his polite goodbye. He needed to end on a composed note, needed to end this marriage. Period.

Sebastian made it to the elevator just before it slid closed. He hammered both hands against the part in the doors until they rebounded open. Marianna's eyes went wide for an instant and he thought, oh yeah, now she'll snap back. Toss a few heated words around and maybe even the leather portfolio she gripped against her chest.

Then boom. Her gaze shot straight down and away, looking anywhere but at him.

He tucked into place beside her, the two of them alone in the elevator chiming down floors. "How's Buddy?"

"Fine." Her clipped answer interrupted the canned music for a whole second.

"Holly chewed up the grip on Matthew's nine iron yesterday."

His brother had pushed him to play eighteen

holes of golf and unwind. Sebastian had won. He always won. But unwinding didn't make it anywhere on the scorecard. "Luckily, Matthew's in a good mood these days with his new fiancée and the senatorial race. So Holly's safe from his wrath for now."

She didn't even seem to be listening. Strange. Because while she'd stopped loving him, she still loved those dogs.

He normally wasn't one for confrontation outside the courtroom, but he'd seen enough divorce cases to know if they didn't settle this now, they were only delaying a mammoth blow up later. "You can't expect we'll never talk to each other again. Aside from having the final court date to deal with, Hilton Head is a relatively small community. We're going to run into each other."

She chewed her full bottom lip, and just that fast he could all but feel that same mouth working over his body until he broke into a sweat.

He thumbed away a bead of perspiration popping on his brow, irritation spiking higher than her do-me-honey heels. "Seems we should have spelled out the rules for communication in that agreement. Let me make sure I get the gist of this right. We aren't speaking anymore except for hello and goodbye. But is a nod okay if we're both walking the dogs on the beach? Or should we section off areas so we don't cross paths?"

Her fingers tightened around her leather portfolio, her gaze glued to the elevator numbers. "Don't pick a fight with me, Sebastian. Not today."

What the hell?

He never picked fights. She did. *He* was the calm one, at least on the outside. So what was going on with her? Or with him, for that matter? "Was there something with the lawyers that didn't go the way you hoped?"

She chuckled, dark and low, a sad echo of the uninhibited laughter that used to roll freely from her. She sagged back against the brass rail. "Nobody wins, Sebastian. Isn't that what you always say about divorce cases?"

She had him there.

Sebastian planted a hand beside her head. Sure he was crowding her but they only had one more floor left for him to get his answer. "What do you want?"

Marianna raised her eyes, finally. That dusky dark gaze sucker punched him with the last thing he expected to find, especially after they'd spent six months sleeping apart. And he saw the one thing he absolutely could not resist taking when it came to this woman. Marianna's eyes smoked with flaming hot...

Desire.

Her marriage began and ended in the backseat of a car.

Marianna had eloped with Sebastian Landis at

eighteen. They hadn't made it to a hotel before hormones got the better of them, and they pulled off on a side road. Now, after the final appointment with their lawyers, hormones—and emotions— once again blindsided her.

And all because of a fleeting moment of regret in his eyes when they put it in writing about splitting up Buddy and Holly. That hint of vulnerability from her stoic-to-a-fault husband had turned her inside out.

Then turned her on.

She'd tried to haul buggy out of the conference room before she did something stupid, like jump him. No such luck. They'd barely cleared the elevator with their clothes on before sprinting through the rain to his car. He'd peeled rubber out of the lot and pulled off at the nearest side road for isolated parking.

Frantic to ease the ache between her legs if not the one in her heart, Marianna hooked her arms around Sebastian's broad shoulders as he angled her over the reclined seat and into the back. The tinted windows offered additional privacy in their wooded hideaway. Spanish moss trailed from the marshy trees like sooty bridal veils, at once both beautiful and sad.

Raindrops pounded the roof in time with her blood gushing through her veins. Lips locked, she tumbled and twisted until they settled into the lengthy backseat, Sebastian's Beemer roomier than the Mustang convertible he'd driven as a teen.

They also didn't have an unplanned pregnancy confining their moves this time.

Sebastian looped his tie around her neck and tugged her toward him. Melting into the familiar feel of him, Marianna inhaled the spicy scent of his Armani aftershave, rich with whispers of how often she'd inhaled the same smell as it rode the steam of his morning shower. Greedy with the need to take all she could this one last time, hungry after months without his body, she explored Sebastian's mouth with her tongue as fully as her hands roved his shoulders, back, taut butt in pin-striped pants.

"Marianna, if you want to stop, say so now." A damp strand of brown hair fell over his brow in a downright blaring statement of rioting emotions from a man reputed to be the most ruthless litigator in the state of South Carolina.

"Don't talk, please." They would only start fighting. About his interminable hours at the law office. About her temper as flamboyant as some of the homes she decorated.

About how they had absolutely nothing in common except physical attraction and the precious babies they'd lost.

Thunder growled and he cupped her face in his hands, electric-blue eyes snapping sparks through her, echoing the snap of lightning overhead. "I need to hear you say it, that you want me inside you as damn much as I want to be there." His low growl spoke of his own strained control. "We have enough regrets without adding one more to the pile."

"I only know this is a heartbreaking day and I have to have *this*." She couldn't bring herself to say she wanted him, not after all the times she'd needed even just his presence only to spend another solitary evening on their balcony with only the rolling surf, a top-shelf wine and her salty tears. "Now, can we put our mouths to better use?"

He kept his gaze firmly on her face while his hand slid down, his thumb brushing a distracting back and forth along the side of her breast. "We can end the conversation, but that won't stop me from telling you just how sexy you are."

His eyelids lowered to a heated half-mast as he dipped his head to nip at the oh-so-sensitive curve of her neck. Knowing every button to push to send her writhing against him, achy, needing. More. Now.

"Or how much you turn me inside out with the way your legs look in those heels. Yellow. God, who wears yellow shoes?" His broad palm slipped under the hem of her skirt, up the length of her thigh in a hot path as he traced the edge of her panties right between…

Her head fell back as words scrambled together in her overheated mind. "Me. I do. And they're lemon-colored."

"They're hot."

If only great sex and a whopping big bank balance were enough, they could have made it to their golden anniversary, no problem. That thought could douse the pleasure brought by his talented fingers faster than emptying a silver ice bucket in their laps.

She tore at the buttons on his monogrammed shirt, popping, opening, scraping back fine fabric until her palms met warm skin. The flex of hard muscles contracting beneath her touch blocked out the world waiting beyond the abandoned forest nook. She kissed, nipped, laved over him while Sebastian tunneled his hands through her hair until it slipped free of the loose twist, tumbling midway down her back.

His BlackBerry buzzed an unwelcome interruption. Her skin started to chill. He tore the handheld off his belt and tossed it to the floor impatiently.

About damn time he did that.

Marianna gripped his shoulders, fingernails digging half-moons into his flesh as she strained to get nearer, desperate to deepen the closeness. Twining her fingers in his close shorn hair, she held his face to hers, devouring him, ravenous after the months of going without.

Sebastian nudged her jacket aside, down her shoulders, and cupped her breast through the satin camisole. He circled a thumb around the tightened crest sending sparks of want through her. When he lowered his mouth to replace his hand, she couldn't control the urge to roll her hips against his.

"Enough." The moist heat of his mouth as he worked the satin over her skin tightened the swirls of pleasure. "More."

And thank goodness he understood the contradiction of impulses that had plagued most every part of their marriage. He angled them both upright again until he sat in the middle of the seat. Marianna straddled his lap, her suit skirt hitching up as she knelt, her toes pressing against the front seats until her Gucci pumps began to slip off.

His hands reached down, gripping both shoes and holding them in place. "Leave them on," he growled low, "I'm suddenly a big fan of lemon."

She fumbled with his belt, just above the hard press of his desire straining against his zipper. Then yes, she found the enclosed velvet length of him, stroking. Never one to lag behind, Sebastian slid his hand beneath her skirt again, fingers twisting in the thin string of her thong, pulling the panties lightly biting into her flesh. She welcomed the pinch on her over-heightened senses and then it…

Snapped.

He pitched aside the insubstantial scrap of yellow silk she'd worn to make her feel like more of a woman and less of a failure at the most important relationship of her life. Marianna positioned herself over him, and he thrust upward. Fast. Hard. No fumbling. No awkwardness. Rather a synchronicity gained from nine years of knowing just how to come together with sex if nothing else.

She grabbed his wrists and moved his hands to cup her breasts. Her fingers stayed with his over her while he pounded into her with an urgency as powerful as the storm outside and the man inside. Marianna rocked her hips against him in grinding circles, milking every ounce of sensation from this last explosive encounter.

One last time to be together.

One more memory to tuck away and torment herself with over a glass of wine by the beach.

If only they could communicate half as perfectly on anything as well as they connected during sex. Even that bond became strained because of the looming "after" time, a free-fall into sadness because there was nothing else left between them.

Sweat slicked his chest, her arms, their kisses turning slightly salty in her mouth. Pleasure built and clawed inside her, the need to finish almost painful. His hands twisted in her hair, his jaw tight in a way she recognized as Sebastian waiting for her, holding back until even his arms shook. Her moans mixed with his, urgent, faster. Exploding through her in a release that satisfied even as it destroyed another corner of her weary soul.

Pleasure rippled over the pain in a bittersweet farewell mix. Wave after wave surged and receded until she sagged against him, his arms still banded around her as his body rocked with aftershocks.

The confines of the Beemer echoed with only their panting breaths and the tapping rain. Marianna knew they had nothing left to talk about. It was over between them. They just had one last meeting before a judge in a few weeks.

It wasn't like they even needed to discuss their lack of birth control. Her miscarriage nine years ago had left her infertile. Not that they hadn't continued to try—and fail.

Then hope had briefly returned. Sebastian had been a hundred percent on board with adoption, and for four blessed months Marianna had been a mother. Little Sophie's face stayed as firmly planted in her memory as in her heart. She and Sebastian had put aside their marital problems bubbling to the surface and poured themselves into parenthood.

Only to have Sophie's birth mother change her mind.

Lying against Sebastian's chest this last time, Marianna ached to cry, for herself, for him, for their daughter. But when a person dried up inside, tears were tough to find. Six months ago, Sophie had been plucked from her arms, their home, their lives.

Marianna's heart broke. Sebastian went to work. And their marriage finally fell apart.

Two

Marianna winced as the judge raised his gavel and—*whap*—cemented everything she and Sebastian had spelled out with their lawyers in the divorce paperwork.

In the span of one day, she'd become both a divorcée and an unwed mother. A baby. She gripped the edge of her chair to keep from flattening her hands to her stomach.

After so many failed attempts at conception, miraculously one of Sebastian's swimmers had managed to circumnavigate all her cysts and scar tissue. She'd only found out this morning—an axis-tilting moment that still left her reeling.

A tiny flutter of hope stirred like the life she looked forward to feeling move inside her. Just maybe this time…

She had considered telling Sebastian before court—for all of five nauseating seconds. This didn't change anything about them as a couple. Custody paperwork would be a separate matter altogether. Besides, she wanted to be a hundred percent certain with a doctor's visit. She wasn't going on the voucher of one pink plus sign, not after nine years of disappointments, after the past months of hell from losing Sophie.

And how would Sebastian feel about the news?

He loomed a few feet away—how could the man loom even when he sat?—thumbing closed the locks on his briefcase. Scowling. At least something was normal in this upside-down day.

She gathered her resolve and crossed the aisle. "Sebastian, I would like to set up a time for us to talk. Perhaps someday next week?"

After she'd visited an ob-gyn. She'd missed the signs at first because of her heavy workload decorating two major Hilton Head homes, then assumed the stress of the impending divorce had thrown off her cycle—even when one missed period became two…. It had been two months since she'd ditched her panties in the backseat with Sebastian.

Standing, he smoothed his silk tie and refastened a button on his suit jacket. "We can talk now. Let's wrap everything up at once."

"I can't today." She had an urgent appointment with a pack of crackers and a flat surface.

"Something more pressing to do?"

"You're the one who's married to his Black-Berry." Bile burned the back of her throat. "I wanted to give you enough notice to wedge three minutes with me in between appointments, court and catching up on your e-mail."

"Nice." His tight smile didn't even come close to reaching his eyes.

But true. And sad. "I'm sorry. I didn't intend to rehash old ground." She pressed her palm to her forehead to ease the swimming dots of frustration swirling in front of her eyes. "This isn't a good time to discuss anything, which is why I want to meet with you next week. I'll call your secretary and set up an appointment."

She spun away on her heels, only just managing not to fall on her face. She grabbed the end of a row for balance until the floor stopped wobbling underneath her.

Sebastian braced a hand on the small of her back. "Slow down and take a deep breath. It's only natural you're still upset from the proceedings."

"Upset? *Upset!*" Glancing over her shoulder at

him, she swallowed a bubble of hysterical laughter. She wanted to cry and pitch plates and rail at the unfairness of her greatest dream being tempered by such a total crap day. "As always you're the master of understatement."

He pinched the bridge of his nose for two of those steadying breaths before looking at her again, his expression a little too close to pity for her liking. Ire kicked up a storm in her already churning stomach.

Sebastian slid his hand from her back to her arm for a tiny squeeze as he stepped closer. "So now you want some kind of goodbye-over-coffee moment."

Her body reacted through instinct to the familiar heat of him, the scent of his aftershave, the strength of his touch. How long would it take for time to dull the sensory memory of just how good he could make her feel?

She plucked his hand off and aside. "We said our goodbyes in the backseat of your car." Anger, hurt and fear all left her itchy and irritable. "Your conjugal rights officially ended about five minutes ago."

He would no doubt have plenty of opportunities to indulge himself with all the starry-eyed students that floated in and out of his successful practice. She'd seen a virtual entourage of admiring females in his law library some nights when she'd come by to pick him up late.

"Okay, okay, take it easy." He backed her into

the privacy of a quiet corner. He flattened a hand on the wall beside her head, his body creating a barricade between her and the onlookers staring at them with ill-disguised interest. "I completely understand that future shoe fashion shows have been canceled."

Marianna scrunched her toes in her silver Jimmy Choo slingbacks and willed down the memories that would only wound her. Heaven knew that when she hurt she let it out with anger. But she would not cause a scene.

It was hard enough getting through these past few hours while her mind taunted her with images of what the day could have been like. If only she'd been able to surprise Sebastian at the office with a mug that read "Real Men Do Diapers" or some other cute coded announcement.

Of course he probably would have been in court or taking a deposition.

Oops, there went her temper again. *Breathe. Breathe. Breathe.* "It's not about a civilized cup of coffee. There are just some, uh, loose ends we need to discuss when we're both calmer. I'll talk to you next week, somewhere neutral and public."

He held his position, almost touching, his gaze assessing her like some witness on the stand for endless seconds.

His BlackBerry buzzed. He ignored it. But still…

"You had that on during our divorce hearing?"

She backed away, all hopes of calm long gone. "We definitely shouldn't talk today."

"Fine, whatever you want."

It wasn't what she wanted by a long shot, but there wasn't any other choice. "Goodbye, Sebastian."

But it wasn't really farewell and she knew it. There would be no clean break for them now. Marianna ducked under his arm and toward the exit. She had one week to shore up her resolve and make plans.

She double-timed down the hall, barely registering that his big wonderful family sat on benches waiting. Just the kind of oversize clan she'd dreamed about as a lonely only child of elderly parents, who'd loved her, yes, but now even they were gone.

She pressed her hand to her stomach, her silver bracelets clinking, and prayed all the harder for the tiny life inside her. Her heart pounded faster. Or wait. Those were footsteps approaching her— Sebastian's, of course. He wasn't letting her off that easily. How strange that while he never fought, he always won.

Sebastian punched the elevator button for her, cocking his head to the side as he studied her with his piercing litigator stare. Oh God, she so didn't want to climb into that claustrophobic box along with resurrected visions of their last ride.

"Uh, thanks, Sebastian, but I think I'll take the stairs."

She turned too fast and the world grew tighter like a narrowing focus of a lens. Her knees gave way, and all she could see on her way down were Sebastian's Ferragamo loafers she'd given him last Christmas.

"We should call EMS," Sebastian's stepfather said for the third time, his voice booming with all the authority one would expect from a three-star general.

Sebastian agreed. But the doctor—at the courthouse to testify in a hearing—seemed to think seven minutes and forty-one seconds of unconsciousness wasn't anything to worry about yet. Dr. Cohen sat on the edge of the sofa, the young professional reading her watch while holding Marianna's wrist in her hand.

After Marianna had landed at Sebastian's feet in a fall as fast as his own stomach, he'd scooped her up and made tracks for an adjacent conference room. He'd stretched her out on a sofa, slipped off her shoes, loosened her pink jacket, while his mother hovered and the General located help in the form of Dr. Cohen.

While he'd asked his family not to come to the courthouse, they'd shown up anyway. It was a good thing after all.

Two of his brothers clumped in a corner with his mom and the General. Standing. Waiting. Sebastian hated inaction, a big part of why he enjoyed his job.

There was always something to do, some way to charge ahead and take control.

Why wasn't Marianna opening her eyes? And how many times would that doc count a pulse? Duke medical credentials be damned—and yeah, he'd asked when she started checking Marianna over. Dr. Cohen would just have to live with being overridden if his ex-wife didn't wake up in the next ten seconds.

Sebastian knelt on one knee beside the sofa, lifting Marianna's other hand, too cool and limp in his grip. "I'm going to take her to the E.R. now. If she wakes up on the way, great. And if she doesn't—" What could be wrong with her? "She'll be at the hospital all the sooner."

The doctor stood, pulling her glasses off to hang from the gold chain around her neck. "That's your call to make, of course, as her husband."

Husband? Now wasn't that a kick in the legal briefs? But he didn't intend to correct the doctor and lose what tenuous ground he held over Marianna's medical care at the moment. He shot a quick "mouths shut" look over his shoulder to his wide-eyed family.

A low moan from Marianna yanked his attention back to the sofa. Her lashes fluttered and he squeezed her hand.

"Marianna? Come on, wake up. You're scaring us here."

"Sebastian?" She elbowed up to look around,

massaging two fingers against her temple. She blinked fast, her gaze skipping around the small room filled with nothing more than a conference table, swivel chairs, the sofa and concerned relatives. "What happened?"

"You passed out in the hall. Don't you remember?" If any day was worth forgetting, this would be it.

She sagged back, her pink suit skirt hitching up her legs. "Oh, right, the courthouse, your Ferragamo shoes."

He didn't know what the hell his shoes had to do with anything, but at least she grasped the gist of the day.

His mother nudged him aside and placed a damp handkerchief over Marianna's forehead. "Here, dear, just lie back until you catch your breath."

"Thank you, Ginger." Marianna accepted the cool cloth with a grateful smile.

Why hadn't he thought to do that? "How are you feeling now?"

She looked away, apparently more interested in the window blinds than in seeing him. "I forgot to eat breakfast. That must have sent my blood sugar out of whack."

"What about lunch?" He pointed to the industrial clock over the door. "It's three o'clock."

"Already?" She peeled the damp cloth from her forehead and dabbed it along her neck. "My nerves must have gotten the best of me. I couldn't bring myself to choke anything down."

If Marianna couldn't eat, something was seriously wrong. This woman loved her food, one of the things he'd enjoyed most about her. Watching her savor oysters on the half shell had landed them in bed more than once. "Have you been sick?"

She sat upright, swinging her feet to the floor beside her silver slingbacks. "Thank you for your concern, but I'm responsible for myself now that we're divorced."

Dr. Cohen's eyebrows rose. "He's your *ex*-husband?"

Marianna nodded, glancing at the clock. "As of about a half hour ago."

The physician brought her red-rimmed glasses to her mouth and nipped lightly on the tip. "Taking that into consideration with a low blood sugar level, no wonder you fainted." She gave Marianna's wrist a final pat. "And here I was assuming you must be pregnant just because that's my specialty."

Marianna winced and looked away as she'd done countless times over the years when people mentioned babies. The purple stains of exhaustion below her eyes broadcast the additional stress she'd been under lately if anyone looked beyond a credible makeup job. Sebastian stepped between her and the doctor, territorial, protective.

Shaking loose of that husband appellation and all the urges that came with it was easier said than done. "That's not what's going on, but we will find the real reason for her fainting spell."

How many times in the past had he diverted conversations from the seeming unending litany of well-meaning and sometimes downright intrusive comments?

When are you going to make me a grandmother?
Isn't it time to start your family?
You and Marianna treat those dogs like children.
I guess not everyone wants babies.

Dr. Cohen backed away, scooping her bag off the conference table. "My apologies for jumping to conclusions. Of course there are plenty of other reasons for fainting besides not eating. If the problems persist, however, I do recommend that you check in with your regular physician." Hitching her bag over her shoulder, Dr. Cohen paused at the door. "Now if you'll excuse me, it's probably about time for my turn in the witness stand."

The General escorted the doctor out with a thank-you while Ginger hovered just off to the side. "Marianna, dear, we're glad you're all right. Please know that you can call on us if you need anything."

Like prideful, strong-willed Marianna would ever show that kind of vulnerability. He was still shocked as hell she'd asked to meet with him next week.

With soft spoken goodbyes, his family cleared out, leaving him alone with Marianna for the first time since they'd torn each others' clothes off in the back of his car two months prior.

Damn, silence sure did weigh a lot.

He leaned back against the conference table, his arms crossed over his chest to keep from touching her. "I don't think you should drive yourself home."

She slipped her slingbacks onto her feet, drawing his attention to slender long legs. "And I don't think it's wise for us to get in your car together again."

"Still want me that much, do you?" he couldn't resist retorting.

"Don't be an ass." Her eyes snapped with barely restrained anger and something else he couldn't quite define. "All I want is a nap."

He needed to focus on her health, not those creamy legs that wrapped so perfectly around his waist. "You should see your doctor or go to an E.R. if he's busy."

"I have an appointment for the end of the week. I called this morning."

His legal eagle instincts piqued, urging him to dissect her statement. "If you're feeling that ill, why wait until the end of the week?"

Silently, she stared back, blinking quickly, her chest rising and falling faster by the second. He'd spent the last three years since passing the bar exam interrogating witnesses, and he had a good knack for spotting when a person was hiding something. And he knew without question, Marianna had a secret lodged somewhere inside that beautiful head of hers.

He intended to discover that secret before they left this room.

Three

"So Marianna? Why wait four days to see the doctor if you can't eat and you're passing out?"

Marianna stared back at her narrow-eyed ex and experienced a total empathic bond with butterflies pinned to a display board. Somehow Sebastian knew she had a secret, and he wasn't setting her free until she ponied up information.

Did the state bar pass out internal lie detectors when awarding licenses? She had two choices here. She could brush him aside and wait for the doctor's verdict that Friday. If she wasn't pregnant, she wouldn't need to say anything to Sebastian.

Except she knew in her heart, against all the

odds, somehow she carried his baby, which brought her to the other option. Tell him the truth now, because if she didn't he would be royally pissed next week.

And rightfully so.

"About that time a couple of months ago, in your car when we, uh…"

"Right, I remember." Heat stirred in his eyes.

Of course he did, but hearing him admit it rekindled the steam of their raw goodbye. She could almost smell the rain and sex in the air. "We didn't use birth control."

His eyebrows pinched together. "Of course we didn't. You're not on anything, and I don't carry any with me because we…" his voice slowed as his forehead smoothed "…don't need it."

She stayed silent.

He shook his head, opened his mouth and shook his head again. "You're pregnant?"

She nodded, shrugging, still not able to form the words after so many years coming to grips with the idea of *never* having the chance.

He sunk into a leather conference chair, his face completely expressionless in spite of the slight paling. "You're pregnant."

"I'm fairly certain I'm two months along."

He scrubbed a hand over his jaw. "I already figured out the two months part."

"Thank you for not asking whose it is." She couldn't have taken the pain of such an accusation on a day when her emotions were already stripped bare.

"I guess I'm not the total ass you seem to think I am."

"You've questioned my hours at work often enough."

He'd quizzed her about time with her boss more than once. Sure Ross Ward had a playboy reputation, but damn it, Sebastian should have known she could be trusted. She'd been hurt by his unfounded suspicions. He vowed he could read the truth in people's eyes, but he'd sure missed the boat on that one with her.

He folded his arms over his chest, the swivel chair squeaking back. "Are you trying to start a fight by bringing up Ross Ward?"

"Of course not. There's no point. With DNA tests, it's easy enough to prove paternity these days."

Sebastian stood and paced away, resting his palms on the window ledge. His broad shoulders stretched the dark suit jacket as they rose and fell heavily. "We're having a child."

It still seemed surreal to her, too. "If all goes well."

He pivoted hard and fast toward her. "Is something wrong?"

"I don't think so, but I only just ran a home pregnancy test this morning."

He closed the steps between them. "You're two

months along and just figured it out today? You haven't even been to a doctor?"

She fought the urge to stand and jab him in the chest. She would probably just faint at his feet again anyway. "Don't raise your voice at me."

He snorted on a laugh. "Now that's a switch. Usually you're the one shouting."

"Sit down and listen, please." She waited until he took his seat beside her, which placed his thigh and arms temptingly against hers.

Marianna swallowed hard and forged ahead. "I know it sounds strange, but at first, I couldn't bring myself to believe I'm actually finally pregnant."

"That's what you wanted to talk to me about next week."

"Yes, once I had a chance to confirm it with a doctor."

She waited while he processed the information. This wasn't going nearly as badly as she'd feared. Maybe in spite of all the harsh and hurtful words they'd tossed at each other over the years, they could be civil when it came to their child.

Sebastian slid his arm along the back of the sofa, almost touching her shoulders. "I still don't understand one thing."

She fidgeted, trying to ignore the warmth of him moving closer. She could not, would not let hormones muddy the waters between them, peace and objectivity all the more important with their child's happiness in the balance. "What's that?"

"If you took a pregnancy test this morning, why didn't you tell me before the final divorce decree?"

Everything went still inside her until her pulse grew all the louder in contrast. So much for hoping this would go well.

She should have known he wouldn't let that part pass, and maybe his driven persistence was the very reason she hadn't told him. What if he'd tried to stop the proceedings? Her heart had been bruised enough by this man. She couldn't have withstood hearing him say he wanted to stay married for the baby, especially since he'd only married her in the first place because of an unplanned pregnancy.

"Sebastian, this doesn't change anything."

"Like hell it doesn't."

She rose, at the end of her tether and in need of distance. "I will be in touch with you after I see my doctor." She scooped up her portfolio and inched toward the door. "We have seven months left to settle visitation and child support."

Just that fast, he stood behind her at the door, his breath hot on her scalp. "That's not what I'm talking about. Do you really think I would have gone through with the divorce if you had told me?" He skimmed his knuckles along the back of her neck with a persuasive gentleness at odds with the terse edge to his words. "Or was that your intent all along in keeping this a secret? Making sure you could cut me out as much as possible?"

"That's not fair." Although she couldn't ignore

the grain of truth in what he'd said, she also knew she'd made the right choice. She turned to face him—and draw his enticing caress off her skin. "We were getting ready to contact divorce lawyers before when we heard about a baby girl coming up for adoption. We stayed together for Sophie, and it didn't make any difference. If anything, we grew farther apart afterward. I can't—I won't—go through that again."

"Don't—" He held up a hand, his face tight, cold. "Don't bring up her name just to derail this discussion."

Eight months ago, she would have given anything to share comfort with him while they grieved over Sophie being taken away without warning. But he'd shut down, shut her out, left her basically alone to deal with the most emotionally-crippling event in her life.

She'd learned to stand on her own and she couldn't sacrifice that hard-won ground now. "Oh, that's right, we can't talk about Sophie." Her voice cracked but she plowed ahead. "We have to pretend the child we both loved for four months doesn't even exist."

"Fighting over the past doesn't change the present." He neatly dodged mentioning Sophie's name yet again.

Marianna bit her lip until she tasted blood. Her chest heaved with emotion and the need to cry out her frustration. Was her well of tears bottomless after all? "Fine, you win on that one. I can't take any more stress today."

"I agree you need to stay calm. We have another more pressing issue anyway."

"What now?" She didn't have any reserves left to combat his doctor of jurisprudence skills at winning.

He reached for the doorknob, his other hand clamping gently but surely around her arm. "We're going to find Dr. Cohen."

She started to argue that she could find her own damn doctor when something he'd said earlier tickled through the anger to taunt her. She unpacked their conversation and realized, hey wait— He'd said he didn't carry condoms because they didn't need them, which led her to a heart-stuttering conclusion.

He didn't carry them because even with their divorce in the works, he hadn't been seeing anyone else.

"There's your baby." Dr. Cohen pointed to the ultrasound machine. "And that's a healthy heartbeat."

Sebastian stared at the screen, unable to take his eyes off the tiny bean shape wriggling around. His *child*. In no universe had he predicted his day would turn out this way. At best, he'd expected his brothers to pour vintage bourbon down his throat until he could pass out and sleep away his first night of renewed bachelorhood.

Not in his wildest dreams had he imagined

chasing down an ob-gyn at the courthouse and requesting she take a surprise drop-in client. And in
the times he'd let himself consider the possibility
of Marianna becoming pregnant, he definitely
hadn't thought they would both work to avoid
touching and looking at each other.

Dr. Cohen typed commands on the keyboard, the
image on the screen freezing as she readjusted
Marianna's gown and sheet. "And that's all for
today." She patted Marianna's arm. "Once you get
dressed, stop by my office on your way out."

Marianna's hands fisted in the crackly paper
covering on the exam table. "Is something wrong?"

"Nothing that I can see." Dr. Cohen slid on her
glittery red glasses and jotted notations on the chart
before slapping it closed. "I need to give you your
prescription for prenatal vitamins. And if you opt
to stay with me as your ob-gyn, we need to set up
your next appointment."

The ob-gyn reached beneath the monitor and
came back with two black-and-white glossy photos.
"A picture of the baby for both of you. Congratulations, Mom and Dad."

Marianna reached to grasp the doctor's hand.
"Thank you for all your help and patience this afternoon. You've really gone above and beyond for us."

"I imagine this has been a roller-coaster day.
I'm glad to be of help." Dr. Cohen pulled the
privacy curtain aside, then in place again a second
before the door clicked open and closed.

Marianna inched up, tucking the sheet around her. "Sebastian, could you please step outside?"

He tore his eyes from the photo to Marianna. The paper "blouse" and sheet strategically covered everything. But now that she mentioned it, he couldn't help but think of her bare beneath those flimsy barriers.

Her breasts seemed fuller—from the pregnancy?—tempting him to test their weight with his hands, explore the swell brought on from carrying his child. No matter how long they stayed apart, he would never forget the exact feel and shape of her.

He'd been her lover since they were eighteen years old. He'd become her husband when they found out she was pregnant. Interesting how life had a way of repeating itself.

"Sebastian—" Her indignant voice pulled him back into the sterile reality of the exam room.

"Relax, Marianna. I've seen you naked, and undoubtedly I'm going to see you that way again at future doctor visits. Then there's the delivery—"

"Stop. You may have rights when it comes to your baby—" she shoved her tousled curls out of her face "—but we're not married anymore, and that means no more naked fashion shows after I go shoe shopping."

"Damn shame." He plucked her slingbacks from the floor and set them on the exam table. "That's a hot pair of silver heels you're sporting."

She opened her mouth, and he held up both

hands, realizing he'd pushed his luck as far as he could for one day.

"I'm going. I'm going." For now. "I'll be waiting in the doctor's office."

He didn't expect they would return to the way things were, but he resented being dismissed so easily. In fact, he didn't intend to be dismissed from his child's life at all. He hadn't walked away from his responsibilities at eighteen, and he sure as hell didn't intend to at twenty-seven.

Marianna might not know it yet, but theirs was going to be one of the shortest divorces on record.

Marianna hadn't expected to end the day riding in Sebastian's Beemer, and she resented being here now. Already he was taking over her life again—the doctor, the half-eaten hoagie in her lap. And while they'd been at Dr. Cohen's, he'd arranged for his youngest brother, Jonah, to drive her car back to her house—their old home.

Sebastian had simply stated he worried about her becoming dizzy behind the wheel even though pregnant women drove every day. Although she had to admit, this day wasn't like any other. Surely when she woke in the morning she could take a calm moment to simply enjoy the photo of her baby, Sebastian's baby.

Moon battling the sun, she studied her ex-husband's stern profile as he drove past the golf course leading into the seaside subdivision where they'd built their two-story colonial dream house. Palmetto trees lined the road, marsh grass just beyond bordering the darkening seashore.

His family fortune and her inheritance from her parents had eased some of their earlier years when they both had been in college. Though they'd both rushed to graduate and start earning their own way. Maybe they would have split sooner if they'd been forced to struggle financially.

Marianna watched as they passed house after house, neighbor after neighbor. She'd been planning to move into a condo, away from memories. Now she didn't know where she would live. She had so many plans to revise.

Plans. For the first time since she'd risen this morning—and promptly tossed her cookies—she felt *happy*. She blinked back tears. "We're going to have a baby."

He cut his eyes toward her. "Appears so."

"I need some time for it to soak in. Then we can start making decisions." Like how she traveled to and from appointments and how much of her body he saw. "My work schedule is more flexible than yours. Let me know when you're free next week, and I'll be there."

"Thanks. And I'll have my accountant deposit money in your checking account tomorrow so you can put in your two weeks' notice."

She sat up bolt right. Surely he couldn't have meant what she thought. "What did you say?"

"You already miscarried once." He paused for a yield sign, calm-as-can-freaking-be, as if he hadn't just ordered her to quit her job. "You need to take things easy."

Stay cool. Try not to think about his jealousy of her boss in the past. They only had a few more yards until she could escape into the house. "That's for the doctor to decide, not you. And I lost the first baby because of an ectopic pregnancy. We already know from the ultrasound that isn't the case this time."

"I have enough money—more than enough—so you don't have to work." He charged ahead with his plan as if she hadn't spoken. "Why risk it?"

Flashbacks of that frightening miscarriage rolled through her head. How she and Sebastian had gone to the mountains for their honeymoon after eloping, both of them realizing their relationship was starting on shaky ground and hoping to cement their feelings with a getaway.

Instead, four days in, the excruciating pain and scary bleeding had started. Then she'd endured the interminably long drive down the mountain road to find a hospital. The surgeon had told her if they'd arrived an hour later, she could have hemorrhaged to death.

She understood full well how quickly things could go wrong.

Marianna gathered her portfolio off the floor mat. "This is the very reason I wanted to wait until next week to discuss anything with you."

"Seven days to line up your arguments."

"Seven days to shore up my defenses against being bullied."

"You're right." He glanced over at her with a curt nod. "You shouldn't be upset."

"I'll take that as an apology."

He stayed silent beside her, slowing the car to turn onto her street. He never apologized. After arguments, he analyzed how they could have chosen their words differently. He left extravagant gifts. He bought her a day at the spa.

But he never said those three magic words: *I am sorry*.

Staring into the night sky, Marianna blinked fast against the moisture stinging again. Sebastian put the car into Park outside their brick home with white columns and leaned across the seat. He pulled her close, and she let herself rest against his chest even if she didn't actually touch him back.

She sniffled, scrubbing her wrist over her damp eyes. "It's just the hormones, understand?"

"Got it." He gave her shoulders a quick squeeze then stepped out of the car.

She opened the passenger door, steeling her will to stop him at the steps. Marianna's hip bumped the door closed and she turned only to slam into Sebastian standing stone still. All tenderness left his face as he stared at the front porch—where her boss, Ross Ward, waited in a rocking chair.

Four

Blood steaming, Sebastian resisted the urge—just barely—to launch up the steps and pitch Ross Ward off the porch on his Italian-jean-clad ass. The bastard apparently wasn't wasting any time making his move on Marianna now that she was a free woman.

Boy, did Ward have a surprise coming his way.

But not now. Marianna had been through enough drama for one day, so Sebastian reined himself in. Hell, a divorce, surprise pregnancy and decision to win her back rocked even him on his heels.

Sebastian pivoted slowly to face her again,

sculpting control into his voice given her boss had been a sore subject between them in the past. "What's he doing here?"

"I have no idea." Marianna shrugged, hitching her portfolio under her arm and brushing by him toward their sprawling porch.

Ward shoved up from the white rocker, smoothing his casual jacket and tie. "What is *he* doing here?"

Sebastian had done his level best to be polite to the guy in the past. Her boss owned the interior decorator firm where she worked, after all. Ward handled the more masculine designs, making a name for himself as the decorator for sports stars across the Southeast. Marianna had been placed in charge of the homes for the *Southern Living* crowd.

He'd been okay with her boss at first, but over the years, he just couldn't get past the sense that Ward harbored feelings for Marianna. He even seemed to schedule her buying trips around the few times Sebastian had free.

His instincts had been validated often enough in the courtroom that he did not doubt himself for a second when it came to Marianna's boss.

Sebastian kept his hand on her shoulder as they walked along the decorative stepping stones winding around patches of flowers and a stone bird feeder. "Why am *I* here? I'm Marianna's husband."

"Ex-husband." Ward lounged against the porch column with a proprietary air that set Sebastian's teeth on edge. "I thought Marianna might need some cheering up after court." He stroked his close-trimmed blond beard as he faced her. "I've made dinner reservations. If we leave now, we can make still make it."

"Oh," she responded, looking flustered for the first time since they'd stepped from the car, "thank you—"

A low bark sounded from inside the house, growing louder and louder until a thud sounded on the other side of the door. Buddy. Marianna hurried past, and Sebastian wanted to dispense of this poaching jerk and go about normal life—walking on the beach with Marianna and talking about their baby, while their dogs bounded through the surf. And yeah, he was being semi-delusional given the workload weighing down his briefcase since he'd been forced to take half a day off for handling the mess his personal life had become.

Sebastian stopped on the porch, topping Ward by at least two inches. "She's already had supper."

Hanging baskets of ferns creaked in the evening breeze as Ward glanced at the half-eaten hoagie in Marianna's hand with ill-disguised disdain. "So I see."

She placed the sandwich on the rocker and unlocked the front door. Buddy bounded out as she knelt to greet the pug-faced mutt. "Hey there, fella. Did you miss me? I missed you—yes, I did."

Marianna adored that dog and by God, so did he.

An image blindsided him of a little girl one day dressing Buddy up in a tutu, and damn, but the mental vision sucker punched him hard.

He was a father again.

The reality of it rolled over him fully for the first time in a day that had moved too fast to let him think. All his lawyerly impulses revved to maximum velocity. He had a case to put forward, a family to win back. Losing was not an option.

Marianna rubbed her face against the dog's short fur, pitching her portfolio onto the hall floor, the long stairway up to the bedrooms beckoning. She reached to grab Buddy's leash draped over the rocker.

Sebastian quirked a brow at Ward. "Looks to me like she's settling in at home. Guess you'd better pull out your little black book and find someone else to share your grilled grouper."

"Hell-O." Marianna waved her hand between them, holding on to Buddy's leash as the dog leapt toward Sebastian. "I'm here, and I can speak for myself."

Ward stepped back from the bounding dog—all twenty-five pounds of "threatening" energy. "Of course you can. You're a single woman now."

Kneeling to scratch Buddy's neck, Sebastian didn't even bother holding back his smile over sharing this with Marianna. As much as they enjoyed their dogs, how much more awesome would it be when they saw their child for the first time? A connection that could never be broken.

Sebastian looked at her stomach, then over at Ward who was busy wiping dog drool off his Prada penny loafers. What would the guy think of Marianna's pregnancy?

She jabbed her finger in the middle of Sebastian's chest. "Don't even think about saying it."

He leaned over Buddy to whisper in her ear. "Shouldn't your boss know?"

She hissed between gritted teeth, "When I'm good and ready. You would be wise to remember it's in your best interest to stay in my good graces."

He didn't think for a minute that Marianna would keep his baby from him, but he wanted the whole package—wife and kid. This called for diplomacy on his part.

Ward looked from one to the other, his smugness faltering for the first time. "Was there some hitch in the proceedings?"

Marianna passed Buddy's leash over to Sebastian and turned to Ward. "The divorce is official." She stepped closer, a smile curving her soft lips. "Thank you for the dinner offer—that was thoughtful— but how about a rain check? I'm really tired."

Concern for her health mixed with relief over Ward being given his walking papers. As she escorted Ward to his low-slung Jaguar, Sebastian looped the leash around his hand, remembering late-night walks on the beach, memorable, but not all that frequent now that he thought back.

Juggling his workload while winning Marianna

over would be difficult, but then he'd always thrived on a challenge at work. And who needed sleep anyway?

The Jag's growling engine drew Sebastian's attention back to the manicured lawn and Marianna coming up the decorative stepping stones she'd picked out. She'd asked his opinion, but he left that sort of thing to her. She'd chosen well.

Marianna flattened a hand to a fat column. "Thank you for not saying anything about the baby. I'm not ready to tell the world yet. I need time for the news to settle in and some reassurance the pregnancy will go to term."

"Understood." The thought of her miscarrying again—the hell of her almost hemorrhaging to death all those years ago—clenched through him. And he refused to think of the daughter they'd lost a few short months ago. He couldn't even bring himself to think her name with the fresh slice those two syllables would bring.

Marianna scraped a fingernail along a smudge on the pillar with undue concentration. "Would you please hold off on telling your family?"

"I think it's something we should do together. But whenever you're ready." It was an easy enough concession, especially since his goal was keeping her even-keeled.

Confusion shadowed through her eyes in the dim porch light. "I can't believe how reasonable you're being about all this. That means a lot to me."

"Your peace of mind is my number one priority."

She looked down and away. "Of course. The baby's wellbeing comes first."

He skimmed knuckles along her arm. "I still care about you, too." And he meant it. He wanted her. Even though she seemed to have some pie-in-the-sky idea of what he should be able to give her, they had made some amazing memories together. That and their baby would be enough this time. It had to be. "It's impossible not to care after nine years of marriage."

She trembled under his touch, her pupils widening with desire as she rocked toward him. How damn ironic that it took a divorce to soften Marianna, but he wasn't one to squander an advantage. His hand slid up her arm to cup her neck—

Headlights swept the driveway as Ward pulled in behind Sebastian's Beemer. "Marianna? I meant to remind you before I left. Don't forget we're meeting with Matthew Landis and his fiancée tomorrow to discuss decorating plans for their new home."

Sebastian eased his hand away. So much for drop-kicking Ward to the curb just yet. But at least Sebastian knew exactly where he needed to be for supper tomorrow night.

The next evening, Marianna drove along the winding paved drive leading to the Landis compound. Palm trees and sea grass parted to reveal a white three-story house with Victorian peaks overlooking the ocean. A lengthy set of stairs stretched upward to the second-level wraparound porch that housed the main living quarters. Latticework shielded most of the first floor, which boasted a large entertainment area.

The attached garage held a fleet of expensive cars for all the family members residing in various suites and the carriage house. She stopped her Mercedes convertible out front by a clump of pink azaleas, having months ago handed over the garage remote she'd been given.

Although exhausted from a long afternoon dealing with a picky society scion with questionable taste, she looked forward to finishing her day here. She genuinely liked Sebastian's brother and his fiancée. She'd asked them repeatedly if they would prefer another decorator from Ross's business, and they'd insisted she was their first choice.

Climbing the stairway leading up to the main entrance, she reminded herself not to be nervous about seeing everyone. She was a twenty-seven-year-old woman with a successful career. She'd redecorated everything from a historic mayoral mansion to an elaborate tree house featured in *Architectural Digest*. She'd consulted on a design show that had been picked up in several regional markets. Besides, her ex-in-laws were wonderful people. They wouldn't skewer her just because she'd initiated the divorce.

She hoped.

Shuffling the portfolio packed with color swatches and sketches of room designs, Marianna started to grab the doorknob—then pulled her hand back as if burned. She wasn't family anymore. With a twinge to her heart, she rang the bell. She just wanted to get through this evening without tapping into more of those hormonal tears that seemed to hover ever-near.

The door swung wide to reveal her ex-mother-in-law, a smoothly beautiful woman with gray-blond hair. In her jeans and a short sleeve sweater set with pearls, no one would guess Ginger was one of the country's most powerful politicians.

Even having been a Landis for nine years, Marianna still found herself taken aback on occasion by so much financial and political power in one family. Sebastian's independently wealthy father had been a U.S. senator, a seat that passed to his wife after his premature death. Now that Ginger was on a short list to be the next secretary of state, her oldest son was running for her soon-to-be vacated senatorial spot.

Ginger wrapped Marianna in a warm hug and urged her inside. "Come in, dear." She smiled openly, easing some of the awkwardness. "You must be feeling better. You look positively radiant."

Pregnancy glow? Awkwardness tingled right back up Marianna's spine again.

"Uh, thank you, Ginger." Her shaky voice echoed up into the cathedral ceiling.

Ginger led her past the main living room, the wall of windows showcasing the stars just beginning to twinkle. Hardwood floors were scattered with light Persian rugs around two Queen Anne sofas upholstered in a pale blue fabric with white piping. Wingback chairs in a creamy yellow angled off the side in a formal but airy, comfortable way.

Marianna considered the decor one of her best works since she'd seen firsthand how the family worked and designed it with their needs in mind.

Ginger squeezed her elbow. "We're having dessert on the balcony. I saved a plate for you. I know chocolate cheesecake's your favorite."

As much as Marianna wanted to keep this businesslike, no mealtime chitchat, her first official pregnancy craving walloped her. She would have walked across nails for a slice of cheesecake. "That was very thoughtful of you."

Ginger paused just before the French balcony doors. "Even though you and Sebastian are no longer married, we still love you." She'd said the same before, but hearing it again after the divorce meant a lot, especially with the baby on the way. Even more so *because* Ginger didn't know about the baby. "You were my daughter for nine years and that's not something I can just shrug off."

Whoops, there went those hormonal tears after all as she studied Ginger with a new perspective—as her baby's grandmother. Why couldn't this have been a happy time of celebration? Heaven knew, she and Sebastian had dreamed often enough of the day they would be able to present Ginger with grandchildren.

They'd experienced this beautiful moment when Sophie joined their family at two days old.

Another tear slipped down her cheek. "I don't know what to say except thank you, and you're all very special to me, too."

Ginger whipped a tissue from a brass box on a cherry wood accent table. "I'm relieved to hear that."

Dabbing her eyes dry, Marianna prepared to face the rest of the group, hoping they would be as welcoming. Ginger swung the glass doors wide to the balcony overlooking the organic pool and rolling ocean.

As an only child, Marianna still felt overwhelmed by Sebastian's relatives at times, even in partial force. The second-born son, Kyle, was serving in the Air Force and had just been deployed to Afghanistan. She scanned the porch, the wicker furniture full of Sebastian's family.

The General, Sebastian's stepfather, slid an arm around Ginger's shoulders and smiled his welcome to Marianna. "We're glad to have a chance to see you before we head back to D.C."

The older Air Force pilot now served on the Joint Chiefs of Staff. Ginger and Hank Renshaw divided their time between South Carolina and the nation's capital.

Sebastian's oldest brother, Matthew, sat at a small corner table with his fiancée, Ashley; the engaged couple feeding each other cheesecake in such a blatant display of love Marianna clenched the damp tissue in her fist.

"Hey, Marianna," the youngest of the Landis brothers, Jonah, said as he flipped a lock of shaggy hair off his brow. Tossing a mint into the air, he bounced it off his head and into his mouth with the seasoned dexterity of a college soccer player. Except now he'd graduated, and he was busy "finding" himself.

A bark drew her attention to the beach to see Holly—running with Sebastian.

He'd left work early? Blinking back her surprise, she allowed herself a second to study him playing Frisbee with their other dog—his dog now. He'd even been home long enough to change into khaki shorts and a polo shirt.

She braced herself for the inevitable wave of attraction. Wind ruffled his brown hair as he sprinted with a lean, athletic grace. What kind of craziness was this that she ached for his body even more now than before the divorce? Was this some kind of weird quirk of nature along the lines of want but can't have?

Or could it be another by-product of the hormonal flood assaulting her system?

Matthew Landis rose from his chair, his hand still resting affectionately on his shy fiancée's shoulder. "Thanks for coming over, Marianna. Hope you don't mind if we look at the plans out here."

As much as she wanted to retreat away from the lure of family life, who could argue with this million-dollar view? The *beach* view that was, not Sebastian, blast it.

Marianna kept her mind focused on business, doing her best to avoid the magnetic pull of her tanned ex thudding up the steps. "I'm glad to be here. Ross will be joining us shortly. He got held up by an accident on one of the bridges."

"Hey, beautiful." Sebastian's voice drifted up the stairs.

An awkward silence settled like a storm cloud on the otherwise clear evening. Holly bounded past him, breaking the tension and providing her with a welcome alternative focus.

Marianna met Holly halfway down the wooden stairs, needing a chance to break the ice with Sebastian before facing him with his whole family in earshot. "You're off work early."

"A guy's gotta eat sometime."

She restrained herself from mentioning how many meals he'd taken at his desk. Was he genuinely making an effort because of the baby? If so, only time would tell whether or not he could maintain the change.

Marianna knelt to rub Holly's ears. The brown-and-black mutt rolled onto her back appreciatively. God, she missed the sweetie and questioned again the wisdom of separating the two dogs. Had she been selfish? Should she have let them stay together with Sebastian? She had given them both to him for Christmas two years ago, after all.

Warm, strong fingers banded around her ankle and she, startled, found herself eye level with Sebastian. His thumb slid between her high heel and foot to stroke her arch, a spot he knew full well to be an erogenous zone.

"Nice shoes." He tapped the strap on her fire-engine-red heels—and no, she hadn't chosen them with him in mind.

Had she?

She inched her foot free, the exact imprint of his fingers still tingling along her bare skin. She wanted more, ached to test the rasp of his five o'clock shadow along the sensitive pads of her fingers. Gauging by the knowing glint in his blue eyes, he understood exactly what he was doing to her.

Marianna leaned closer, whispering, "Touch me that way again and the heel goes through your hand."

"You sure don't pull any punches." He tugged a lock of her dark hair, stroking his fingers down its length and finishing with a gentle pull.

"You're a big boy. You can handle it." She eased her head away from his tempting caress. Too easily she could be wooed by the warmth of his touch and the welcome of his family.

"Can *you* handle it?" His hand grazed hers under the guise of petting Holly.

"Do I even want to?"

"You tell me." His warm blue eyes turned lazy. "The Beemer's out front."

She swatted his hand aside, all too aware of his family working overly hard at conversation on the porch. "Stop flirting."

"'Scuse me. Were you talking?" His gaze fell to her chest. "I was busy checking out your new curves."

She rolled her eyes, sighing, not sure whether to be miffed or charmed by his teasing. At least he was trying in his own way to smooth over this awkward moment.

Regardless, she wasn't sure how much more of his sensual teasing she *could* handle tonight. Marianna climbed back up the steps just as Ross Ward strode onto the balcony in his signature jeans and jacket.

Sebastian palmed her back.

Frustration simmered low, battling with the urge to press more firmly against his hand. Hadn't she just told him to stop touching her? She looked over her shoulder at her ex and found he wasn't looking her way at all. His eyes were narrowed and locked firmly on Ross.

Damn. So much for her hopeful thoughts of a pleasant evening with a reformed Sebastian. Her ex-husband hadn't changed in the least.

Sebastian was marking his territory.

Five

Sebastian was in the doghouse and he knew it. He'd been there often enough in the past to recognize the signs of Marianna's fast blinking and tight lips. But having been intimately acquainted with the inside of said doghouse provided the handy benefit of knowing how to get back out.

Marianna had a temper, no question, but she also usually had a forgiving heart. Yet somewhere along the line in their marriage, he'd stopped caring about making up and she'd stopped caring that he didn't try anymore.

Tonight, however, with a baby to consider, he decided it was time to capitalize on those old making-up skills with a walk along the beach. He just needed to persuade her to join in before she had time to fish out her keys and climb into her Mercedes.

She'd been ticked off with him since her hippie boss had arrived. Not that anyone else would have noticed. Sebastian had gone through the motions of a pleasant dessert meeting, pretending interest as Matthew and Ashley chose the decor for the home they were having built.

Sebastian was genuinely interested in seeing his brother and happy new fiancée, of course, but he didn't know squat about decorating. He spent most of the evening trying to pinpoint what it was about Ward that set off his protective radar. Yet no matter how closely he watched the guy, there was never anything overt. Ward didn't touch Marianna too much, was always deferential to her opinions and eager to hear what she had to say.

About a year ago, he'd tried to spell out his concerns about the guy to Marianna and she'd about blown a gasket explaining that just because Sebastian never wanted to have a conversation didn't mean every man felt the same way. This proved, once again, that her boss was a topic they couldn't discuss rationally.

Now as Ward drove down the driveway, Sebastian stood with Marianna outside her convertible prepping his strategy to divert her anger before it erupted into an argument. "Let's let Holly run for a few minutes so we can talk away from my family."

She was always on him about spending too much time at work and not enough time relaxing together. A walk should fit the bill.

He kept his hands in his pockets. She wouldn't be receptive to touches yet, not until she cooled down. With stars winking overhead, the backdrop of the opaque night ocean would set the romantic mood well enough.

Hesitating, she twisted her key ring. She didn't look quite ready to forget her anger…

Finally, she nodded an acceptance of his offer and tossed her keys on top of her portfolio on the front seat. Nobody would steal her car inside the gated confines of the Landis family compound. "A walk sounds nice. I should start getting more exercise, and there's something I need to discuss with you."

Yeah, he figured as much, but he would sidetrack her before she had a chance to start that "Ross Ward Fight" again.

She picked her way alongside him, heels sinking into the sandy lawn as he circled the main house toward the beach. Sea oats rustled in the distance along with the gush and roar of the waves on the shore. Holly bounded ahead and into the surf, the more playful of their pets. He'd been insistent on Marianna keeping Buddy because of the dog's pro-tectiveness.

Thinking of Marianna alone in the big house…

Sebastian stuffed down thoughts certain to frustrate him at a time he needed to keep his cool more than ever. It proved to be a tough enough job already with her exotic perfume scenting the breeze, reminding him of times that same scent clung to their sheets.

Marianna kicked off her shoes and jogged ahead to join their dog. Her short suit skirt left plenty of leg bare to splash through the waves, her hair tumbling down her back. The wind plastered her untucked blouse to her breasts with an intimacy his hands ached to copy.

He scooped up her heels and watched. She'd gone from angry to laughing in the span of two minutes all because of a pup's playfulness. Marianna's exuberance entranced him. How long had it been since that happened? A few years into their marriage, he'd become irritated with her distractibility, no longer seeing the charm of her capricious moods.

As if she felt his eyes on her, she glanced back over her shoulder and stopped. Her arms fell to her sides again, moonlight playing with all those different shades of brown in her hair.

Tiny sand crabs scuttled past his feet as her smile faded. Once again she wore her defensive cloak of awareness from their past fights. Countless times he'd asked her to stay on topic while she demanded he quit using his lawyer logic on her and shout back, damn it. The past threatened to suck him under again with its old numbing anger at a time *he* needed to stay on topic. Maybe he should slip off his own shoes and—

"All right." Marianna approached him and said, "What do you need to say now that we're away from your family?"

He wanted the dancing Marianna back. "Is it a crime to spend time together?"

"We're divorced, not dating." She began walking at least, if not dancing.

He eased closer to her side as they left the house farther behind. "We have to establish neutral ground before the baby is born. Tension isn't good for a kid."

"I agree," she conceded graciously—then her eyes sparked with renewed anger as bright as the starlight in the clear black sky. "I just don't want you to think this child provides you with a magical key to resume our marriage."

Were his plans that damn transparent? And what happened to her anger about Ross Ward? "What makes you believe I want to remarry so soon after the kick-in-the-teeth of a divorce?"

Her eyebrows pinched together, her lips pursing into a bow he burned to nip. "Sebastian, do you realize that's the first time you've expressed any kind of emotional feelings regarding the divorce?"

"What kind of robot goes through something like that without being affected?"

She stayed silent, giving him his answer with a

shocking clarity. He was about to explode into flames from wanting this woman and she really *did* see him as some kind of emotionless machine. He might not shout and pitch a fortune in crystal and dishes but he felt things. He just didn't waste energy ruminating about them.

"Marianna, let's get back to what you said before…" and crap, he'd just fallen into his old habit of steering things on topic. Too late now to change course, though. "Why would you assume I've already got a new wedding-ring set tucked and waiting in my pocket?"

"The last time I got pregnant, you insisted on doing the 'right' thing and I want to make sure you understand this is different."

"We were in love then."

She sure hadn't labeled him a robot in those early days.

"Love?" Marianna stumbled, and he caught her elbow before she could trip to her knees in the surf. "I, uh, didn't expect you to be this understanding of the difference between now and then."

"Did you want me to fight for you?" Of course, this was what he was doing. She just didn't know it. Yet.

"No, no, of course not." She scraped her wind-swept hair from her face to reveal her confusion. "I only thought that with the baby… I don't know what I thought anymore. Except that I don't under-stand why you went all green-eyed monster with

Ross again. He's just a friend, but even if it was more, we're divorced."

A friend? Sebastian didn't doubt for a minute the man wanted to be a helluva lot more. What did Marianna want? "Are you planning to go out with him?" He held up his hands before she could go on the defensive. "I'm honestly just curious."

She wrapped her arms around her waist, emphasizing her lush new curves. "I'm planning to have a baby."

"Pregnant women date, and I'm absolutely certain you will be one of the sexiest pregnant women on the planet."

She glanced up at him through her lashes. "You're flirting again."

"I'm stating the obvious." And he'd probably pushed as hard as he could for one night. It was time for a strategic step back in the interest of staying on track with his real goal—getting a ring on her finger before the pale patch of skin had time to tan over.

He didn't have the new diamond bought yet— even he wasn't that organized—but he didn't intend to let grass grow under his feet while he waited around. "I realize the marriage is over," he lied, but hey, he was a lawyer after all. "Still, I hope that we can use these next few months to rebuild our friendship. For the baby's sake, of course."

Stopping, she toyed with her untucked blouse grazing over her stomach. "No more nitpicking me to death about Ross?"

Any other time he would have pressed that point, but right now was about slipping into Marianna's good graces, then back into her life. "I hear you and will do my level best to lock away all caveman tendencies."

She laughed lightly and picked up her pace along the water's edge again, heading toward the house. Well, damn, her temper could be diffused that easily? Either he'd missed the boat in the past or pregnancy hormones had mellowed her.

He slowed his strides to stay even with her as they walked through the ebb and flow of the tide, time passing in a semicomfortable silence. He wanted to kiss her, lower her to the sand behind a dune and celebrate their baby news the good old-fashioned way, but no doubt even a hint of that would only cut the walk short. For now, he would settle for this slice of time with Marianna that felt like a replay of their early days together.

Too soon they were nearing the house.

Marianna tipped her face into the wind. "This isn't the way I expected things to be after we divorced. When do you think we will start fighting?"

"I hope no time soon, but I'm not counting on it." He scooped up a piece of driftwood and tossed it ahead for Holly.

"That's a fair assumption. Especially if you keep talking about me quitting work."

"So warned."

She stopped on the beach, waves lapping around

her ankles. "Thank you for suggesting this. You were right. It was a nice way to unwind after work."

"I wish I had taken the time to do it more often." And this time he wasn't lying.

Her eyes widened with surprise. She opened her mouth a couple of times as if searching for words before she finally said, "I should leave now."

It was time to shift off serious footing before she resurrected the walls. "Aw, aren't you going to walk me to my door?"

"You've got to be kidding."

"I feel so cheap."

"Sebastian…" she warned, but a hint of laughter softened her scowl.

He passed Marianna her shoes. "Now *that* was flirting."

Smiling, she snagged her heels from him. "You do it well."

"Thanks." He would have offered to walk her to her car, but she was safe enough on the secured property and he needed to run off the edginess from being so close to her yet being unable to touch her the way he wanted. "You go on ahead. Holly needs to exercise for a while longer."

"Good night, Sebastian." She leaned down to give their dog a final ear ruffle—and provide him with a too clear and tormenting view down the front of her blouse before she straightened. Waving as she turned away, she picked along the shore those last few yards toward the house.

Watching the sweet sway of her hips proved a double-edged sword. The sight completely rocked his socks, but he would have to run at least a couple of miles if he planned to sleep at all tonight.

He snagged another piece of driftwood and turned to Holly. "Hey, girl, are you ready to race?"

The mutt leapt higher, trying to snag the wood from his hand. He arced his hand back, ready for a long pitch—

A scream cut the air and clean through him. That wasn't just any scream.

It was Marianna.

Marianna barely had time to hop on one foot out of the surf before Sebastian sprinted up beside her. He scooped her into his arms, not even panting, yet sweat dotted his brow. "What's wrong? Is it the baby?"

No wonder he'd broken into a cold sweat. She squeezed his shoulder reassuringly and tried to resist the temptation of sinking deeper into his hot, muscled arms. "I'm all right. I just got stung by a jellyfish."

It hurt like a son-of-a-gun, but the hard play of Sebastian's flexing biceps under her hand offered a welcome distraction. The tense furrows on his face eased somewhat but not completely as he carried her up the incline and past the white-iron fence into the patio area. He lowered her to sit on the edge of the pool, submerging her calf in the cool water for a few soothing seconds before pulling it back out to examine.

Sebastian cradled her foot in his hand, turning it from side to side and studying the slight pink color of her skin around her ankle. "Let's go inside, and I'll get something to take the fire out."

She wasn't heading back into the warm and wonderfully welcoming Landis home. Especially not on an evening when she was already too weakened by memories of the good times they'd shared, recollections she'd somehow forgotten over the past couple of years as the chill had settled deeper and deeper into her marriage.

"It's not that bad. The sting is already fading, and the water really helps." She lowered her foot into the pool again. "I bet if I sit here for a couple of minutes I'll be fine to drive home."

He eyed the house, then her, the wheels of his logical brain almost visibly turning. The remaining tension finally eased from him, and he took off his shoes as well.

Now that was a shocker.

Then he lowered his feet into the pool. Who was this man, and what had he done with her brooding ex-husband?

His leg brushed against hers and all distracting thoughts took flight on the next gust of wind, leaving her free to focus only on the sensation of his skin against hers. His thigh teased her with each tantalizingly brief swish. An ache settled low inside her that had nothing to with the jellyfish burn and everything to do with the man beside her.

Damn him for reminding her of things she'd enjoyed about him before, of happier times. And she couldn't even blame him because still she sat here beside him, swaying closer. Her body had been weak willed around this man since she was eighteen years old.

His shoulders seemed even larger, if possible, shaded by the darkness of the seashore behind him. She waited, transfixed by a desire greater than she wanted or needed with him again.

Sebastian's hands slid from the edge of the pool onto her head, his fingers trailing along her hair. Her eyes drifted closed as his touch brushed down. He clasped her shoulders, pulling her against his broad chest, anchoring her with the caressing pressure of one palm.

Grasping her hair in his other hand, he wrapped its length around his wrist and tipped her head back with a gentle tug. The light sting echoed the tingle in her breasts pressed against him. She gasped in surprise when his lips skimmed her exposed neck, nipped her earlobe and grazed her cheekbone before hovering over her mouth. He gave her hair a more forceful tug until her lids flickered open.

"What the—" Sebastian jolted as Holly nudged between them. He gripped the mutt by the collar.

She slumped against him, gasping in hot humid gulps of sea air, relief and regret jockeying for control inside her. "Holly just saved us both from making a big mistake."

Sebastian didn't confirm or deny her statement, just stared back at her, his eyes flecked with the flinty blue she only saw during sex. Regardless of any regrets, she knew what she had to do.

Marianna angled away from him, snagging her shoes. If they'd kissed much longer, she would have been following him…anywhere. In fact, with the flush of desire still hot on her skin, she couldn't race back to her car fast enough.

Gasping, Sebastian bolted upright on the leather sofa in his office. He swiped an arm over his sweat-drenched face and swung his feet to the carpeted floor. At least he didn't have to worry about Marianna chewing him out for working too late—again.

Reaching down, he rubbed his mutt behind the ears. He wasn't sure why he'd brought Holly with him when he'd come into work after his walk with Marianna. He'd never done it before. For some reason it just seemed the thing to do when Holly had barked at the door as he headed for his car at ten in the evening.

"Hey, girl." Rough as freshly laid gravel, his voice scratched the air.

He eyed the grandfather clock in the corner—three o'clock in the morning. He'd only been asleep for an hour—long enough to sink into the night-marish night nine years ago when he'd driven Marianna down the mountain pass to the hospital, scared as hell she would die before he could get her help. And during the whole seemingly endless drive, kicking himself for choosing such a remote locale for a getaway with his *pregnant* new wife.

The scent of mountain air and her perfume still clung to his senses. How many times would he have to relive it in his sleep? Maybe Marianna was right, and they really were flat-out wrong for each other.

Sebastian rose, working the kink from his neck that had been there long before he slept on the sofa, and lumbered through down the dim hall and into the small kitchenette without pausing to flip a switch. Why bother? There wasn't much risk of bumping into anybody at the firm at this time of night.

And he spent enough time here that he had the layout memorized.

He opened the refrigerator door, the slim light knifing through the darkness. He plucked out a leftover foam container from his favorite rib restaurant—a place that knew him well after he and Marianna split. They even regularly delivered him meals after closing. One hip resting against the sink, Sebastian lifted the lid and pulled out a dry cold rib, picked it clean, tossed the bone to Holly, then started the unsatisfying process over again. More from habit than hunger, Sebastian ate, all the while thinking about the ultrasound photo in his wallet.

Sebastian threw Holly another bone. "Little different than how things used to be, huh, girl?"

There had been good times, damn it.

Sifting through the leftover dinner, he scavenged up a memory to replace the nightmare. Nearly two years ago, Marianna had surprised him at Christmas with the pair of puppies. How could he forget the power of her infectious smile as she set loose both boisterous animals with red bows around their necks, complete with adoption papers from the local animal shelter?

Sebastian looked down at the now full-grown mutt with her pug face and terrier body. Holly growled as she gnawed a bone, and he could almost hear Marianna giving him hell for feeding the dog table scraps.

She'd been right tonight about the divorce not playing out the way either of them could have predicted. Their whole marriage hadn't played out the way they expected, first with the miscarriage and then with losing Sophie.

Damn. He cut that pathway to more of the doubts that had led him to divorce court in the first place. He had to stay focused. Life had changed directions, and that was a fact—accept it and deal with it. He had a baby on the way now, and he wasn't going to be a long-distance dad.

And he sure as hell wasn't going to turn over his child to be raised by some guy like Ross Ward.

Wooing Marianna was a solid place to start. But if that didn't work, he would resort to any means necessary. Nightmares be damned, the stakes were just too high to waste time on anything less than a full press ahead.

Six

Tossing and turning all night from dreams of making love with Sebastian on the beach had left Marianna tired, cranky. And late for work. Her bout of morning sickness hadn't helped her stay on schedule either. Juggling her portfolio and sacked breakfast she hoped to be able to eat now that her stomach had settled, Marianna opened her office door only to stop short.

Sebastian was sprawled on her Queen Anne, Jacobin print sofa—asleep.

She started across the room to boot him off her couch and out of her office. What if her boss walked in? Or the receptionist?

Why couldn't Sebastian understand they weren't married anymore? He didn't have the right to waltz in and out of her life at his leisure. He needed to call in advance, make an appointment.

Dropping her portfolio and insulated food bag onto a wingback chair, she stopped inches away from his propped leather loafers. Had they really come to a place in their lives where they needed to schedule a time to talk? How damn sad.

Marianna snagged a tissue from the silver box on the end table and polished a scuff off the tip of his shoe, her eyes traveling up his toned long legs in a slightly rumpled suit. It wasn't fair that her body should be raging with hormones that left her achy and wanting at a time when Sebastian was officially forbidden territory.

Her eyes scanned along the taut muscles of his chest, suit coat parted as his hand lay on the floor. Then her gaze reached his face. Taut lines along the corners of his eyes and his jaw showed his exhaustion. From too much work? Would he continue this pace after their baby was born?

Old instincts stirred inside her, concern for how hard he pushed himself mixed with frustration at his uncompromising ways. She tried to tell herself she only cared because he was the father of her child, but couldn't ignore the extra twinge to her heart. Her feelings for him weren't as easily cast aside as she had thought while pursuing the divorce in her numbed state of grief.

She thought about waking him—but reconsidered. Let him sleep. She had plenty of work to keep her busy. And, yes, maybe she was trying to prove something to herself by staying in the room with him and successfully stifling the urge to stroke the stress lines from his forehead.

Marianna settled into the wingback, her feet on the ottoman. She spread an antique auction catalog open on her lap while she peeled back the foil top from her yogurt.

Fifteen minutes and a carton of boring dairy goop later, the grandfather clock in the corner chimed eleven o'clock. Sebastian startled awake, gripping the side of the sofa to keep from pitching off.

"Hi there, gorgeous." He scrubbed a hand over his face, his gravelly voice sounding too temptingly like numerous shared mornings over the years. "How are you feeling?"

"We're doing fine." She smiled, placing the catalog on the ground beside her. "Just putting my feet up for breakfast and a little professional reading."

He sat at the end of the Queen Anne sofa, scooped up her feet and swung them to rest in his lap. She started to protest, but then he pressed his thumbs into her arches and she had to focus all her energy on not moaning in ecstasy. "The pregnancy books say you should get plenty of rest."

She tried not to bristle at him stating the obvious. She wasn't the scatterbrained artsy eighteen-year-old he'd married. "I'm not likely to forget since you texted me instructions often enough yesterday."

Sebastian leaned forward, angling close to her stomach. "Your mama's getting feisty, so she must be feeling good."

"Actually, I'm still hungry." Which perhaps accounted for her irritability. Eating healthy sucked when her body screamed for other treats—edible as well as sexual. "Do you fully comprehend the power of an estrogen-induced craving?"

"It just so happens, I brought you dessert."

"Thanks, but I already ate and I want to be careful about eating healthy," she said as her sweet tooth ached.

"Lady, I've known you for nine years and that includes the foods you prefer. As a matter of fact, the way you enjoy your food is more than a little hot."

A tingle of awareness spread from her feet and up her legs at a time when her heated dreams were still too close to the surface. "So you like the way I pig out."

"Put your feet up again, and I'll surprise you with a brunch you'll never forget."

He reached over the arm of the sofa and pulled up a canvas shopping bag. One at a time, he set out an array of plastic containers filled with strawberries and kiwi and pear slices. She pressed her lips tight to hold back her frown.

The fruit looked beautiful, but she really wanted

a slice of fudge. Or, hey, maybe a Milky Way. Didn't that at least *sound* healthy since it contained the word *milk?*

Since he'd obviously tried, she forced a smile on her face, reminding herself of the stash of mini-pralines in her desk drawer. They had nuts and that equaled protein. "This was really thoughtful of you."

He'd taken great care to make sure the baby had exactly what it needed.

"And last but not least, we have…" He pulled out a jar.

"Peanut butter?" she asked, more than a little disappointed. Couldn't he have at least gotten her some peanut butter truffles?

"My dear, this is white chocolate raspberry peanut butter."

Her mouth watered while her heart fluttered with a scary hint of softening over the romantic thoughtfulness directed at *her.* "Really?"

He pulled out another. "And café mocha peanut butter. Last but not least, coconut-banana flavored." He winked. "Stay in good with me and I'll hook you up with the gourmet section in the all-night store where I found this to slather on your fruit."

Suddenly the strawberries looked a helluva lot more enticing. She grabbed for the jar. "Pass it over pronto, big guy."

He held the peanut butter out of her reach and opened the lid with one of those smooth male moves. Such a simple domestic thing—can you open this jar for me?—but it tweaked at her already-vulnerable heart. He pulled out a silver butter knife and smoothed some of the white chocolate raspberry peanut butter onto a fat strawberry.

She thought for a moment that he would try to feed it to her, and she would have to draw a line at a time when she really just wanted to enjoy the moment. Then he speared the strawberry with a toothpick and passed it over.

Marianna bit the treat in half, the juicy taste of fruit and chocolate exploding over her taste buds in a near-orgasmic flood. Her eyes fluttered closed so she could shut out all distracting sensations and focus fully on the intense flavor. She *so* didn't care about those truffles anymore.

She bit at the rest of the strawberry, but it bobbled on the toothpick. Sebastian reached at the same time she did, their fingers meeting at her lips.

Glinting blue eyes locked with hers. His gaze fell to her mouth, her breath coming faster. Marianna's thumb twitched as if trying of its own volition to connect with Sebastian. Then she snatched her hand away.

Sebastian relaxed back onto the sofa, surprising her when he didn't relentlessly push for more. They had nearly kissed last night, yet he seemed willing to respect her boundaries now.

She should be happy, not disappointed and achy.

He stretched an arm along the back of the sofa

with casual ease. "Will you be coming to my brother's campaign party this Sunday evening?"

So much for laid-back. Her master strategist ex had worked his timing well. Marianna hesitated, unsure of what to do with this confusing mix of charming and maneuvering.

Besides, facing his family had been tough enough last night, and that had been business. What would they think if she showed up for a social occasion? "I hadn't planned on it."

"It'll be a good promo opportunity for you professionally as well as a chance for us to show the world we can still be civil before we spill our secret."

He kept his body loose and lanky on the sofa, the perfect nonthreatening posture. It was a little too perfect, like he'd studied just such body language in a calculated bid to win his point.

"You're a good lawyer."

"I try."

She opted for honesty and let him do with it what he would. "What will your family say?"

"Absolutely nothing. They're all diplomats—comes from being politically inclined."

"True enough." She would be having far more contact with them than she'd expected because of the baby. "Through the whole divorce proceedings, your mother never said anything untoward to me."

"Lucky for you. More than once she demanded to know what I did wrong."

"Really?" That surprised her—and it didn't. Ginger adored her boys, but she'd never hesitated to call them on the carpet, even as adults. They all came by their driven natures honestly. "I'm sorry you caught flak. I hope she understands this is as much my fault as it is yours."

He stiffened, some of the studied ease of his body slid away. "You've never said that before."

"I'm sorry about that too then." She stared at his thoughtful breakfast offering. "I guess in spite of any attraction, we're just unsuited to live together. Our temperaments are too different."

He leaned forward, elbows on his knees, within touching distance. "I'm having a tough time remembering what all those differences are."

And right there blared the whopper difference beyond his workaholic tendencies. He'd never wanted to confront their issues, unbending in his insistence they didn't exist or would fade with time. Like how he wouldn't talk about Sophie while the wound of her loss festered to debilitating proportions.

Of course he would say she wanted to discuss things to death and pick at those sore spots. She stared at the jar of gourmet peanut butter in her white-knuckled grip. Eight months ago, she would have thrown it. Instead, she just wanted to cry over all they'd lost.

As much as she still found him infinitely desirable, she needed to steel herself to touch him without letting him seduce her back into his bed.

She lightly tucked her hand in his, still resting on his knee. "Sebastian, let's not ruin this momen—"

The door swung open and they both jolted back, the strength of Sebastian's fingers still imprinted on her senses. Ross filled the doorway, and for once, she resented his presence. She shot a wary glance at Sebastian. He sat calm as could be gathering up the food from the coffee table.

Ross lounged in the doorway tucking his hands in his jeans pockets, parting back his forest-green jacket. "Just wanted to check in and make sure you arrived all right."

"Sorry I was late." She scooped the antique auction catalog off the floor. "The evening meeting with Matthew and Ashley must have set my mental clock behind a bit."

"No problem." He strode deeper into her office space. "Working on the future senator's home is a top priority."

Sebastian shoved to his feet. "Thanks for your confidence in my brother's electability."

"You Landis men have a reputation of getting what you want."

Marianna tensed but Sebastian didn't snap back, and she actually found herself wanting to scowl at her boss.

Then Ross's easygoing smile returned. "I appreciate the overtime Marianna has been putting in lately. We're really excited about the company's expansion."

Sebastian's hands fisted by his sides. "What expansion?"

Oh, damn. She hadn't told him. Of course there hadn't been a need during the divorce proceedings as they were working to establish separate lives.

"Southern Designs is opening another branch upstate in Columbia. It is my hope that Marianna will be the acting manager and chief decorator."

Sprawled in a poolside chair, Sebastian tipped back a glass of seltzer water at his brother's campaign party, wishing for something stronger to drink but needing his wits around his tempting ex.

All this time he'd been concerned about Ross making a move on Marianna, and instead the guy had been working on flat-out moving her. Columbia wasn't at the end of the universe, but the three-hour distance stretched a helluva lot longer when he thought of the constraints it would put on his plans to be a daily presence in his child's life—and Marianna's. Would he even get any reassurance on that issue from her tonight?

Chamber music played lightly from a band off to one side under a lighted gazebo. The ocean breeze rippled across the pool scattered with magnolias and floating candles. His mother and Ashley had gone all out in planning this exclusive gathering at the Landis compound.

Invitations to their home were rare and coveted.

Ginger valued her privacy, however gathering political movers and shakers at her house would prove advantageous for Matthew. For the General and Ginger too, for that matter, as they entrenched themselves deeper and deeper into D.C. affairs of state.

He preferred his behind-the-scenes role of managing the family's fortune and taking on cases that spoke to his inner convictions. Marianna used to say she admired that about him.

And just that quickly, Sebastian felt it all the way to his bones the minute she walked out to the pool area. The sound of nearby conversations and polite laughter faded to zilch as that same tingling sensation he'd experienced throughout their marriage returned, even surprising him with its strength. Straightening in his chair, he saw her talking with his mother by a champagne fountain and a crystal bowl of iced shrimp.

God, he was glad she'd come. While he didn't begrudge his brother's happiness, listening to Matthew and Ashley make wedding plans wasn't always pleasant to do while in the middle of a divorce.

Marianna's wine-red dress hugged her body in quiet elegance, draping her curves from the high neckline down to midcalf. Tendrils of dark hair escaped the soft bundle of curls on top of her head, gently framing her face. When she turned to lift a canapé from a waiter's silver tray, Sebastian nearly choked on his drink.

The damn dress didn't have a back. Well, it did, but not much of one.

A single lock of hair trailed down her spine, brushing her pale skin as she tilted her head to listen to Ginger. Marianna's skin glowed with a translucent quality reminding him of the magnolias and candles floating in the pool.

"Hey, Mom, great party," Sebastian called as he grabbed his drink and strode closer to the women. "Hello, Marianna."

Setting his seltzer glass on the table behind her, with careful nonchalance, he traced a path down each vertebra, his callused finger snagging against her silky skin. Holy crap, was that silver glitter sprinkled along her shoulders?

"Good evening, Sebastian." She stepped away and crossed her arms over her breasts, shielding her response to his caress. "I was just asking your mother for the name of her caterer."

"And I was telling Marianna we're glad to have her here." His mother eyed the two of them with ill-disguised curiosity.

He wouldn't be able to dodge an interrogation much longer. His mother could be quietly relentless—the epitome of a steel magnolia.

And while he was on the subject of strong-willed women... When would Marianna want to tell the world about the baby? He preferred waiting until that announcement could be made along with their intent to get back together. He didn't want her settling too comfortably into the single-parent role.

He sure as hell didn't want her moving to Columbia.

Donning the perfect hostess smile, Ginger gestured across the patio. "There's Judge Johnson arriving with his new wife. I need to say hello. You two go enjoy yourselves." Ginger tossed the couple a wave as she located her husband and began the required social circulation.

Marianna faced him, the moon casting shadows through her long lashes. "I appreciate that you're willing to hold back on talking to your family. I know that can't be easy."

"They'll start pushing soon, but I'm a big boy. I'll talk when I'm ready."

"I know that firsthand."

Dangerous territory. She'd frequently complained about his reticence. Although she'd used stronger words—like stubborn jackass—to describe his refusal to discuss something before he'd had a chance to sort it out in his head. Growing up with talkative brothers, he'd found it easier to keep his own counsel and go his own way.

She crooked a finger and whispered, "I'll let you in on a secret, but you have to promise not to tell."

He brushed his finger just over her left breast. "Cross my heart."

Marianna pinched his wrist none too gently and moved his hand away. "That's not yours anymore."

As if he needed reminding of all he needed to win back. "What's the secret?"

"I'm really getting addicted to that gourmet peanut butter. Thank you."

"You're welcome." Sebastian leaned back, his arm resting behind her without touching. Checking out her body glitter and imagining how far it dusted beneath her dress proved plenty enjoyable for the moment. "You can uncross your arms now that Mom's gone."

"And you can pack away the flirting."

"As long as you're not packing your bags for Columbia."

"I was wondering how long it would take you to bring that up."

Matthew and Ashley burst onto the back porch, breaking the thread of tension. Sebastian retrieved his seltzer water for a much needed cooldown.

Ashley edged closer to the group. She was quiet but a surprisingly funny woman who Marianna had once mentioned she looked forward to calling sister. The bride-to-be filled a champagne flute from the fountain while Matthew slung an arm along Marianna's shoulder. "Is my brother behaving?"

"Sebastian's behavior has been borderline acceptable." Her smile tempered the words.

Sebastian tapped his glass against her arm. "Only borderline?"

She shivered as he lightly caressed the rim against

her bare skin. "I haven't shoved you in the pool yet, but it's going to be a near thing if you keep that up."

He pulled his glass back and drank from the spot that touched her. "There's an idea about the pool." Sebastian turned to his wide-eyed brother watching the two of them with ill-disguised confusion. "Matthew, you better watch your back because I'm thinking I owe you one for when you dunked me at that party Mom threw right after Marianna and I eloped—"

Ashley hooked arms with Matthew. "The photographers would love the chance to sell those pictures to the tabloids."

"Spoilsport," Sebastian mumbled. His soft-spoken future sister-in-law had an understated approach to getting her way, he would do well to study. Perhaps he needed to ease up on touching Marianna for the night. "So, Matthew, do you still have time in your campaign schedule for golfing next weekend?"

With some luck, Marianna would pick up on his mention of taking downtime, something she'd requested often enough in the past.

Matthew turned toward Ashley. "Do I?"

"Don't look at me. I'm not your boss."

Matthew snorted.

Ashley rolled her eyes. "Yes, Sebastian, Matthew may come out and play next Saturday."

Watching Matthew and Ashley, Marianna couldn't help but envy their ease together, their obvious love and compatibility. While she wouldn't begrudge them one moment, all that happiness and hope flat-out hurt right now.

But damn it all, she was tired of feeling sorry for herself. She was weary of grieving and crying. Her life wasn't perfect, but she had a helluva lot going for her right now. She had a baby to look forward to.

And a rekindled passion with her ex-husband.

Did she dare touch that fire again? They'd both been burned so badly. But, God, when had she become so timid?

It was after losing Sophie. The fight seemed to have gone out of her then. What a sad legacy to carry in the name of a precious little girl who'd brought so much joy.

Marianna stood taller and wondered how long she'd been slumping. Too long.

She didn't know where things were headed with Sebastian. Likely nowhere, although she imagined he had some honor-driven notion they should re-marry for the child. She disagreed. They'd taken off their wedding rings and turned the page on being married. Not even a relentless pursuit on his part could change that.

But in spite of any divorce decree, apparently they still had unfinished business between them—business they needed to sort through before the baby was born. Marianna took in the breadth of his shoulders, the slightly aloof tip of his head, her body already humming with awareness and an urge to explore the renewed attraction.

She was growing tired of his flirtatious strokes then pulling back. She was sexually frustrated and totally knew it. It was time Sebastian either quit the touching dance or own up to the fact that he wanted her, too.

Seven

Sebastian sprawled in a poolside chair for the bulk of the engagement party, making political chitchat as people strolled by. Mostly he used the spot as the perfect vantage point to watch Marianna while she helped his mother befriend wallflowers, give instructions to the waiters…

And open up the dance floor under the stars.

His body thrummed as he watched her sway to the music with his youngest brother, her laughter teasing his senses from across the patio. His decision to lay off touching her for a while was already playing with his sanity. Her smile tonight sliced right through the distance they'd put between them over the past months. Sebastian hadn't seen her happy like that in a long time. It must have something to do with that famed pregnancy glow.

A big band–era song struck up next and the General approached her. As Hank began to take her hand, his arms stopped in midair as he searched for a place covered by fabric. Sebastian stifled a smile.

Another hour passed until he watched Marianna sit alone for the first time, relaxing in a poolside chair. His no-touching decision was about to take a temporary hiatus. He deserved at least one dance, damn it. He strode over to her just as the strains of the final tune of the night played, a slower song as the band wound down.

"I think I'm the only man left who hasn't danced with you."

"You haven't asked me."

So she'd noticed his backing off. Good. At least he could gain some satisfaction from his restraint. Although right now, he wondered just how long that restraint would last.

He extended his hands. "May I have this dance? In the interest of being friends."

Marianna gulped as the full impact of Sebastian's appeal washed over her. The Southern gentleman to the hilt, he wore a navy jacket with his khakis in spite of the eighty-degree weather, a conservative maroon tie neatly knotted at his neck.

Odd thing, though, there were plenty of men

dressed much like him, equally attractive and powerful men, but none of *them* stirred her interest for even a second.

She placed her hands in Sebastian's, rising from the chair, stepping into the circle of his arms. His other palmed the bare skin low on her spine, his calluses calling to mind his strength. Marianna let him draw her near, his cheek just barely brushing her hair.

Slipping her fingers over his shoulder, she began to move her feet in rhythm with the music. Her breath twined with his in the sliver of air between them. He traced small, hypnotic patterns as he hummed along with the music.

Marianna's eyes drifted closed, and she let the attraction have its way with her senses, hot and steamy like the South Carolina heat. She leaned closer, her breasts heavy and full pressed against his chest. Their legs skimmed as their bodies mimicked a more fundamental dance, bringing back memories of better times.

She looked up at him, seeing all too clearly the desire in his eyes and becoming achingly aware of every inch of him. She knew that look well, and if they'd been anywhere else but in public, he would have her stripped down in seconds. As it was, she could only sway against him, hypnotized by the fierce want in his gaze, her whole body begging to be with him.

"Marianna, all flirting aside, you have to know

you're a beautiful, sexy woman," he whispered, his hands skimming tantalizing figure eights up and down her back.

Again, she felt the draw to take this window of time before the baby's birth to jump in and simply enjoy the urges her body demanded be filled. Even though Sebastian had given her space during the party, he didn't seem likely to tell her no.

He'd seemed calmer about her possible move than she'd expected, but she knew how well he could hide his steely streak. Maybe she needed to learn to trust her own strength of will in letting him know—calmly—where she stood. That sounded reasonable, especially for a woman with sensual longing supercharging through her veins.

She inclined her head just a hint, gazing at him for an electrified moment. "What do you think of a short-term arrangement as sex buddies?"

Sex buddies?

Stunned mute, Sebastian stared at Marianna in his arms on the starlit dance floor. She actually wanted to have sex with him. Now.

The rest of her words sunk in. She said something about a short-term arrangement, total BS in his mind, but he would deal with that later. He wasn't stupid enough to let this opportunity pass. "My place is more than a little crowded tonight. What do you say we go back to the house?"

She stared back at him with an unmistakable craving her eyes. "I say yes."

Restraining the urge to pump the air with his fist, Sebastian palmed her back and eyed the nearest exit. To hell with tossing around niceties on their way out, she seemed as determined as he was. Would they even make it to the house, or would they be pulling off the road again?

Five interminable minutes later, the valet had unearthed her car from the rows of guest vehicles. Sebastian snagged the keys and had the engine in Drive.

He eyed a convenient side road along the way but decided he wanted to take his time with her in the privacy of their house—in *his* bed. He could almost convince himself things were normal between them. Again?

Had they ever been normal? Their life together had started off at such a frenetic pace. They married three months after meeting. Marianna lost the baby on that hellish night in the mountains.

Then it was a breakneck pace through college and law school. The ups and downs of failed fertility treatments, and the adoption… He cut off thoughts that solved nothing. The past had no bearing on the present. He needed to forge ahead, build on what they had—the baby.

And a smoking-hot passion for each other that had ironically grown stronger during their divorce.

Sliding the car into Park outside their house, he lifted a stray lock of hair gracing her shoulder. "Have I told you how beautiful you look?"

"You mentioned it."

"Just checking."

"Sebastian."

"Yeah?"

"Shut up and kiss me."

"Yes, ma'am."

Urgency built with a need to roll free. He nibbled along her soft hand, vulnerable wrist, making short order of the trek up her arm to claim her mouth, hot, hard and fast. The familiar grip of desire that always simmered below the surface around Marianna roared to life.

He tangled a hand in her hair, combing through until her curls fell free, pins pinging along the gearshift. His other arm locked low around her waist and lifted her flush against him. Her soft curves fit against him, her hips rocking a promise he fully intended to accept.

"Inside," he whispered against her lips. "We've already done the sex-in-a-car deal. Let's take this to a bed."

"Yes," she gasped, her fingernails pressing through his jacket and into his shoulders with urgency, "but soon, please."

He reached to open his door while she held on to their kiss until the very…last…second. Sprinting around the hood of the car, he made it to her side just as she stepped out and back into his arms. Her feet tangled with his as they stumbled along the pavers.

She lost a shoe. He started to retrieve it, and she gripped his wrist, bringing his hand back to her waist as she kicked off the other high heel. "I'll get them later."

If Marianna didn't care about her precious shoes, she must mean business.

He scooped her off her bare feet and carried her up to the porch. Her fingers tunneled under his collar to tease his neck, her lips following suit while he fumbled with the keys.

Finally, the door swung open and he angled her into the cool hall. She slid down his body in a sensuous glide until she stood flush against him again. He booted the door closed and dodged Buddy zigzagging around them before curling up beside the door.

Sebastian backed her toward the stairs, his coat somehow falling off and landing on a Persian rug as he hit the first step. Damn, he adored her quick and efficient hands. And her eager mouth moving under his. Her soft breasts brushing against his chest.

Right now, he liked just about everything about her. She arched deeper into the kiss, her fingers making quick work of his tie, sending the strip of silk fluttering through the air.

Halfway up, he pinned her against the wall, needing to touch a lot more than they could with most of their clothes still on. His hands tunneled under her dress and up her legs while he kissed his way down her neck. Her head fell back against the wall with a thud as loud as her gasps of pleasure.

Sebastian caressed higher, along her hips then around to find she wore a skimpy thong. A possessive growl rumbled up and out as he thought about her dressed this way all evening long. He gripped her soft bare flesh and pressed her closer against him. Still not near enough to ease the throbbing in his pants—and not near enough for her either, if her urgent wriggles and breathy whimpers were anything to judge by.

Who the hell needed a bed anyway?

He slid a hand around front again, teasing along the edge of her thong, back and forth, just grazing her moist heat. The feel of her desire alone was almost enough to send him over the edge, but he held back. Wanting, aching to see her come apart before he gave in to his own driving need to be inside her.

"Sebastian," she gasped, hooking a long leg over his hip, "you're not playing fair. You promised we would hurry."

"Be patient." He blew lightly along her shoulder, some of her body glitter taking flight. "We'll get there."

He slid two fingers inside her panties for a firmer stroke followed by a slow dip inside her. Then out. Repeating again and again while imagining just how good the sweet moist clamp of her would feel around more than just his fingers.

Her other knee buckled, and he anchored her against the wall. She gasped as fast as his heart pounded inside his chest, each breath faster as he could see her nearing completion. She rocked against his touch while slipping her hand to his belt buckle and damn but she already had him buzzing...

Except wait—that was his cell phone, clipped to his waistband, set on vibrate.

"Ignore it." He circled his passion-slicked fingers around her tight bud of nerves.

"Probably just work trying to intrude on our love life for the four hundredth time."

"Work can go to hell tonight," he grumbled between tight teeth.

His BlackBerry buzzed. He pitched it to the floor and kissed her quiet, his tongue stroking the inside of her mouth as thoroughly as his fingers playing lower. The cell phone buzzed again.

Marianna nipped along his lower lip. "Maybe we should just check the caller ID."

"Not so inclined right now."

She reached to tip the phone's LCD screen upward and instantly stilled in his arms, her foot sliding back to the stairway. "Sebastian, it's the General. What if it's a family emergency?"

As much as he wanted to think she was overreacting, he couldn't ignore the fact that the General never called late. Ever.

Sebastian grabbed the phone just as it stopped ringing, then hit Redial. He picked up after one ring.

"General? Sebastian here. What's up?" Besides him.

"You know I wouldn't bother you this late if it wasn't important, but your mother needs you. Kyle's plane has been shot down in Afghanistan." The nightmarish words feared by every family with a military relative echoed through the airwaves. "They don't know if he survived the crash."

Marianna pressed a hand to the dashboard, her brain struggling to change gears as quickly as Sebastian shifting into fourth on her car as he raced back to the Landis compound. There'd been no discussion of leaving her at home. Kyle had been a part of her family for nine years. Just thinking of Sebastian's lighthearted brother possibly lying out there somewhere dead…

She wanted to be with the family. She *needed* to be there, could only imagine how terrified his mother must be. Her own heart ached so deeply over losing Sophie, yet she had the reassurance that her daughter was still alive. What kind of hell it would be to fear for your child's life?

And Sebastian… Yes, she had to be there for him, even though he would never ask, much less acknowledge he had needs. What must be churning inside him right now? His jaw flexed in what had to be a teeth-grinding clench as he powered down the four-lane road. His fist stayed tight around the gearshift. In spite of the muscles bulging beneath his shirtsleeves, he held steady at the speed limit.

Just barely.

Maybe if she could get him to talk. "What else did the General have to say?"

"Only that Kyle was working some kind of covert operation with the Air Force's Office of Special Investigations. The transport plane that was carrying him went off radar. Radio transmissions indicate they were shot down. They're searching for the wreckage now."

"God, Sebastian, I'm so sorry. Your mother must be frantic."

"I'm not borrowing trouble. Kyle's tough. He's a survivor."

He was also just the reckless, selfless kind to die saving everyone else. But that didn't need to be said. Sebastian knew his own brother well enough.

"Anything else?" she asked, more to keep him talking than out of any expectation to discover more.

He shook his head. "The media hasn't gotten hold of the story yet. The Air Force is trying to keep Kyle's name out of the news in case he's evading."

She shuddered at the possibility of him in the hands of enemies. If they realized they had the son of a politically influential family in their grasp… The horrendous possibilities were unthinkable.

Sebastian stopped for a red light, revving the engine as if willing the miles between them and the compound to go by all the faster. The light turned green and he accelerated.

Headlights blinded her through her window. Brakes squealed. Her muscles tensed in anticipation of the likely crash. She braced her hand more firmly against the dash, her other arm hugging her waist, her baby, with a fierce maternal drive to protect—

Cursing, Sebastian twisted the steering wheel, jolting the car. Her body flung to the right, rapping her head against the passenger window with a painful snap.

Then everything went dark.

Eight

Sebastian paced in the emergency room waiting area, still not certain if Marianna and their baby were all right.

Damn it, why had he let himself become distracted while driving? Sure he managed to avoid the other vehicle—barely. The drunk driver had embedded his car in a telephone pole, then staggered around without so much as a scratch. Marianna, however, had been knocked unconscious.

The present resembled the past too closely for him to shrug it off. Again, he was in an E.R. waiting to hear if Marianna and their baby were all right. Even thoughts of the ride itself made him break out in a cold sweat. As with nine years ago, he'd driven like a bat out of hell with Marianna in the car. He was lucky he hadn't killed her then. But what about now?

He still didn't know because the doctor had banished him from the room out into this damn small space where he kept knocking his legs on metal furniture every time he turned around. And the noises, God, they jangled in his ears. The older lady two gurneys down the hall who kept up a steady stream of complaints whenever a nurse walked by. A teenager crying quietly as she spoke into a cell phone. The occasional drum of the EMTs' feet as they raced in with a new patient.

How much longer would he have to cool his heels? He kicked an end table aside, which drew his attention to his shoes, the ones Marianna had given him for Christmas. Shoes that would have been beside her bed if this night had gone differently.

He couldn't even wrap his brain around what might be going on with his brother. Somebody needed to cough up good news. Soon.

The sliding doors swished open to admit more of the late-night crowd, except a much-better dressed new batch—his family. They must not have had time to change out of their party clothes before the call about Kyle came in. His mother rushed toward him, Matthew and Ashley close on her heels.

He bolted forward and slid an arm around his

mother's shoulders. "Have you heard anything about Kyle?"

Matthew shook his head. "Nothing yet. The General's out in the parking lot making more calls, trying to tap into his military contacts. Jonah stayed at the house to man the phones."

Sebastian exhaled hard, wishing for more information while grateful that at least there hadn't been bad news. Still, his mother must be feeling torn in two tonight. Her clothes might be camera-ready perfect, but the rubber gardening clogs on her feet declared how frazzled she must have been as she rushed out the door.

"Mom, you didn't need to come here." He gave her a light one-armed hug. "You've got enough to worry about right now."

"You're my son, too." She pressed a maternal kiss to his cheek, the strain around her eyes painfully evident. "Every child is equally important in my heart."

"I'm okay. It's Marianna—" and their baby "—that I'm concerned about."

She gripped his arm, her eyes searching his face. "You said on the phone that you were with Marianna, but you didn't say what happened to her."

"She's still in the exam room." He scrubbed a hand over his face. "She hit her head on the passenger window when I swerved to miss a drunk driver."

"Son, I can't even begin to understand what's

going on between the two of you lately. I'm just glad you're both all right."

Half the time *he* didn't even know where things stood between him and his ex-wife. "Thank you for coming, but you really can go home. I've got this."

She cupped his cheek. "You of all my boys understand the fears of a parent's heart."

For a second he thought she'd found out about the baby, then he realized she meant Sophie. He stood stock-still, frozen from the inside out. No one other than Marianna had dared mention his daughter's name around him, not after he'd cut off conversations often enough. That his mother would bring her up now only proved how stressed she must be. He stayed silent and let his mother keep talking.

"Even though you know Sophie's well cared for, it's difficult not to worry about our children when they're out of our sight, much less when you know you can't see them again. You and Marianna have been through so much these past months."

Now that part, he had heard from his mother— her softly spoken suggestion that he and Marianna not go through with the divorce so quickly. Which only proved how well he and Marianna had hidden their problems from even those closest to them. The lead up to ending their marriage had been protracted and painful, dragging out over the past two years.

"Sebastian, did you hear what I said?" his

mother's worried voice yanked him back into the cold, antiseptic present.

"Sure, Mom, absolutely." He hoped he hadn't just agreed to something too outrageous.

Matthew took her elbow, angling her toward the exit. "You've seen with your own eyes that he's okay. Let's go back to the house."

The doors leading to the exam rooms swished open and Sebastian pivoted fast, his family pretty much fading away. Dr. Cohen strode through with brisk efficiency, her red glasses hanging from her neck. "Mr. Landis, Marianna is awake. By all indications, she and the baby are both perfectly fine."

He gripped the back of a chair, his legs suddenly not too steady under him. "How much longer until I can go back to see her?"

"In a few minutes. She's getting dressed, then you can take her home. She'll need someone to check on her through the night, just to be on the safe side with that bump on her head." The doctor tapped his arm with the edge of the chart. "You've got a tough one there, both her and the baby."

"Thank you again, Dr. Cohen. I appreciate your coming to the hospital so quickly." The E.R. docs had said they could handle Marianna's case. But with the nightmare of that long-ago miscarriage still so starkly fresh in his mind, he'd demanded they call Marianna's ob-gyn to check her over.

The doors slid closed after Dr. Cohen, and he

turned around to find his family gawking wide-eyed back at him. Even the General had arrived just in time to hear everything, his arm already around Ginger to steady her. Ah, crap. Wrapped up in his need for news about Marianna's condition, he'd all but forgotten his relatives were even there.

"Baby?" his mother whispered, her smile quivering in time with a tear.

So much for waiting to tell everyone about the pregnancy. At least Marianna wouldn't be able to blame him for spilling the news.

Matthew scratched his head, cheeks puffing with a long, slow exhale. "That sure answers a lot of questions, like why you two have been so chummy all of the sudden."

Sebastian rocked back on his heels. "That day she fainted at the courthouse, we found out about the pregnancy when she saw the doctor afterward." He figured it wasn't any of his family's business that Marianna actually had known a few hours *before* the divorce, a fact that still grated. "Marianna and I wanted to find the right time to tell you—once we've had a chance to make plans."

His brother clapped him on the shoulder. "Congratulations, bro."

His mother rushed to hug him. "I'm happy for both of you. A baby is always cause for joy."

All the emotionalism started to make him itchy. He just wanted to see Marianna—and holy crap—there was still the uncertainty with his brother. How could he have forgotten about Kyle for even a second? "About Kyle, Marianna and I will be over as soon as—"

His mother held up a hand. "You need to be with Marianna, and it sounds like she should rest. We'll keep you posted the second we hear anything."

He hesitated, his need for news about his brother at odds with concerns for Marianna. "You're sure?"

"There's nothing any of us can do now except wait." She nodded toward the door leading back to the exam rooms. "Go be with Marianna."

His mother was right. He couldn't help Kyle, but he could take care of Marianna. "We'll be by tomorrow to talk more."

And once his mother didn't have so much worrying her, he intended to make it clear Marianna would be a part of their family in every possible way. He would get his life on track.

He couldn't get Sophie back. But he damn well wasn't going to let anyone take a child of his away again, not even his stubborn ex-wife.

Marianna rested her forehead against the cool glass of the car window and looked out at the homes in their neighborhood. *Her* neighborhood, since Sebastian had moved out.

Had it really only been a couple of hours since she and Sebastian had raced into the house expecting to be sex buddies? Now they didn't know if

Kyle was alive or dead. They themselves could have died because of that drunk driver.

Life had a way of reshuffling cards faster than she could think. Like with her teen pregnancy and how her elderly parents had been so disappointed in her. Would things have turned out differently—better—for her and for Sebastian if she'd pushed him for more time to get to know each other rather than rushing into marriage?

As he pulled into their driveway, she slid her hand over her stomach and her eyes toward him. The two most important people in her world were okay. She should take great comfort in that, yet she still felt so unsettled. Yes, Sebastian mattered to her and in a way that went beyond sex buddies. But what had changed between them? Feelings weren't so easily cut off simply because they'd signed their names to a divorce decree.

None of which she could deal with or resolve tonight, not with the fear of that near-wreck leaving her emotions raw. And certainly not while concerns for his brother loomed.

Sebastian opened his door and met her as she swung her legs out. She couldn't help but compare this somber walk along the pavers with their frantic rush up the porch steps earlier. Her senses hummed with the memory of his arms wrapped around her, carrying her inside. She could use the comfort of his embrace again.

What if he wanted to pick up where they'd left

off on the stairway earlier? She wasn't sure if that was wise or not, but she did know she needed to be honest with him.

She stepped inside, kneeling to catch Buddy before he sprinted outside. She glanced up at Sebastian as he secured the front door. "I don't know if we should have sex tonight."

He pocketed the keys, studying her with inscrutable eyes. "You need to rest. I'll wake you every couple of hours."

He'd given in so easily that she didn't know whether to be relieved or insulted. "I'm sorry to keep you from your family. You must be worried sick about Kyle. *I'm* worried sick about him."

He reached down to pat Buddy, calming him with the slow, steady dog-whisperer way of his. "There's nothing I can do for Kyle, and Matthew promised to call if there's any news." Buddy circled them once more then trotted away, nails clicking on the hardwood floors before she heard the doggie door swish open and closed. "I'm where I'm supposed to be right now. You and this baby are my family."

The sincerity of his words whispered over her like a breeze stirring the water at night, disrupting and enticing all at once. "The baby's fine. You can stop worrying about that much, at least."

His jaw flexed as hard as the muscles bulging along sleeves of his jacket. "I shouldn't have let the news about my brother compromise your safety."

He blamed himself? That was so unfair—and such an awful burden to carry. "Good God, Sebastian, it wasn't your fault. The other guy was drunk."

He gripped her shoulders, his face tight with unmistakable pain. "I thought you were going to die tonight."

His words now echoed words he'd spoken nine years ago after she'd woken from surgery after the ectopic pregnancy had ruptured her fallopian tube. Suddenly she realized the hell he must have gone through tonight, experiencing what must have seemed like a replay of the past. Could he somehow have blamed himself for that night as well?

Damn keeping her distance.

Her hand gravitated up to caress his neck, her thumb stroking his tensed jaw. "Sebastian…"

She didn't even know what else to say to him. Then his mouth sealed over hers with a fierceness that touched her heart and rekindled her banked yearning from earlier. Each tender stroke of his hands over her shoulders nudged aside the emotional boundaries she'd tried to put in place with him. His one admission of fear for her made her more weak-kneed than the velvet sweep of his tongue.

Sebastian slipped a hand behind her head and cupped her neck. With the other, he palmed her waist, his fingers hot along her back exposed by the party dress she'd chosen hours ago. Marianna slid her hand inside his jacket, her fingers spreading wide against his chest, digging past his shirt.

He guided her face to his, flicking his tongue along the seam of her full mouth. She opened, begging for more, needing the reassurance of connecting on any level, even if just the physical. With a whispery moan, Marianna slid her arms around Sebastian's neck, deepening their kiss. Their mouths mated with the familiar, yet unexplainable frenzy she'd come to accept as inevitable.

His hand crept up, cupping the curve of her breast, his calluses rasping against the silky fabric as he caressed the added fullness brought on by pregnancy. The tightening bud of response echoed a thread of longing pulling tauter inside her.

Sebastian paused, his mouth hovering a scant breath away. "Are you all right, with the baby—"

"I'm fine." Marianna plucked at the buttons down his shirt. "The doctor said so. In fact, it's a good thing for me to stay awake. Remember?"

"Let me know if—"

"I will," she said between kisses as they started up the stairs, trailing clothes behind them, his jacket, their shoes, the undressing going faster this go-round.

As the stairs turned, he stopped on the landing, pressing her to the wall again. She didn't want to think about tomorrow or their failed past. She wanted to dive into this craving for Sebastian and never climb back out. Apparently, his feelings weren't too different from hers because he kissed her with a fierce passion that had her legs going weak while her arms conversely grew stronger as she held on.

A white flutter snagged her attention as Sebastian tossed his shirt down the stairs. When had he peeled it off? She didn't care as long as her hands got to explore more of him.

Her dress slid down her shoulders, and she couldn't recall how it got there. Again, not that she cared as long as he swept it aside and away...ah, yes. She pressed her near-naked body to his.

He bracketed her with his arms, his hands flat on either side of the wall. Sebastian leaned forward, his breath steaming over her skin, sending shivers down her spine, making her all the more aware of the chair railing at her back.

His lips crashed down on hers again. She met his power, gripping his hair to bring him closer. Her mouth opened, wide and hungry as she tangled her tongue with his in a battle of wills that promised much for both of them if neither gave up.

That last flight of stairs looked like a never ending trek. Marianna sagged, her arms locked around his neck and his arm hooked around her back, the only restraints keeping her from sliding to the...

The floor. Yes, the floor of the landing was perfect and immediate, taking away those last few steps that would give her time to reason her way out of something she wanted, needed so damn much.

Sebastian eased her to the thick wool rug on the landing. "Now? Here?"

"Absolutely."

She rocked her hips against his, moaning at the

glorious sensation of being intimately close to him again. His leg wrapped around hers, bringing her nearer, nestling her against the throbbing length of him. He slipped a restless hand inside her bra. His thumb caressed tantalizing circles over her swollen breasts. She arched her back to fill his palm, the increased pressure only making her crave more. More of this. More of him.

He growled low and hot against her ear. "I thought you didn't want to have sex."

"I don't." The real reasoning for her words earlier flowered in her mind. "I want us to *make love* again."

And yes, she wanted that even as she knew it could well be impossible for them to recapture.

She saw his eyes shift, the blue cooling to that shade that meant he was working to distance himself from deeper emotions. Emotions he'd called wasted drama in the months leading up to their divorce. If she let him think too long now, they would lose what little chance they had to connect on any level tonight.

"Hurry." Marianna worried her bottom lip between her teeth as she struggled with his belt. She freed him with a caress too slow to be anything other than deliberate. Sebastian throbbed in her hand as his fingers skimmed aside her bra and panties.

He propped on his elbows to keep the bulk of his weight off her, his gaze sweeping down her body with an admiration a woman would have to be comatose not to enjoy.

Comatose. Just the word brought that fearful moment in the car, those frightening seconds when she'd woken up in the hospital. All of it reminding her of what she could have lost tonight.

Making her determined not to take whatever she could.

She guided him inside her, carefully, slowly, then slid her hands inside his pants to urge him deeper.

He pulled his mouth from hers. "Look at me."

Her lashes fluttered, but didn't open. She guided his face closer, bowed up to meet him.

He inched away, tightening his grip on her hair, her curls draping down a step. "Marianna, look at me."

She nuzzled his neck before staring up into his eyes, half afraid of what she would find. "Okay. I'm looking."

He tipped her face, his pupils so wide with an intensity that pushed the blue to a thin ring. He thrust into her. "My name."

"What?" What was he talking about, and how he could even think, much less talk?

He stroked again, his hand grazing over her hair as it trailed down the wooden stairs. "Say *my* name."

She pressed her lips to his, refusing to let jealousy ruin this moment. "Sebastian." She raked her fingers along his shoulders. "Sebastian."

Marianna circled her hips against him, willing

him to toss aside some of his seemingly endless supply of control. So damn frustrating when any semblance of control seeped from her the minute he touched her with his hands, his eyes, even his words. She closed her eyes, locked together by something stronger than she even wanted to fight anymore. She simply let their need with its own special frenetic rhythm have its way, driving her closer to completion with each thrust of his body.

Release exploded through her and she repeated his name arching her back until her toes curled. With a hoarse shout, he knotted his fingers in her hair and shuddered against her until finally he dropped to his side and pulled her to him.

Their bodies bound by sweat, tangled legs and a strange bond she couldn't shake free, she knew traveling up that last flight of stairs was the least of their worries.

Nine

Sebastian lay in his own bed again for the first time in eight months. Wide awake. Not that he could have slept even if he didn't need to wake up Marianna every two hours.

Waiting for the phone to ring with news about his brother was hell.

He'd tried to distract himself by going downstairs and logging on to Marianna's computer. He'd accessed his bank account, looking into different kinds of trust funds to set up for the baby. And sure, he'd spent much of that time trying to figure out a way he could persuade Marianna to quit her job and take things easy. Was it so wrong of him to want to care for her, especially on a night like this that brought to the fore how damn fragile life could be?

The gauzy stuff that twisted around the canopy railing swished with the gusts from the ceiling fan. They no doubt needed the cooling relief after their workout on the landing and again in bed.

He twined a lock of her hair around a finger, careful not to twist too tightly and risk waking her early. He checked the clock. 4:25 a.m. Another five minutes to go, and he didn't intend to rouse her a second before.

He studied her face and how the soft puffs of breath between her lips feathered the strand of hair draped across her cheek. After so long apart, he welcomed the opportunity to look his fill. A pale shoulder peeked from beneath the sheet draping along her curves, and he resisted the urge to sweep it away.

What the hell had happened between them on the way to the bedroom? He'd wanted sex, along with a forgetfulness he'd always been able to find in her body in the past.

Their coming together had been anything but peaceful. She'd pinned him with her eyes, held him in some kind of intense moment that stoked his craving for her even as it made him want to back the hell away. She needed something more from him—she always had.

He would just have to keep her distracted with what they did well long enough for her to forget the parts they seemed destined to mess up. He glanced at the clock.

4:30 a.m. on the dot.

Sebastian peeled away the Egyptian cotton sheet inch by inch, kissing every revealed patch of her—her breasts, her stomach, her hips—until she wriggled beneath him. Marianna stretched with a feline grace that almost had him sliding inside her again. Almost. He needed more time to haul his defenses into place around her before she ambushed him with another "make love" line.

He looked up the length of her body, his hand grazing down to tease behind her knee. "Are you awake?"

"I am now." She smiled back at him with heavy-lidded arousal.

He brought his hand up and in front of her face. "How many fingers?"

"Three."

"Perfect."

She lightly stroked his jaw. "Has there been any word about Kyle?"

He turned to kiss her palm. "Nothing yet, but I'm going with the no news is good news philosophy." Wanting distraction from a subject that frustrated him with how little he could do, he turned his attention to something he could fix. "How about a snack before morning sickness has a chance to kick in?"

Marianna studied him with concerned eyes for

a second beyond his comfort level before she gave him the smile he needed.

"You're a man after my own heart." She sat up, clutching the blue-and-yellow-striped sheet to her chest. "I'm craving some of that raspberry chocolate peanut butter in the fiercest way."

There she went with the heart talk again. He tamped down the twinge of unease and swung his feet off the bed. He retrieved his boxers while she wrapped the sheet around her body, toga style.

She grinned over her shoulder. "Last one to the kitchen has to feed the other one while naked."

"Sounds like a win-win situation to me," he called after her as she raced ahead of him.

He took his time following her, already looking forward to the pleasure of bringing food to her lips and watching near-ecstasy spread across her face. Even the computer room with its glowing screen couldn't compete with what Marianna had to offer right now.

Once in the kitchen, he clicked on a single band of track lighting, illuminating the state-of-the-art cooking space. She'd taken the most time decorating here, a place to indulge her culinary prowess. Memories ambushed him.

Of her excitement over picking out the mammoth cooktop.

Of her on a ladder hanging pots from the rack attached to the ceiling.

Of their newborn daughter snoozing in a baby

seat on the floor beside the table, Marianna rocking the tiny chair with her foot while chopping vegetables on the island.

Definitely different from his late-night snack in the dark office kitchenette. "Have a seat and prepare to be fed."

She perched on a bar stool at the tiled island while he opened the stainless steel refrigerator. How long had it been since they'd indulged in a post-sex snack? He honestly couldn't remember when. Any lightheartedness had left their relationship a long time ago.

He wondered now how he'd let that happen when Marianna's uninhibited laugh was one of the things he enjoyed most about her. He could use some of her brightness tonight with the past dogging his heels and concern for Kyle kicking in his gut.

Sebastian snagged a bottle of sparkling water and set it on the kitchen island by the fruit basket. He checked the pantry, and yes, she'd stored all the gourmet peanut butters there, in a line, in front of anything else on the shelf. Each one had been opened for more than just a sample.

He passed her the chocolate raspberry, then pulled a knife from the block. He sliced an apple and handed a piece to her. "What is it about peanut butter that calls to a person regardless of income level?"

She scooped it through the gourmet mix. "Must be something to do with tapping into memories from when we were little."

More so than she could have realized. Damn. It was one helluva a time to dredge up childhood memories. But talking about Kyle was a lot easier than even thinking about Sophie, especially since he *had* to believe that his brother was fine.

His knife slowed along the apple. "Kyle and I used to eat peanut butter and marshmallow sandwiches when we were kids."

She looked up, surprise widening her eyes before a sheen of tears hovered on her lids. "You two have always been close."

"More so when we were younger, before we got caught up in our careers."

He paused, waiting for the snappy comeback about him putting his job above everything else. But for once, she didn't take the shot. His shoulders relaxed, and he hadn't realized until that moment he'd even tensed them.

"This one time when we were about nine and ten, we spent most of the summer playing in a forest behind our house. Well, it seemed like a forest, anyway. It was probably just a few trees with a walking path."

He sliced piece after piece from the apple until only the core remained. "We hung out there all day long. We'd pack peanut butter and marshmallow sandwiches, take a gallon jug of Kool-Aid. And we dug tunnels."

"Tunnels?" She leaned forward on her elbows, intent and ever elegant even in a sheet.

"We dug deep trenches, laid plywood over the top, then piled a layer of dirt over that." The fun of those times wrapped around him again. "We were lucky we didn't die crawling around in there. We could have suffocated. Or our whole roofing could have given way if someone had unknowingly stepped on one of those boards."

"What did your mother say?"

"She never knew." No doubt she would have grounded both of them for all of eternity, and they'd deserved it. They were too fearless as kids. Kyle was still too damn reckless for his own good. "We made Jonah stand guard and let us know if she was coming."

"What did you have to pay him to get him to go along with that?"

"Who said we paid him?" Chuckling, he pitched the apple core in the trash. "He's the youngest. He did what we said."

Her gentle smile warmed her eyes and the room. "And Matthew?"

"He's too much of a rule follower. We never let him in on the secret." He tried to make light of the memory, but still, it sucked him under. "Kyle was especially into it. I should have known then he would go into the military."

Marianna slid off the bar stool and slipped her

arms around his waist, resting her head on his bare chest. Concern for his brother damn near choked him, but no way in hell was he going to let it cripple him. Especially not in front of Marianna.

He glided his hands up and down her back, trying to keep himself in check when he wanted nothing more than to try and recapture some of that forgetfulness she offered. She tipped her head up to press a kiss against his neck, her arms clenching tighter around him. The lump in his throat grew larger. He had to do something and do it fast, or she would cut him right open.

Sealing his mouth to hers before she could blindside him by saying something sympathetic, Sebastian cupped her bottom and lifted her against him. Pleasing her would most definitely please him.

Marianna wanted to sink back into their old habit of losing themselves in sex. Falling into an old pattern was so much easier than forging a new one. His story about playing with Kyle still twisted her already vulnerable heart.

His hands low on her buttocks, he lifted her, setting her onto the island. The sheet slithered from her shoulders to pool around her hips in a cool glide against rapidly heating flesh. The silence of their house swelled around them, reminding her of how lonely the past months had been.

"Hey there, you," Marianna said, more to chase away the silence than to talk. "You lost the race to the kitchen. You were supposed to feed me while naked."

"So take them off," he whispered against her ear.

She thumbed along the waistband of his boxers with a snap, then sketched her hands up to his defined pecs, honed from hours on the water and golf course. She brushed her cheek across the sprinkling of bristly hair on his chest, kissing and blowing dry paths down to his stomach and back up again with teasing restraint.

Staring straight into his heavy-lidded eyes, she teased along the elastic in his boxers again. She hooked her thumbs in his waistband, scratching a light trail over his hips until the underwear slipped down his legs. His low growl of appreciation urged her to continue.

He kicked the boxers aside, molding their bodies flush against each other. Marianna couldn't contain her moan of pleasure at the sensation of skin against skin.

Sebastian pressed his forehead to hers. "You can't know how good you feel."

She slid her hands along his five o'clock shadow and up to cradle his face. "I think I do because it's probably much the same as how you feel against me."

He sealed his mouth to hers and nudged her knees apart. He stepped closer, the throbbing length of his arousal pressing against her slick core. She wriggled, sending sparks through her, showering faster than she would have expected after the pleasure he'd already brought her tonight.

His hand trailed lower, dipped, teasing the bundled center of nerves, launching her over the first threshold too soon, too fast, scaring her a little with how much power he held over her responses. She couldn't imagine being with anyone else, which left only the option of working things out with Sebastian— or being alone for the rest of her life.

Then a second wave of pleasure ripped through her, stealing her ability to think, to doubt. Tremors shook through her, convulsing her fingers around the hot length of him tearing mingling groans from them both.

Settling himself more firmly against her, Sebastian slid inside with a tantalizing slowness. Deeper, he filled her. Her eyes drifted closed and she arched her back, feeling her body stretch with a pleasurable ache as she accommodated him. Hooking her ankles behind his waist, she savored being joined with him again, having as much of him as she wanted tonight.

And tomorrow? She couldn't let the chilling thought encroach on what she felt right now. And she did feel so much.

When he didn't move, Marianna looked up into his face. She wished she hadn't. Sebastian's blue eyes sparked familiar intensity that unsettled her all the way down to her painted toenails. He hadn't changed any more than she had, and foolishly, she still wanted him.

Marianna buried her face in his neck and rocked her hips until he joined in the rhythm. Relentlessly, he drove her to the brink and then slowed. Taking her there again, he hurtled her over with a force that ripped cries of release just before he followed her into the explosion of sensation.

She sagged limply against him, gasping for breath, losing track of how long they stayed locked that way before he gathered her into his arms. Marianna relaxed against his chest all the way up the stairs and into the bedroom they'd once shared.

He placed her on the bed again gently. His back to her, he set the alarm clock. For work?

Then she remembered the bump on her head and the doctor's orders to wake her up every two hours. The car wreck seemed like days ago, so much had happened in such a short time. She hadn't thought of the tender spot on her scalp since coming home.

Marianna stared at the gossamer shadows flickering across her bedroom ceiling as the moonlight filtered through her lacy canopy. The cloudy shadows danced across the spackling, shifting, merging, changing, just like her turbulent life. Turning her head on the pillow, she gazed at the cause of her turmoil sleeping beside her.

She couldn't escape the niggling doubts grabbing

hold in her mind, threatening what little ground she and Sebastian had found here tonight. When he'd carried her up to the bedroom again, she'd seen the computer screen glowing and knew she hadn't left it on. She didn't have to ask if he'd been working.

Marianna pressed a hand to her stomach, visualizing her—their—child. She wanted this baby, needed him or her. She just wasn't sure how to handle the father, this complex man who evoked tantalizing whispers of emotions she'd thought were lost to her.

The ringing telephone jarred Marianna awake. Reality blazed through her as brightly as the early morning sunlight slanting through the blinds.

The phone rang again. With information about Kyle?

She reached beside her to shake Sebastian awake. Her hand smacked through empty space before thumping the mattress. Where was he? Back at work on the computer again?

She rolled to grab the phone just as the ringing stopped. The light on the handset showed another receiver was in the use somewhere else, the caller ID confirming the call had come from his mother's house.

Sebastian wasn't gone. Relief seeped through her even as she worried about Kyle. She scraped away the covers and snatched her silk robe from the closet. Whichever way the conversation went, she needed to be with Sebastian when he heard the news.

She yanked the tie closed around her waist and started down the hall toward the stairs. The near-by sound of Sebastian's voice slowed her feet. She turned to follow the sound, not far, coming from…

Sophie's old bedroom.

Her stomach clenched tight at the thought of his stepping into that room of tiny roses, ruffles and memories. Had he simply gone in there because it was closest when the phone rang? That had to be the case, because Lord knew he had never set foot over that threshold since the day Sophie left their lives.

She paused in the open doorway, her bare toes curling on the cool hardwood floor. She studied his profile as he sat in the rocking chair where they'd both wiled away nights soothing Sophie back to sleep.

"Uh-huh…" Sebastian spoke into the receiver. "That's great news, General. And when will Kyle be able to call?"

She sagged against the door frame in relief. His brother must be fine. Thank God. She kept her eyes on Sebastian, not yet ready to look around the space she'd decorated with love and hope. Still every detail of the vintage cabbage rose nursery stayed in her mind from the glistening cherry wood furniture to the yellow and pink patterns.

Even Sophie's sweet scent remained in her memory long past when it faded from the room—baby detergent mingled with mild soap. She swallowed down a lump swelling from her chest to her throat and focused on Sebastian.

His head nodded in time with whatever the General was saying. "Thanks for calling. Make sure Mom tells him I'm glad those trench digging skills of his worked out so well."

A half smile tugged at his face in spite of the weary hunch of his shoulders.

"Good night then—uh, or rather, good morning." He disconnected the phone, his hands falling to his knees, his head thudding back against the rocker.

She almost rushed in to comfort him, but she recalled how he'd frozen in the kitchen when she'd hugged him. Then he'd shifted quickly to sex as a distraction—not that she could blame him when she'd been a willing participant.

Somehow, even sex had seemed better than a total rejection, another reaction she'd experienced often enough right after Sophie was taken. She could already see the way it would play out. He would straighten back into big strong man mode, impervious to silly things like emotions or pain.

So she would let him have his private moment to deal with whatever was going on inside that mind of his. Marianna backed a step away as Sebastian turned his head toward her.

"Don't go," he said.

For once his face stayed open, no walls in sight. Just an intense and slightly weary man, and yet somehow he looked stronger than ever to her. Had something shifted between them in the kitchen after all? Could everything she'd begun feeling again be flowing both ways?

She hovered in the doorway warily. "I didn't realize you knew I was here."

"I always know when you walk into a room."

Now wasn't that a nerve sizzling notion?

She eased deeper inside until her feet padded along the soft give of the pink and yellow braid rug. "I take it from what you said on the phone that all is well with Kyle."

"Yes, not even a scratch on him," he confirmed. "Apparently someone lurking around on a mountain shot down the plane. Everyone survived the crash landing, but they'd abandoned the site to hide out from rebels. So the rescue mission took a while longer."

"Those hours must have been horrifyingly long for your brother."

"I don't even want to think about it."

Of course he didn't. Sebastian was all about closing down the past and moving ahead as if it never happened. She trailed her fingers along the large armoire, door open with Sophie's baptismal gown on display. With the ache so fresh again in this room, she actually wanted some of Sebastian's selective amnesia.

He pointed toward the bags filling the crib. "I see you went shopping for the baby."

She looked at those sacks full of all things pink and thought of the tears that went into that recent shopping trip. Forgetting be damned. She just couldn't hold back any longer. If he truly wanted to try at some kind of renewed connection between them, he would have to accept who she was and how she dealt with life. He would have to learn how to change.

Her hand leaving the silky baptismal dress, she turned to Sebastian, letting all the grief flow freely through her, and asked, "Do you ever think about her?"

Ten

Do you ever think about her?

Marianna's question burned through Sebastian's ears to sear his insides. He didn't need to ask who Marianna meant. Just the hint of Sophie seemed to bring her back into the nursery so tangibly he could have sworn her heard his daughter cooing from the crib. He forced his grip to loosen on the arms of the rocker before his fingers went numb.

The instinct to end the conversation pounded through him. But only momentarily. If he ever wanted to make things right with Marianna, he couldn't keep repeating the same mistakes. He needed to accept that Sophie—and his unwillingness to share the grief with his wife—dug half the chasm in their marriage.

"I think about Sophie all the time." The words grated all the way up his throat.

Even as he'd tried to forget her, tried not to even think her name, still he found himself wondering if she was fed, held, warm enough, cool enough. Loved enough.

Marianna stopped in front of the crib, her hands gripping the lowered railing that would never be raised again for their daughter. "Her first birthday is at the end of this week."

"I remember."

She reached into one of the shopping sacks and pulled out a tiny pink dress, tracing the white daisies stitched along the collar and hem. "I went shopping a few days ago to buy things for her."

Marianna snapped off the tag and dipped into the bag again. "I know she can't have them, but I needed to… I just couldn't let her birthday go by without celebrating it in some way."

A fabric doll came out next, tag snapped, toy placed to the side. "So I shopped." She cradled a little bathing suit—pink with yellow, blue and green fish. "I'm going to donate everything to charity."

"That's a really nice gesture." He should have thought to set up some kind of annual donation to a charity in Sophie's honor. It certainly wasn't too late, and he was learning that as much as he tried not to think about her, she still sprung into his mind at unexpected times. "What else did you pick out?"

"More clothes, of course. Smocked dresses and practical outfits too, for playing at the park. Bibs and shoes." She pulled out a traditional-looking teddy bear and hugged it to her chest. "Oh, and I bought her a stuffed animal from that store where you pick the pet and they stuff it for you."

"We had a discussion about the place once." He remembered Marianna going whimsical over the dream of having a birthday party for Sophie there one day.

Her eyes took on a faraway look as she stroked her thumbs along the plush fur. "Before they stuff it, you get a tiny red fabric heart to make a wish on then place inside the toy." A tear sparked in her eyes as her arms bit deeper into the stuffing. "So I prayed that she's happy and safe."

His chest felt heavy, his breath growing labored from the weight of trying to shore up the dam against images from the past. "You're killing me here, Marianna."

"I'm sorry." She turned slightly away and tucked the bear into a corner of the crib with heart twisting tenderness. "I shouldn't have rambled on so much. I know you prefer not to talk about her."

"No, it's not that," he finally admitted to himself and to her, even if the truth might push her away again. "It's killing me that I wasn't there for you how I should have been when she was taken away."

She angled back toward him, blinking fast. "You were grieving too, even if you didn't show it."

Marianna had been more magnanimous than he'd expected or probably even deserved. "Thank you for that."

"I know I should just be happy about this baby." She paused, her hands sliding over her stomach. "And I am, truly."

"Each child is just as important as the other." Hadn't his mother said much the same words at the hospital? He'd heard and comprehended in theory, but this time, the meaning sunk in with a deeper resonance.

"You understand." She extended a shaky hand, her eyes wary.

He hated that she had reason to doubt him when all he wanted was to make life easier for her. Sebastian clasped her fingers and tugged her forward until she sank into his lap. He gathered her closer, not sure how much time passed but at some point realizing he was staring at a framed photo on top of the armoire.

A picture of Marianna, Sophie and him at the baby's baptism.

Would he recognize his daughter if he passed her on the street? He liked to think so but couldn't be sure—babies changed so much so fast. Regardless, the time had come to accept that even if he saw her and knew her, she wouldn't remember them anymore.

"Sebastian?" Marianna's hands slid around him, linking behind his back. "You did hold me then, sometimes really late at night when I couldn't sleep."

"God, I don't even remember. That time is such a blur of..." He searched for the right word and could only come up with "...anger."

"You held me. You just wouldn't let me hold you." She tipped her face up to his, streaks on her face broadcasting the tears she'd cried silently. "But it's okay now. I know you miss her, and I know it's scary thinking about loving another child."

He grazed a kiss across her lips, keeping his hands firmly planted on the arms of the chair. Resisting the urge to pull out of her embrace because for some reason it made her happy to tear their hearts out this way.

And actually, simply kissing his wife had an appeal he hadn't fully appreciated until the privilege was taken away. His wife. While he hadn't doubted that he could win her back, he was damn glad things were moving along faster than he'd predicted when it came to bending her will.

The sooner he had his family together and taken care of, the better for all of them.

Sitting in Sebastian's car as he drove her to work, Marianna could barely believe all that had happened since they'd gotten into *her* car last night.

Kyle being shot down and recovering.

The car wreck and trip to the E.R.

Making love with Sebastian—and yes, she'd begun to hope they were beginning to make *love* with each other again.

The way he'd opened up to her in the nursery still took her breath away, filling her up again with hope. Sure, he hadn't spilled a wealth of words or emotionalism, but what he had shared felt like a fortune coming from her stalwart husband.

Ex-husband?

She wasn't quite ready to think in terms of marriage again so soon after their divorce, but for once, she wasn't completely crossing out the possibility. If he would just be patient with her, proving he'd changed his ways.

Sebastian chose a spot in the parking lot outside her office building, a quaint cottage on the beach. "I'll pick you up after work. I should finish with my court case on time. This judge has a reputation for keeping a tight stopwatch on proceedings."

She thought about asking him what sort of case, but work—his and hers—had been a sore spot between them. She didn't want to risk ruining their tenuous truce. "I appreciate your taking the evening off."

"I'm trying, Marianna."

"And that means a lot to me." She stared down at her clasped hands. "I noticed you spent some time at the computer last night."

He didn't miss a beat. "I couldn't sleep, not until I heard about Kyle."

That sounded reasonable, and she wouldn't have thought twice about the whole thing if it hadn't been for the past. Marianna reached across to cup his freshly shaved face, leaning to kiss him. He'd done so much of the pursuing lately that it was time to show him she was willing to meet him halfway. Inhaling the scent of his aftershave, tasting his mouthwash on his tongue, she savored the feel of his mouth against hers, familiar, yet with an edge of something new and exciting.

His hand slid to her stomach, palming just over where their baby nestled. She wanted to languish in the warm weight of his touch as much as she wanted to enjoy the sentimental gesture. But she couldn't shove aside the doubts that they were simply replaying the past. They'd gone through this dance when waiting to adopt, putting happy faces on the deeper troubles until the issues wounded, festered, left so many scars they'd eventually become numb.

She cut short the embrace, working to cover her unease. "We'll draw a crowd if we keep this up." She tapped his mouth. "But I promise we'll pick up where we left off. Tonight, I'll feed you while naked."

"It's a date." He winked his promise before stepping out of the car and around to her. He dropped a final quick kiss on her forehead, then climbed back behind the wheel.

Could she actually be watching his car pull away like the love-struck teen she'd once been? The twinge of uncertainty stirred inside her again, the fear he was playing along simply because of the baby as he'd done when Sophie entered their lives.

When would she believe he pursued her for herself? It all circled back around to trust taking time.

She backed toward the entrance, spinning along the door as she pushed inside. The lounge area buzzed lightly with piped in Muzak, their receptionist off to the left—and to the right, Ross waiting in her office door.

He shot her a wave. "Marianna, I need to speak with you for a minute."

"Sure," she answered, snagging her mail from the receptionist on her way to her office. "What do you need?"

Her boss closed the door after her, shutting them in the warm décor of her space, a place she'd decorated as a haven, complete with a soothing view of the Atlantic Ocean.

Ross followed her with lazy but even steps. "You can't actually be planning to take him back."

"You were watching us?" She tossed the mail and her purse onto her desk.

"Difficult to miss when you're right outside the building in broad daylight." He stroked his beard, his face tightening as if he was searching for words. "I just wanted to make sure you're all right."

Her skin prickled and not in a good way. This

wasn't playing out like a professional meeting. Could there have been something to Sebastian's suspicions? "While I appreciate your concern, this really isn't any of your business."

"I like to think we have more than a boss/ employee relationship. I consider you a friend."

Friend. She relaxed a little at the word. But not even for Ross could she hold back the tide of her emotions and the habit of speaking her mind. "As do I, but even friends need to be careful where they tread in offering relationship advice."

"See, here's the thing." He hitched his hands on his jeans loops, parting his jacket. "I did my level best to keep my emotions in check and my hands to myself while you were still with him. Married women are off-limits in my book."

Holy crap. Her feminine radar blared. "As they should be."

She crossed her arms over her chest, and if he knew anything about body language, he should read her back-off stance. Sebastian's sensors about Ross had been right. The man had feelings for her, even if he kept them to himself. How could she have missed picking up on that all these years they'd worked together?

Ross ambled a step nearer. "But you're not married now. I had planned to wait for you to get over the divorce, but I'm getting the sense that I may be short on time."

She swallowed down a hint of resentment for the

sake of professionalism, even as it angered her that he would tread into this terrain when she'd never given any indication she harbored those kinds of feelings for him. And he had seen her kissing Sebastian not five minutes ago.

"Please, don't say anything more." This conversation was spiraling out of control as fast as her spinning thoughts. She needed to make him understand he didn't have a chance with her—and she needed to do it before he messed up their working relationship forever.

"I will regret it for the rest of my life if I don't speak my mind." He crowded closer to her, backing her until her legs smacked an end table. "He doesn't appreciate you that way I do. Just give me a chance to show you how it could be between us." He pulled her to his chest.

She flattened her hands to his lapels to shove him away before he did something he would regret—or she said something she couldn't take back because it was getting harder and harder to put a cap on her mouth. "Ross, let's talk reasonably for a minute—"

The door clicked open, almost thudding against her as it swung wide. God, what would the receptionist think? Marianna shoved harder but Ross wouldn't budge.

"Hey, beautiful," Sebastian's voice echoed along with his footsteps against the carpet. "You forgot to eat breakf—"

She looked over Ross's shoulders as Sebastian came into sight. His gaze went from open to angry in a flash of dawning realization.

Marianna twisted free, searching for something to say other than the too cliché: *This isn't what it looks like.* She gripped Sebastian's arm, still so flustered at Ross's physical play for her she could barely comprehend this new turn of events. "Let's be reasonable adults—"

Sebastian shook his head without taking his gaze off the other man.

She felt so damn bad for Sebastian and how angry he must be over walking in on them, basically confirming for himself what he'd feared all along. "If you'll just step outside with me, we can sit in the car and talk."

"Talk?" Sebastian turned narrowed eyes toward her. "I don't think so, but I do think it would be a good idea if *you* step out of the room."

"Ross?" Again she tried to intercede. "Leave my office, please."

Her boss loped closer. "You're not going to be alone with him, not when he's in this kind of mood."

Sebastian eased his arm from her grip and turned his full attention to Ross. "Are you daring to insinuate I would ever hurt Marianna? You're the one hurting her by hitting on her in the workplace."

She stepped between the two men, certain neither of them would actually harm her. "Both of you, please take the testosterone level down a notch."

But neither of them was listening to her anymore.

Sebastian set her to the side with gentle hands at complete odds with the fury on his face. He pivoted on leather loafers to confront Ross. "I'm only going to say this once. Stay away from my wife."

Her boss didn't advance but he didn't back down either. "She's not yours anymore."

"Like hell. She's carrying my baby."

Marianna might have been tempted to laugh at the stunned expression on Ross's face—*if* she wasn't so steaming mad at the pigheaded father of her child for telling about the pregnancy. Even if he'd been right about Ross harboring feelings for her, she still stuck to her guns in believing Sebastian should know he could trust her.

How much better this would have played out if he'd simply put his arm around her and said they were working on their problems. Apparently Sebastian could only change so much at a time. She opened her mouth to demand Ross deliver an apology and explanations for stepping out of line.

Only to stop short as her ex-husband hauled back his fist and decked her soon to be ex-boss.

Sebastian might have been tempted to smile over how fast and hard Ross fell back onto the sofa.

Might have.

But rage steamed too hot and furious. The bastard wasn't wasting any time moving in on Marianna. Having all those jealous convictions confirmed only served to fuel Sebastian's anger.

He shook out his fist, angling toward Marianna, who must undoubtedly be shaken by what her boss had done. From the corner of his eye, he spotted a flurry of movement. Ross Ward surged up from the floor, tackling him at the waist. What the—?

Sebastian slammed back against the wall, rattling the Monet print by his head. Nose to nose with the object of too many marital fights, he couldn't hold his fury in check any longer.

In some distant part of his brain, he heard people gathering in the open doorway as Marianna shouted, "Stop!"

He stole a quick glance to make sure she was staying a safe distance away. Ward clipped him across the jaw.

Damn, that actually hurt. Sebastian threw all his muscle into sending the poaching jackass crashing back into the tapestry chair.

The fight visibly slid out of Ward as he sagged into the seat. "Baby?"

Marianna nodded, her lips tight with unmistakable frustration. "It's true. I'm two months along."

Frustration? If anyone deserved to be mad, he did. Ward had plastered his slimy hands all over

Marianna. Even thinking about seeing her so close to the other guy sent Sebastian seeing red. He kept an eye on Ward in case he decided to launch a surprise attack.

Gasping in the armchair, her boss worked his jaw. "I'm going to sue your ass for assault." Ward looked over at the three people standing in the doorway— the receptionist and two strangers who must be clients. "You're all witnesses to what happened here."

Sebastian stepped closer, staring the man down. "Go ahead and try it. I'll smack a countersuit against you so fast it'll fry that overly groomed beard off your face. Even a first-year law student could see your behavior constitutes sexual harassment in the workplace."

Marianna's mouth went tighter as she strode across the room to close the door on the now gaping onlookers. She pivoted back around, her hands behind her on the brass knob.

"Both of you, stop it. I don't *belong* to either one of you." She turned to her boss. "I intend to speak with you later, but not now. Will you please step out so I can talk to the father of my child?"

As Ross left the room, Sebastian blinked back his surprise at Marianna's words. Hearing her officially acknowledge their child for the first time sent a charge through him like nothing he'd felt since…since they brought Sophie home. And damn, that thought sideswiped him far harder than any punch from Ward. Except for once, Sebastian didn't want to close off that thought.

He willingly let a happy memory of his daughter flood his brain until Marianna slid into his line of sight, cutting short the moment.

"Sebastian, you were right about him having feelings for me. I'm sorry I didn't listen to you."

He hadn't expected that to come out of her pretty mouth. "Okay then. We're on the same page. Do you want me to get moving boxes or are there some around here that we can use to load up your office supplies?"

She patted his chest softly, unmistakably conciliatory. "You're steamrolling me again. If I decide to quit, I can pack up my own office."

"If?" His frustration shifted from Ward to Marianna. "What the hell are you talking about? Your boss just hit on you."

"You seem to be missing the most important point." She smoothed his tie, tightening the knot, which must have gone askew during the fight. "You had absolutely no reason to be jealous."

He grasped her wrists to stop her nervous motions. "The guy wants to have sex with you. That's reason enough."

"There are women out there who want to have sex with you. Should I tear their hair out? Of course not." She eased her hands from his grip, the six inches between them suddenly seeming a helluva lot wider. "I need for you to trust me, trust that I will make the right decision here. I'm not an unsure teenager anymore. I can take care of myself."

"You're turning this all around." Some lawyerly logic would serve him well right now, except logical was the last thing he felt around Marianna. "Listen, it's not as if we need the money. While I was on the computer last night, I came up with some ideas for investing in a trust fund for the baby. I can set up an account for you by the close of business today."

"Do not go there, Sebastian," she snapped, her chest rising and falling faster and faster with each breath. "Nothing's changed, has it? What makes you think we can just go back to the way things were?"

Her words seeped into his brain, and he wasn't liking the implication one bit. "So you're saying that's it. No trying, not even for the baby."

"I'm saying because of the baby we have to find a way to communicate without tearing each other apart." Marianna stood her ground even as her jaw trembled. "And if that means we can't be together anymore, then that's the way it has to be."

All her talk of making *love* had been just that. Talk.

"You're taking that job in Columbia, aren't you?"

"It's not about the job or the damn money." Anger crackled from her as she all but stamped her foot. "I don't care about your bank balance. This is about your trying to manipulate me into doing things your way. This is about you and me and the way you don't trust me to have handled what happened today."

"Did you ever think maybe you don't trust me?"

That stopped her short and he couldn't miss the hint of guilt that clouded her eyes. She didn't even deny what he'd said. She hadn't trusted him. He kept his hands jammed in his pockets, calling up all restraint. He wasn't the type to shout down any woman, much less a pregnant woman he loved.

Loved?

Hell yes, he loved her. He'd loved her since they were teenagers, and yet they still ended up in this same place time after time.

But that knowledge didn't stop him from pushing the issue. Fighting for this one last bit of understanding from her about a major cause of arguments in the past. "I was right about Ross Ward. All this time he's had feelings for you."

"Of course you're right." Tears welled and she scraped her wrist over her face. "You're always right and I'm just the emotional explosion waiting to happen. You never seemed to consider that I'm a big girl. I can handle a man being attracted to me and keep him at arm's distance."

"Yeah, you were doing real well with that when I came in here."

If he'd hoped to wound her—and hell, maybe

he had—he could see he'd done a damn good job of it. Her face paled. Her lips tightened into a hard, flat line.

"Get out, Sebastian." She turned her back to him, the set to her shoulders making it clear she was done talking, likely done with *them*. "Just leave."

Eleven

The door closed in her now-empty office with a finality that reverberated all the way to Marianna's toes. Even in the quiet aftermath with only the swoosh-swoosh of the grandfather clock to keep her company, the sounds of Sebastian's fight with her boss—the sounds of her fight with Sebastian—lingered.

How had things gone so wrong so fast? Her heart squeezed tight in her chest as she thought of the brief hope she'd felt earlier. How she'd actually thought because he spoke Sophie's name everything else might magically fall into place.

They'd taken a long time getting to this sad and

confusing place in their relationship. She'd been foolish to think that years of problems could be solved in the span of a few days. God, it hurt loving such a quietly immovable man.

Marianna sank onto the sofa, exhausted, and it wasn't even lunchtime yet. She considered going after Sebastian before he could pull out of the parking lot—for all of two swooshes of the pendulum. She didn't even know where to begin sorting through this.

The only fact she knew for sure? She needed to turn in her notice. What Sebastian had wanted from the start.

Had he let things get out of control with the fight, knowing that would leave her no choice but to resign? Could he be that manipulative? He'd tried to maneuver her about the money and stopping work altogether. In fact, from the moment Sebastian had heard she was pregnant, he'd launched in about her quitting her job—any job. She hated the creeping suspicions that he could be so calculating in getting his way.

She looked around her office and said her mental goodbyes to this corner of her life, which suddenly didn't feel all that important when she thought of everything else she could lose today. Sebastian. The possibility of a future with him.

Marianna shoved to her feet, resigned to getting past her meeting with Ross. She ignored the curious stares as she strode through the lobby and into the sleek blues and silvers of Ross's office.

Leaving the door very wide open.

He seemed to size her up as he finished a phone call and replaced the receiver into a cradle on his mahogany desk. From the dark rocks in the waterfall fountain sculpture along one wall to the stark, structural paintings over the couch, everything about his space underscored a quiet masculinity that had won him awards for his designs.

How much of her own success had trickled down from opportunities he'd given her out of a need to slide into her good graces? She would never know for sure, but it presented yet another reason she couldn't work here any longer. She deserved to realize her own strengths, to test how far she could go on her own merits.

Ross tipped back his chair with a creak, his jaw already purpling from the impact of Sebastian's fist. His gaze flicked from the lobby, then back to her. "What can I do for you, Marianna?"

Her heart drummed in her ears, adrenaline pumping through her veins, urging her on. "I appreciate the opportunities I've had here, and I've always respected your talent. But I can't work for you any longer."

He leaned forward with a long squeak of the chair. "Marianna, please take a seat so I can expl—"

Her sense of rightness about what she was doing forced her to interrupt.

"I won't be here long enough to sit." She stopped well shy of his desk, anger simmering anew at the way he'd backed her quite literally into a corner earlier. "I'm only here to tell you I'll be turning in my written two weeks' notice this afternoon."

He started to rise and she took another instinctive step toward the door. Ross sank into his seat, angling forward, his voice low. "I told you I never would have made a move on you as long as you were married, and I meant it. If you and he are getting together again, I won't be happy, but I won't interfere."

He seemed to be telling the truth, and in that moment she felt a twinge of sympathy for him. She understood well how painful it was to have feelings for someone only to be shut out. However she couldn't let that understanding affect her decision.

She bit back the urge to chew him out for causing such chaos in her life. For not listening when she'd told him to stop. None of which would help any of them. She needed a clean cut here, regardless of how things worked out with the father of her child.

"Sebastian has a problem with my working here, and I should have respected his feelings. He and I need to find a more level footing for the baby's sake."

"Does that mean you two *are* back together?"

Were they? She wasn't sure. How they would build a future with each other still seemed unclear to her. However, a sense of peace settled inside her as she stood here *calmly* fighting her own battle.

A sense that she was strong enough to stand on her own, to make hard decisions for her and for her child.

"I honestly don't know, Ross. But I do know I'm not available."

She turned away, her head high as she walked past the people in the lobby now trying too hard *not* to look at her. Marianna strode back toward her office to call a cab and retrieve her purse, reveling in her own strength and the knowledge that she would be okay. People respected her and her work, and just because Ross had been a jerk to her wouldn't change that.

Snatching the phone up, she turned as she punched in the stored number she used to set up rides for clients. Mid-dial, she noticed a flash of white across the room. A small white bag. Had it been there when she arrived?

Lowering the phone and thumbing the off button, she plucked up the sack, the logo solving the mystery. The bag had come from the store where Sebastian bought the flavored peanut butters. Hadn't he said something about her missing breakfast when he arrived? He must have packed the snack for her while she rushed to get ready for work.

Their day could have turned out so differently if she'd been alone in her office. But she also knew they would have only been delaying the inevitable. At some point, this showdown would have erupted.

She opened the fold and looked inside to find…a

cinnamon crunch bagel with a little plastic container of spiced peanut butter. Tucked in the bottom of the bag was one of Sebastian's business cards with a scrawl on the back.

"Love, S," she whispered rubbing her thumb along the simple note.

Love. It felt like forever since he'd used that word. Was he trying to apologize for not saying it last night? Of course she hadn't told him either, only hinting at the subject.

The bag seemed to grow heavier in her hand, its significance weighing on her conscience. She thought of other thoughtful gestures he'd made in the past that she'd chalked up to calculation. What if maybe, just maybe, those could have been attributed to affection rather than manipulation?

She turned the possibility over in her mind. He'd said often that being a lawyer led him to deal with deceitful people on a regular basis. That could certainly wear at a person's ability to trust in words. Actions would count more for him.

It stood to reason her reserved ex would have tried to *show* the love he couldn't voice.

She wasn't sure how she would persuade Sebastian to open up or how they would wade through the mess they'd made of their love for each other. But she wasn't going to quit trying if there was a chance he still wanted to save what they had together. Marianna stuffed the tiny sack into her purse and hooked the leather handbag over her shoulder.

Now she just needed to find which courtroom he was in—and figure out a way to make her own case to Sebastian in a way that would win over one of the best litigators in South Carolina.

Marianna sat in the back row of the courtroom, energized by her new determination even more than by the bagel she'd devoured on the way over.

Sebastian rose from his seat behind the table, buttoning his suit coat. A charcoal gray suit she'd chosen for him a week before they'd split. She'd never had the chance to see him wear it before today. The lightweight summer fabric hugged his broad shoulders even more perfectly than she'd expected. His close-trimmed hair only just kissed the top of his collar, calling to mind the silky texture.

He didn't appear to notice her, not even missing a beat in questioning the witness. Something to do with defending a mother and her son against an abusive father. Looking at his clients, it was obvious Sebastian had taken this case pro bono, and seeing the flame of hope in that young mother's eyes, Marianna admired him for the choice he'd made.

Sebastian went after the witness—the hulking father with fists clenched on his thighs—keeping a calm drive and focus that subtly shifted to a more heated push for the truth. Again and again he challenged the witness with questions that probed

free unwitting admissions, each nugget strength-
ening his case.

She got lost in watching Sebastian at his fiery
litigator best, this man she didn't see at home. Even
knowing he was reputed to be tops at his job hadn't
prepared her for the full impact of seeing him in
action. He poured all that emotional energy into
fighting for a child who couldn't defend himself.

Marianna inched to the edge of her seat, the
deep power of Sebastian's voice filling the courtroom. In a flash of inspiration, she realized he
hadn't been avoiding his feelings at all. He was
pouring his frustrations over losing Sophie into
defending this child. And just as surely she knew
he delivered the same intensity for all his clients.
He'd become the kind of lawyer he'd always said
he wanted to be back in the days when they'd
dreamed.

Maybe as his plan played out, he hadn't expected
to use up most of his best arguing here. Was it any
wonder he wanted peace at home?

The new understanding swelled inside her, along
with a sense of how she could fit into his life in an
unexpected way. God, she would enjoy playing
devil's advocate for a case. Or perhaps showing up
in the courtroom now and then, being a part of *his*
world instead of always waiting for him to be a part
of hers.

She hadn't been wrong in thinking it would take

time to trust each other again. But now, seeing this dazzling glimpse of the man she'd fallen for in the first place, she was willing to do whatever it took, for as long as it took.

Sebastian knew the minute Marianna walked into the courtroom. Even with his back turned, he got that unmistakable sensation telling him she was near. He hadn't missed a beat in his case, but he'd sure been counting down the minutes until they broke for lunch.

His watch showed him noon just as the prompt judge rapped her gavel for a recess. Sebastian took a moment to reassure his client before finally shifting his full attention to the back of the court-room.

He charged down the aisle, Marianna waiting there in the last row, not moving toward him or even standing. Was she here to finish venting her anger at him? He'd lost his cool with Ward, but even with his fist throbbing and Marianna's anger in his ears, he wasn't sure he would do anything differently. The way he saw it, he'd been protecting his wife and child.

He paused midstep, realizing that just because he was right about Ward didn't mean Marianna's day had sucked any less. Sebastian had known all along that the guy had been gunning for her, but she'd been caught off guard, disillusioned and man-handled to boot. And while he'd felt justified in firing off his anger on her employer, maybe he could have offered her some kind of…comfort.

Guilt nipped at his heels. He could almost see his mother shaking a well-manicured finger at him for not making time to take better care of Marianna. Of his family.

Then Marianna smiled. And he knew, deserved or not, he'd been given a reprieve, one he damn well intended to use to the fullest.

She crooked her finger for him to lean toward her. "Sebastian," she whispered, "find a broom closet or empty conference room pronto, please."

He didn't need to be told twice. Even if he'd found some aspects of marriage to a feisty female a challenge, he's always savored this side of her. Marianna might never back down from a fight, but then again, she never held back when she wanted *this*.

Sebastian clasped her elbow and guided her toward the same conference room where he'd carried her just a few short days ago when she'd passed out after their divorce decree. Once inside the room, *she* flattened *him* to the door, arching up to kiss him before he could so much as say hello. Of course who was he to argue with a greeting that beat the hell out of any words?

He met and answered the bold sweeps of her tongue against his, only the lack of a lock keeping him from lowering her to the sofa. God, this woman had been knocking him on his butt for nine years and counting. No problems between them had ever changed that.

She gasped against his mouth. "I gave my two weeks' notice right after you left."

And he'd thought her kisses knocked him flat.

"Because of what I did?" He stared down at her, trying to gauge every nuance of her mood.

"I should have listened to your concerns about Ross earlier." Her fingers toyed with the hair along the back of his neck. "But I quit because it was the right thing to do. He was out of line."

"What do you plan to do now?"

Tension pinched lines along the corners of her eyes, stealing some of the spark. "I hope this isn't a lead-in to you offering to fill my bank account."

He stayed silent, weighing the best answer. He'd been so focused on winning, somewhere along the line he'd forgotten about the power of compromise. The best lawyers realized some instances called for bargaining. She'd made a major concession in giving notice to Ward. Time to reciprocate. Keeping her in his life was too important to screw up again.

"How about I fill your refrigerator with things to tempt your palate instead?"

"Thank you." Her smile provided a bigger payoff than he could have predicted.

Sebastian cupped her face. "I'm sorry I made a scene at your office."

He'd always respected her work, admiring the way she brought beauty to everything she touched.

He hadn't intended to mess any of that up for her. With a cooler temper now, he sincerely hoped he hadn't compromised her ability to take her professional skills wherever she chose.

She stilled against him, her eyes wide and unblinking so long he started to worry about her.

"Marianna? Is something wrong?"

She shook her head slowly. "Do you realize that's the first time you've ever apologized to me?"

What was she talking about? "That can't be right. I've worked like crazy to get back into your good graces more times than I can count."

"I do see better now how you've tried over the years. But I have to confess, counselor, that sometimes it's still helpful to hear the words."

"Makes sense, I imagine. You are a woman who likes a good, long discussion."

Then it hit him. She needed the words when it came to more than apologies. She wanted more than signs of his love.

She had to hear the words.

"I love you, Marianna." He worked with speeches all day long. How could he have missed the boat so thoroughly when it counted the most? "Not just because you're the mother of my children—Sophie and this baby and any others we may have or adopt. But because you fire me up, challenge me to be more, and God knows I have a reputation around the courthouse for enjoying a good challenge."

Since he was also a man of action, he cemented his declaration with another kiss. Marianna leaned into him, her soft curves melding against him. The need to make love, seal their commitment, burned inside him, something he intended to follow up on the minute he got her home tonight.

Marianna took two steps back, keeping their fingers linked until the very...last...second. Hands on her waist, she jutted one hip forward, her leg extended to show off just how hot she made pink designer pumps look. His body tightened with the familiar jolt of desire.

With a defiant toss of her tangled curls, she met his gaze dead-on, with complete honesty and conviction. "I love you, Sebastian Landis. I love your sexy body when it caresses mine. I love your brilliant mind when it challenges mine. I love your peanut buttery thoughtful soul when it touches mine. I love you, unconditionally, forever."

Sebastian felt the waves of her healing love wash over him, chasing away the last whispers of that old nightmare. "Where do you see us going from here?"

She nibbled her lip, and he hated that he'd made her hesitant in voicing what she wanted. He looped his arms low around her waist and brought her close again.

Marianna smoothed the lapels of his suit, her hands tempting even through layers of clothes. "I would like to take time to get to rediscover each other."

Rather than hearing criticism because somehow he'd come up short in giving her enough, he heard her desire for both of them to have more. "Ah, you want to date."

"We did sort of skip over that when we met."

Theirs had been a quick trip to the altar. Had she been carrying around insecurities from that all these years? Something he definitely needed to fix, because he knew, without question, he would have walked this fascinating woman down the aisle, baby or no baby.

He skimmed his knuckles down her cheek. "How about we get a start on that the minute the judge wraps up for the day. No working late for me tonight. I have a special lady to take out who happens to enjoy fine dining."

Her brown eyes glinted with wicked promise. "Lucky for you, I just bought a new pair of shoes to model on our first date."

Epilogue

8 1/2 months later:

Marianna always welcomed the chance to buy a new pair of shoes. And today's event provided the most exciting reason for a shopping spree yet.

Searching for Sebastian among the small crowd at the reception, she wove by the guests milling around the Landis compound pool. Rose petals floated along the surface, the afternoon sunlight sparking prisms off the water while family and a few close friends finished an after-lunch cocktail.

As she walked along the glazed brick, her French pedicure peeked from her cream-colored open-toed heels, a Chanel purchase that had paid off more than once during the day with heated looks from Sebastian. Her off-white silk dress wrapped around her new curves, caressing just below her knees with each swishing step.

The months with Sebastian hadn't always been easy, but the time spent getting to know each other again had proved the *best* investment either of them had ever made. Without question, Sebastian would always be a powerfully driven man, but she no longer doubted her ability to stand up to him and win her point on occasion. She'd learned to lean a bit more on logic, and he'd learned to listen to his heart when it counted.

Today's gathering, however, wasn't about them. It was all about someone else.

This afternoon, they celebrated the baptism of Edward Sebastian Landis—all healthy seven pounds, eleven ounces of him at birth, heavier now, of course with little Edward hitting his six-week birthday.

Her feet slowed as she paused for a glance across the pool to check on her son—she couldn't look at his precious face often enough—and found Edward still sleeping soundly in his grandmother's arms. Ginger held court at a poolside table, showing off her new grandchild from under the shade of the protective umbrella. His traditional, long baptismal gown would go on display next to Sophie's at the end of the day.

A warm palm flattened to Marianna's waist, pulling her back to the moment. She didn't even have to look over her shoulder. She knew that touch intimately well.

Sebastian slid his arm around to lean her back against his chest. "You and Mom sure do know how to throw a great party."

His breath caressed her ear, the low rumble of his voice sending a shiver of excitement tingling along her skin as she remembered just how well and often they'd come together over the past months. They'd stayed away from the subject of marriage though. More than once she'd appreciated his patience in giving her the time she needed to lay her fears to rest by working out some of their problems before saying *I do* again.

She tipped her head to look up into his face, the angular lines that could be so forbidding in court eased by unmistakable happiness. "I have to commend you for giving feedback on the menu for the first time since I've known you."

"Hmmm…I didn't realize that providing you with a list of candies from the peanut butter store constituted feedback."

"I thought it was a sweet and sentimental gesture."

"Sweet? Shhh…" He turned and tugged her away from the crowd and under the privacy of a rose-covered wooden trellis. "Good God, Marianna, don't let my brothers hear that. They'll give me hell on the golf course."

Something he did more often now—golfing and hanging out with his family. He even vowed the extra downtime made him more effective at work.

She teased her pointer finger along his mouth, the ocean breeze wafting the sweet smell from roses clinging to the arbor overhead. "Your secret is safe with me."

They'd both made adjustments in their professional lives. Her decision to stop working with Ross had actually unchained her creativity beyond anything she would have ever dreamed. After considering a number of job offers, she'd decided to branch out on her own. She'd spent the past few months building an online business for interior decorating. People sent photos of their homes, and she offered simple improvement plans for a wide range of budgets—including using furniture already in place as well as listing items for purchase in their area and over the Internet.

She'd also been inspired by how Sebastian allowed his financial security to free up time to represent clients who couldn't otherwise afford even an hour of his billable rate. Her booming new business also took on special interest homes on a sliding scale according to client need. Just last week, she'd finished plans to revamp a house for a family financially stretched from the birth of quadruplets.

She'd found so much fulfillment organizing the space to give those children as much room and privacy as possible, while ensuring the parents had some special retreat spots, too. She'd come to realize how important it was to nurture your love relationship and not take it for granted for even a moment.

Sebastian plucked a rose from the trellis and grazed it along her cheek before tucking it behind her ear. "I've been thinking that perhaps we can tap Mom to throw another party for us."

Without question, the Landises had much to rejoice about lately. Matthew had won his senatorial seat; he and Ashley now married and settled into traveling between their D.C. residence and South Carolina home. His mother was a dynamo in her Secretary of State position. She and the General made the news on a regular basis as one of the U.S.'s most powerful political couples.

"What kind of party?" Marianna smoothed his lapels, thinking of how they almost hadn't managed to get dressed in time this morning with the mattress tempting them both after six weeks of abstinence.

"An engagement party." He pulled his hand from his pocket, along with a ring box.

"The timing is perfect." She reveled in the hard-earned joy of this union, so much different from the first rushed proposal based on circumstance and need.

They'd had chance after chance to walk away from each other, but this marriage would be based on the knowledge that their love was too great to be denied. Too special ever to be taken for granted again.

He hauled her to his chest, his heart picking up speed against her ear, broadcasting how important this was to him in spite of his seeming calm. She breathed in the familiar scent of his aftershave mixed with a hint of Edward's baby powder freshness.

"Marianna, will you marry me—again?" He creaked open the box to reveal a pear-shaped diamond alongside a diamond-studded band. "It's a new ring, but with an anniversary band."

She traced along the line of gems, counting. "This would have been our tenth year." They'd come a long way from two near strangers marrying as teens. She let tears flow that had nothing to do with postnatal hormones and everything to do with pure, undiluted happiness. "I like the blending of the old and new together. It's perfect. Yes, I will marry you, Sebastian Landis."

He thumbed her cheeks dry. Then slid the engagement diamond onto her finger where it settled with a perfect rightness, waiting for the band to be placed beside on their wedding day.

Sebastian closed his hand around hers in a grip as strong and steady as the man. "Just so we're clear. We're not getting married because you were pregnant, although I certainly wouldn't complain if you got pregnant again someday."

Marianna thought of the new photo on their mantel, a picture of Sophie that her birth mother had sent through their case worker. There wouldn't be any contact, and at this point Marianna feared confusing her anyway. She would always ache to hold her, would miss her every day, but she'd found a peace in seeing the happiness in Sophie's eyes—the eyes of a little girl well-loved.

She had to ask, "And if we never have another child?"

He was an amazing father, so patient in walking the floor at midnight with Edward cradled in his strong arms.

Sebastian brushed a windswept lock of her hair behind her ear with the flower. "I'm okay with that, too. I want *you* in my life."

"What a wonderful coincidence." The bloom's sweet scent mingled with the ocean breeze carrying the voices of the happy guests. "That's exactly where I want to be."

He hooked an arm around her shoulders, slipping a teasing finger just under the strap of her dress. "How about we retrieve our son from his grandmother and head home to Buddy and Holly?"

"We do have a lot to celebrate." She slid her hand under his suit jacket, his hard, lean body tempting her to explore him without the barrier of clothing. A pleasure she knew she would enjoy for the rest of their lives together. "In fact, I was thinking an intimate celebration is definitely in order."

His eyes glinted with the promise of deep and leisurely kisses to come once they were completely alone. "So who gets to feed whom naked this time?"

"That all depends on who gets their clothes off first."

* * * * *

2 FREE BOOKS
AND A SURPRISE GIFT

We would like to take this opportunity to thank you for reading this Mills & Boon® book by offering you the chance to take TWO more specially selected books from the Desire™ 2-in-1 series absolutely FREE! We're also making this offer to introduce you to the benefits of the Mills & Boon® Book Club™—

- **FREE home delivery**
- **FREE gifts and competitions**
- **FREE monthly Newsletter**
- **Exclusive Mills & Boon Book Club offers**
- **Books available before they're in the shops**

Accepting these FREE books and gift places you under no obligation to buy, you may cancel at any time, even after receiving your free books. Simply complete your details below and return the entire page to the address below. You don't even need a stamp!

YES Please send me 2 free Desire stories in a 2-in-1 volume and a surprise gift. I understand that unless you hear from me, I will receive 2 superb new 2-in-1 books every month for just £5.25 each, postage and packing free. I am under no obligation to purchase any books and may cancel my subscription at any time. The free books and gift will be mine to keep in any case.

Ms/Mrs/Miss/Mr_____ Initials _____

Surname _____

Address _____

_____ Postcode _____

Send this whole page to: Mills & Boon Book Club, Free Book Offer, FREEPOST NAT 10298, Richmond, TW9 1BR